D1165598

HARDCASTLE'S ARMISTICE

HARDCASTLE'S ARMISTICE

Graham Ison

This first world edition published in Great Britain 2004 by
SEVERN HOUSE PUBLISHERS LTD of
9–15 High Street, Sutton, Surrey SM1 1DF.
This first world edition published in the USA 2005 by
SEVERN HOUSE PUBLISHERS INC of
595 Madison Avenue, New York, N.Y. 10022.

Copyright © 2004 by Graham Ison.

British Library Cataloguing in Publication Data

Ison, Graham
   Hardcastle's armistice.
   1.   Police - England - London - Fiction
   2.   Detective and mystery stories
   I.   Title
   823.9'14 [F]

   ISBN 0-7278-6146-8

Typeset by Palimpsest Book Production Ltd.,
Polmont, Stirlingshire, Scotland.
Printed and bound in Great Britain by
MPG Books Ltd., Bodmin, Cornwall.

One

The maroons had been detonated at precisely eleven o'clock, set off by a constable experienced in such matters, from the roof of Cannon Row police station opposite New Scotland Yard. Across Bridge Street, the chimes of Big Ben sounded the hour, for the first time since the outbreak of war.

In his office on the first floor of that police station, Divisional Detective Inspector Ernest Hardcastle sighed, took his watch from his waistcoat pocket, glanced at it and stepped into the corridor. 'Marriott!'

Detective Sergeant Charles Marriott appeared in the doorway of the detectives' office. 'Sir?'

'How many on duty in there, Marriott?'

Marriott glanced back into the office over which, as the first-class detective sergeant, he presided. 'Seven, sir.'

'Get them all in my office and tell 'em to bring their own glasses.'

'Yes, *sir*,' said Marriott, unable to disguise his astonishment.

Moments later, those members of the detective staff of the A or Whitehall Division of the Metropolitan Police who were stationed at Cannon Row filed into the DDI's cramped office, each clutching a glass and shuffling noisily on the bare boards.

'The Armistice has been signed,' said Hardcastle gruffly. 'There's a bottle of Famous Grouse in that cupboard over there, Marriott. Get it out and pour it. Look lively now.'

Quickly, Marriott dispensed the whisky, being careful to serve the DDI first in case he changed his mind.

Hardcastle raised his glass. 'Well, lads, it's all over,' he said, and took a sip. 'Thank God.'

1

'I'll drink to that,' said Marriott earnestly. Each of the eight men in the room had lost at least one relative in 'the war to end all wars' and now, on the eleventh of November 1918, none of them could really believe that the fighting had finally stopped.

Hardcastle in particular was relieved. His sister's boy, Harold, had been killed on the first day of the battle of the Somme, back in 1916, but Hardcastle's only son, Walter, had been too young to enlist. His threat to put up his age and join the army had been countered by Mrs Hardcastle's own threat that she would 'march down to the War Office with your birth certificate and get you out again if you ever do anything so foolish, my lad'. But with his nineteenth birthday looming – next January – there would have been nothing to stop him. Save the Armistice.

'How about a toast to Ted Kimber's memory?' suggested Marriott.

Ted Kimber, a promising young A Division detective, had been commissioned into the Suffolk Regiment within weeks of the war starting, and had fallen while leading his platoon in the desperate attack on Neuve Chapelle in March 1915.

There were murmurs of 'Ted' as Hardcastle and the others raised their glasses to their former colleague.

Breaking the brief sombre mood, Hardcastle glanced at the bottle. 'Well, no sense in leaving any. Do the honours, Marriott.'

Marriott, astounded at his boss's generosity, to say nothing of his open incitement to breach the draconian discipline code, hurriedly poured more whisky. But this was, after all, a special occasion.

'Excuse me, sir.' An ageing station sergeant stood in the doorway and glanced, somewhat thirstily, at the bottle.

'Yes, what is it, Skipper?'

'There's a woman in the front office, sir. Seems vexed about her lodger what's gone missing. Seems to think she's been done in.'

Hardcastle scoffed. 'Well, it's Armistice Day, Skipper. I daresay she's out enjoying herself.'

'I suggested that, sir, but she says she's never done the like

2

of it before. Been adrift for a few days apparently and she seems to think that something dreadful might have happened to her.'

Hardcastle laughed. 'Aye, I wouldn't wonder at that neither,' he said, 'what with all these soldiers and sailors about. I shouldn't think any woman's safe out there today.' He turned to Marriott. 'Nip down and put her mind at rest, Marriott. And you'd better leave your glass on my desk where I can see it, or one of your leery comrades'll have it away.'

'Right, sir.' Marriott nodded. He could not recall ever having seen the governor in such an affable mood.

'I've put her in the interview room, Charlie,' said the station sergeant, when the pair reached the public part of the police station. 'Seems quite upset, she does.'

'What's her name?' asked Marriott.

The station sergeant glanced at the pad on his desk. 'Mrs Kathleen Dyer. Lives in Davos Street, off of Horseferry Road.'

'I wonder why didn't she go into Rochester Row, then,' mused Marriott. 'That's the nick that takes Davos Street. Duck-shovelled it off on us, have they?'

'I asked her that, Charlie, but she said as how this nick was more convenient.'

'Oh well,' said Marriott, 'I'd better go and see what it's all about.'

Mrs Dyer was about forty years of age. Seated demurely in the interview room – a cheerless, draughty room – she was attired all in black: a hat of Spanish straw, a shapeless, faded, full-length coat and button boots. She had a sad look about her, and Marriott deduced, correctly as it happened, that she was one of the thousands of war widows to whom the Armistice would bring little comfort.

'I'm Detective Sergeant Marriott. Mrs Dyer, is it?'

'That's right.'

'And you live at Davos Street, the station officer tells me. What number?' Marriott sat down and opened his pocket book, resting it on the scarred and ink-stained wooden table.

'Number twenty-seven.' The woman frowned as the noise

of cheering in nearby Whitehall penetrated the small room.

'And I understand that you're concerned about your missing lodger, Mrs Dyer.' Marriott looked up.

'She's more than a lodger, she's a friend. We used to work together on the trams, you see.'

'Perhaps we'd better start with her name, then.'

'It's Fanny Horwood, and I'm very worried about her, Sergeant.' Kathleen Dyer had a grave expression on her face, and her hands, clad in black woollen gloves, were clasped tightly together. 'I'm sure something dreadful's happened to her.'

Marriott wrote down the name. 'And when did you last see her?' He knew what the station officer had told him, but he wanted to hear the precise details for himself.

'Saturday morning, about ten o'clock, I s'pose it must have been.'

'Oh, I see.' Marriott closed his pocket book. He had assumed that Mrs Horwood must have been missing for a longer period than that to have alarmed Mrs Dyer so much. 'Is it possible that she's out, celebrating the Armistice? Everyone knew it was coming off, so to speak, and the celebrations have been going on for a day or two now. In advance, like.' He paused, as a thought struck him. 'She's not, er . . . she's not a war widow, is she?' That, he knew, would have made revelry on the missing woman's part unlikely, though not out of the question.

'No, she's not. At least, not as I know of. Come to think of it, she's never mentioned a husband. And when I told her about my Gerald – he was killed last year at Arras, you know – she never said nothing. I mean, if she'd suffered the same way as me, she'd have said, I'd've thought.'

'Well, Mrs Dyer, there's probably a satisfactory explanation for her not coming home on the Saturday night—'

'Oh, I knew she wasn't coming home on the Saturday night, but it's *two* nights now, Sergeant, not just the one,' said Mrs Dyer. 'She's a sober woman and she's never done nothing like it before. I'm sure she's been murdered.'

'Dear me, Mrs Dyer, I do think you're worrying too much,'

4

said Marriott. 'Now, you said you weren't expecting her back on the Saturday night. Why was that?'

'Because she said she was going to Brighton and staying the night.'

'Did she mention that she was going with someone, a man perhaps? Or did she say where she'd be staying?'

'I never asked,' said Mrs Dyer sharply. 'I'm not one to mind other people's business.'

'So, she's only been missing the one night. Last night, in fact,' said Marriott, rising to his feet. 'People do go missing, often for a quite good reason, you know. Like as not, she fancied staying down a second night. Bit of a lively place is Brighton. She's probably out enjoying herself, what with the Armistice and all. I'm sure she'll turn up, and we can't very well start searching for her, not this early, if you take my meaning. For one thing, we wouldn't know where to start. Brighton's a big place and, as you don't know exactly where she went . . .' He smiled, attempting to lighten the woman's obvious distress. 'I daresay quite a few people will get themselves mislaid over the next few days, but she'll turn up, you mark my words.'

'Well, I don't know.' Mrs Dyer stood up too, shaking her head. 'Like I said, she's never done aught like it before.'

'How long has she lived with you, Mrs Dyer?' asked Marriott, putting his hand on the knob of the interview-room door.

Kathleen Dyer gave the question some thought. 'It must be about six months now, I s'pose. She come to live with me straight after the baby died.'

Marriott relinquished his hold on the door handle. 'Baby? She had a baby, did she?' His detective's mind was starting to take an interest in what could be a possible motive for murder: a woman who had never mentioned a husband, but who had had a baby, might just be expecting another.

Mrs Dyer nodded. 'Only a tiny mite, it was. Barely two months old when it died. It was the 'flu, you know.'

Marriott did know. Thousands had already died in the influenza pandemic, and more were to do so before the outbreak

5

was brought under control. 'What was the child's name, d'you know?' He brought out his pocket book again.

'Blanche, I think. But why d'you want to know that? It's Fanny as is missing.'

Marriott smiled again. 'It's a policeman's failing, Mrs Dyer,' he said. 'We take notes of all sorts of things. Just in case.' He paused, pencil poised. 'Did she have a man-friend, at all? Walking out, was she?'

'Not that I know of. She'd have mentioned it, I'm sure, if there'd been someone.'

'And no husband that you know of?'

'No.' Mrs Dyer paused, thoughtfully. 'Mind you, what letters she had was always addressed to *Mrs* Horwood, but, like I said, I never heard tell of no husband.'

'She wasn't pregnant, I suppose?' Marriott floated the question lightly.

'No, she was not,' said Mrs Dyer adamantly. 'I told you she was a sober woman, and she knew how to behave herself.'

'Well, if she's not home by tomorrow, you'd better let us know,' said Marriott, sensing that the woman was unhappy that the police seemed unwilling to do anything about finding her friend.

'I shall, Sergeant,' said Mrs Dyer, with a show of spirit, 'you can rest assured of that.' She wrinkled her nose slightly, certain that she could smell alcohol on the detective's breath.

'Well, Marriott, anything in it?' asked Hardcastle, when the detective sergeant returned to the DDI's office.

'Difficult to say, sir,' said Marriott, picking up his glass. He summarized what Mrs Dyer had told him, and shrugged. The police knew only too well that the war had upset the normal pattern of social behaviour, and missing persons were not uncommon, even women. They had been known to run away with soldiers, or had got themselves in the 'family way' and, too ashamed to admit it, had left home to have the child somewhere where they were not known. And Marriott was not wholly convinced by Mrs Dyer's denial that Fanny Horwood was pregnant, a denial that had come a little too readily. But even when such people were eventually found, regulations prevented the police from telling worried friends and relatives, just in case the missing person did not want them to know. 'I had the station officer make a note of it in the occurrence book, sir.'

Hardcastle nodded. 'Just have to wait and see,' he said. 'No doubt she'll turn up in a month or two, more than likely with another kid.'

But the next day, the matter of the missing Fanny Horwood took a much more serious turn.

At nine o'clock that following morning, Detective Sergeant Marriott had no sooner taken off his jacket and settled himself behind his desk than the station-duty constable appeared in the CID office. 'Excuse me, Sergeant,' he said, 'but there's a Mrs Dyer at the counter asking for you.'

With a sigh, Marriott donned his jacket again and went downstairs to the front office. Mrs Dyer was waiting, dressed exactly as she had been the previous morning.

'She's not back, Sergeant.'

'All right, Mrs Dyer,' said Marriott, 'I'll get someone to look into it. Will you be at home if I send an officer round?'

'*I'm* not going anywhere,' said Mrs Dyer tartly. 'But what d'you want to send someone round for?'

'To have a look at her belongings, see if there's anything that might tell us where she's gone.'

'I told you where she'd gone. She went to Brighton.'

'Yes, Mrs Dyer, but she might not have been telling the truth.'

'She always told the truth,' said Mrs Dyer with a toss of her head.

But Marriott was far from convinced of that. 'Do you have a photograph of her, by any chance?' he asked.

Mrs Dyer thought about that for a moment. 'Yes, I think there is one. She had one of them studio pictures took with the baby, poor little soul.'

'I'll have an officer round to you in about half an hour, then.'

'Good,' said Mrs Dyer, and turned on her heel, satisfied

7

that, at last, the police had been goaded into doing something about her missing friend.

Back in the CID office, Marriott looked around for a suitable officer, his eyes eventually lighting on Detective Constable Henry Catto. 'What are you up to, Catto?'

'Dealing with a string of thefts at the Army and Navy Club in Pall Mall, Sarge.' Catto contrived to look busy. 'They reckon it's one of them new maids they took on a week or two back.'

'That can wait. Get round to twenty-seven Davos Street, see a Mrs Dyer. Her lodger, Mrs Fanny Horwood, is missing from home. Have a look round, see if you can see any indication of where she might have gone. Like as not, she's gone off with some bloke, a swaddy probably. Oh, and Mrs Dyer reckons there's a photograph of the woman there somewhere,' he added, as Catto rose from his chair. 'Make it look good, like we're doing something, but try not to waste too much time on it.'

'Right, Sarge.'

But as Catto opened the door of the office, he was confronted by the DDI. 'And where are you off to in such a lather, Catto? If it's Bow Street Court, you're late.'

'No, sir, I'm just going to Davos Street. Job for Sergeant Marriott. Missing-person enquiry.'

'Well, just you hold on.' Hardcastle looked beyond Catto to where the first-class sergeant was seated behind his desk. 'Marriott, come into the office. You too, Catto. I've just had word from the Brighton police. They found a body underneath Palace Pier the day before yesterday that they reckon is this Fanny Horwood. She'd been strangled apparently.'

Hardcastle led the way back to his office and, sitting down behind his desk, took his pipe from the ashtray. He spent a moment or two teasing tobacco into it and then lit it, filling the office with the dark smoke of his favourite St Bruno. Somewhere beneath them an underground train rumbled out of Westminster station.

'Seems some lunatic ventured down on to Brighton beach on Sunday morning at about six o'clock, intent on going swimming.' Hardcastle shook his head. 'Must be raving mad, going sea swimming in November. Anyhow, he came across this body underneath Palace Pier and called a copper straight away.'

'How did they know it was Fanny Horwood, sir?' asked Marriott.

'I'm coming to that. She never had any belongings on her. No handbag or jewellery. Nothing like that, but apparently' – he picked up a sheet of paper from his desk and glanced at it – 'a Mrs Phyllis Edwards – she's a landlady who keeps lodgings in Sussex Street in Brighton – went into the nick on the Sunday, a bit later on, and told them that one of her lodgers, a Mrs Fanny Harris, hadn't come back on the Saturday night.'

'How's that tie up with Fanny Horwood, then, sir?' asked Catto.

'Just hold on, Catto,' said Hardcastle testily. 'The Brighton lot went round to Sussex Street and searched her room. Apparently they came across a photograph which they promptly identified as the dead woman. They also found some letters addressed to Fanny Horwood at twenty-seven Davos Street, London SW – in her suitcase they were – and they put two and two together. Not bad for those yokels down there.' The DDI had no great opinion of the Brighton Borough Police.

'But that still doesn't make a connection, sir,' persisted Catto. 'How did they work out that letters addressed to Fanny Horwood in this Fanny Harris's belongings mean that she was actually Fanny Horwood? I mean, she could have nicked them.'

Hardcastle nodded slowly. 'I can see you're coming on a treat, Catto,' he said. 'You're right, of course. Somewhere along the line, we're going to have to get someone to identify the body.' He stood up. 'So, look up the times of the trains from Victoria to Brighton, Marriott. You and I are going to the seaside for the day. And you, Catto, get on round to Davos Street and see what you can find. But don't mess anything up and don't tell Mrs—' He broke off. 'What's that woman's name, Marriott?'

'Mrs Dyer, sir. Kathleen Dyer.'

9

'Right. And don't say anything to Mrs Dyer about her friend having been found dead at Brighton, Catto, because we're not sure. Not sure by any means. All right?'

Two

It had begun to snow when Hardcastle and Marriott arrived at Brighton's central railway station, but a fierce wind deterred the flakes from settling. Outside the station, pedestrians bent against the biting weather as they struggled along the narrow pavement, one of them wrestling with an umbrella that had blown inside out. Near the station entrance, a staggering drunkard – doubtless still celebrating the Armistice – was attempting to sing 'Pack Up Your Troubles'.

Hardcastle turned up the collar of his Chesterfield overcoat, and muttered angrily as he and his sergeant clambered into a waiting taxi.

The headquarters of the Brighton force was above the police station next to the town hall in a road called Bartholomews. Within walking distance of Palace Pier, where Fanny Harris's body had been found, it was little more than half a mile from the Sussex Street lodgings where she had stayed the previous Saturday.

Hardcastle, already in a bad mood at having had to make the journey from London, strode into the public entrance of the police station and, failing to receive an immediate response from the sergeant on duty, rapped sharply on the counter with the handle of his umbrella.

The sergeant looked up, frowned, and then ambled across to deal with this apparently troublesome caller. 'Dear me, we are in a sweat this morning. So, what can I do for you?' he demanded sarcastically.

'I'm Divisional Detective Inspector Hardcastle of the Metropolitan Police, and I don't have any time to waste. I

11

want to see whoever's in charge of this murder. Detective Inspector Watson, I believe.'

'Yes, sir, certainly, sir.' The sergeant became immediately sycophantic in the face of firm authority and raised the flap of the counter. 'If you'll come this way, sir, I'll show you to the inspector's office.'

Hardcastle grunted, and he and Marriott followed the sergeant up the back stairs to that part of the station occupied by the criminal investigation department of Brighton's A Division.

Detective Inspector Percy Watson was about fifty years of age. His pomaded hair was smoothed back from a widow's peak and his black moustache was neatly trimmed. Between his waistcoat pockets was an albert from which was suspended a device in the shape of a square and compasses. His office, much larger than Hardcastle's own at Cannon Row, was wood-panelled and carpeted. On the walls were the usual group photographs of policemen sitting in serried ranks, and a certificate showing that Watson had, at one time, been commended by the chief constable. The cynic in Hardcastle wondered if it was for furnishing his office so sumptuously.

Watson carefully appraised the two men who had entered. 'You must be the Metropolitan officers,' he said, standing up.

'That we are,' said Hardcastle, and introduced himself. 'And this here is Detective Sergeant Marriott.'

'How d'you do, gentlemen,' said Watson, and shook hands with each of them in turn. 'I'm very pleased to see you.'

'I'll bet you are,' said Hardcastle. 'Come to pull your chestnuts out of the fire, most likely.' He put his bowler hat and umbrella on the inspector's hat stand and then took off his heavy overcoat.

Watson blinked at Hardcastle's bluntness. 'Er, well, yes, your assistance will be greatly appreciated.'

'Not much option really,' said Hardcastle grudgingly. 'She might have been topped on your manor, but I'll wager her killer lives on ours.' Uninvited, he sat down in one of Watson's comfortable armchairs. 'But it must be clearly understood, Mr Watson, that I'm here only because of the London connection, not to investigate this murder for you. That's down to you. Now then, you reckon this Fanny Harris is Mrs Fanny Horwood. How d'you come to that, then?'

'I'd better begin at the beginning, Mr Hardcastle,' said Watson, and started to explain about the correspondence that had been found among Fanny Harris's sparse belongings.

'Yes, that's all very well, Mr Watson, but how d'you *know*? For certain, I mean? No one's identified her, have they?' Hardcastle raised a quizzical eyebrow.

'I had Mrs Edwards – Phyllis Edwards, that is – come down to the mortuary and look at her. She's the one that keeps the boarding house in Sussex Street where the poor woman stayed. And she says that the deceased was definitely Mrs Harris.'

'And how long has this Mrs Edwards known Fanny Harris?'

'The Harris woman had arrived from London that morning – Saturday – according to Mrs Edwards.' Watson was beginning to feel like a probationer detective in the face of Hardcastle's incisive questions. But then, Hardcastle had investigated many more murders during his twenty-seven-year career than had Watson, who, Hardcastle accurately surmised, had spent at least half of his service in the Uniform Branch.

'Yes, go on,' said Hardcastle.

'On Saturday, Mrs Harris had a bite of lunch at Mrs Edwards's place and then went out, to the beach she said, and returned to her lodgings at about five o'clock.' Watson opened a file and removed a photograph. 'This was found in her room.' He pushed the print across his desk. 'I should say it was taken by one of the beach photographers.'

The poor-quality photograph showed a young girl – probably no more than twenty – wrapped in a dark coat and wearing a flat wide-brimmed hat. Around her neck was a chain choker.

'Has he been traced, this beach photographer?' asked Hardcastle, returning the print to Watson.

'Er, no, not exactly.'

'Well, either he has or he hasn't.' Hardcastle was growing increasingly impatient with Watson's casual approach.

'I, er, didn't quite see the need to trace him, Mr Hardcastle. I mean, what's he going to tell us?'

13

'We shan't know until we ask him and we can't ask him till we find him, can we? Might I suggest that some attempt is made to track him down, Mr Watson? Sooner rather than later.'

'Yes, of course.' Watson made a note on a pad. Carefully putting the cap on his fountain pen and pocketing it, he reached for a pile of letters bound by an elastic band. 'And these were the letters I mentioned, addressed to Mrs Horwood, that we found in Fanny Harris's room at Mrs Edwards's place,' he said, handing them to Hardcastle.

'But that don't necessarily *make* her Mrs Horwood, does it?' said Hardcastle patiently. 'Not till someone who knew Mrs Horwood says it's her.' He was beginning to wonder if Watson was up to the job of investigating a murder.

'No, I suppose not,' said Watson thoughtfully. 'That was where I was hoping you may be able to assist.'

'I've a Mrs Dyer in London who says that a Fanny Horwood was living with her at this Davos Street address.' Hardcastle tapped the letters with his forefinger. 'Mrs Dyer came into the nick on Monday complaining that she'd disappeared. I'll have to get her down here to Brighton to see if she can identify the body. Now, what about the post-mortem?'

'That was carried out yesterday afternoon,' said Watson, relieved that he was able to come up with a positive answer for this demanding London detective. 'Death was due to manual strangulation and the woman was two months pregnant.'

'Aha!' said Hardcastle triumphantly. 'We might just have stumbled on a motive there, Mr Watson.'

Watson appeared slightly bemused by this proposition. 'Really?' he exclaimed.

'Yes, really.' Hardcastle sighed. 'Fanny Horwood, and for the moment I'm assuming your corpse *is* Fanny Horwood – and might even be *Mrs* Fanny Horwood – had a child previously, but according to her landlady in London, she never spoke of a husband. Now, if she hasn't got a husband and she's been up to a bit of hanky-panky – and her pregnancy would seem to point to it – it might just be that there's a man

14

somewhere who was the father of this unborn child that was discovered at the PM, and we might benefit from having a talk with him. But, of course, that all depends on whether your victim is Fanny Horwood or not.' The DDI gave Watson a sadistic smile. 'And if she's not, then this murder's your problem, rather than yours and mine, if you take my meaning.'

Watson was not at all comforted by that truism. 'Yes, I see,' he said, brushing lightly at his moustache.

But Hardcastle was by no means sure that the Brighton detective did see. 'It looks as though Marriott and me will have to stay the night,' he said. 'Maybe there's a half-decent hotel hereabouts that you can recommend, Mr Watson.' He stood up. 'And perhaps my sergeant here could make use of your telegraph to get a message to London.'

'Yes, of course.'

Hardcastle turned to Marriott. 'Get a wire off to Catto. Tell him to escort Mrs Dyer down here, preferably tomorrow, to see if she can identify this poor bitch.'

It was typical of his sort that, having been made to look an incompetent fool by Hardcastle, Detective Inspector Percy Watson had gone into a towering rage after the departure of the London detectives, and had immediately set about his own officers, lambasting them for their inefficiency.

The following morning Hardcastle and Marriott arrived from their hotel at nine o'clock to find that the beach photographer had been traced and was waiting in the interview room at the police station.

Hardcastle sent Marriott up to Watson's office to get the photograph that had been found in the dead woman's room at Mrs Edwards's boarding house.

'I'm DDI Hardcastle of the Metropolitan Police,' said Hardcastle as he entered the interview room, 'and I'm assisting the local police in a murder enquiry. So I don't want any nonsense from you, my lad.'

The beach photographer rose from his chair. 'I ain't done nothing wrong, guv'nor,' he whined.

'We'll see about that,' said Hardcastle, taking off his hat

and coat and handing them and his umbrella to the Brighton constable who had shown him into the room. He was a firm believer in going on the attack, even with an ostensibly innocent witness. 'What's your name?'

'Danny Hoskins, sir.' The photographer was dressed in a grey check flannel suit with a loud tie and two-tone shoes – upon which Hardcastle gazed with some distaste – and, despite the weather, held a straw boater that he constantly revolved between his fingers.

'I'm told you took a photograph yesterday afternoon, lad.'

'I take lots of photos,' said Hoskins, grinning.

Hardcastle fixed the photographer with a stern expression and the smile vanished. 'I've no doubt you do, but I'm interested in only the one.' He half turned as Marriott entered the interview room. 'Got it there, have you, Marriott?'

'Yes, sir.' Marriott placed the photograph on the table.

'That one.' Hardcastle pointed at it.

Hoskins moved forward to stare at the print. 'Yeah, I think so.' He paused before eventually agreeing. 'Yeah, I did. I took that one, guv'nor.' He looked up. 'What about it?'

'What time did you take it and where?'

'Blimey, guv'nor.' Hoskins looked thoughtful and ran a hand round his chin. 'Let me see now. Yeah, I've got it. Must have been about half past three. I knocked off for a cup of tea and to do a bit of developing round about four, I s'pose. Trade's none too good at this time of the year, and there's too many of us at it anyway, even in winter. This girl was sitting on the beach about halfway between the piers, all huddled up in a coat.'

'On her own, was she?' asked Hardcastle.

'Far as I could tell, guv'nor. Well, I never saw no one with her, like.'

'And how come you remember taking this photograph more than any other you took?'

'She was a pretty-looking thing, weren't she?' Hoskins smirked. 'Bit of a waste that, I thought, being there all on her own. Matter of fact, I had half a mind to ask her for a drink, sort of later on when I'd finished, see.'

'And did you?'

'Nah! Bit short of cash, see, so I thought better of it.'

'Did you indeed?' Hardcastle gazed reflectively at the photographer. 'And did you see her again? After you'd had your cup of tea?'

'No, she was gone when I got back.'

'And what time was that?'

Again Hoskins appeared to give the question some thought. 'Round about five-ish, I reckon.'

'When did you develop this photo?'

'About four o'clock, like I said.'

'Did you really?' Hardcastle slapped the top of the table with the flat of his hand. 'D'you think I'm bloody stupid, boy?'

'No, sir,' said Hoskins, shifting back in his chair with alarm.

'Then how the blue blazes did she get a hold of it, if you never saw her again, eh?'

'I asked her where she was staying, sir, and I promised to drop it in. And I did, round about half past six.'

'And did you see her, when you dropped it in?' said Hardcastle, sarcastically emphasizing the last five words.

'No, sir. I give it to Vi Gunn. She's the lass who works for Mrs E.'

'You know Mrs Edwards, then?'

'I know most of 'em as keeps boarding houses hereabouts,' said Hoskins.

Hardcastle made a mental note to check the photographer's story when eventually he visited Mrs Edwards. 'And how many times had you seen this girl before you took her photograph on Saturday afternoon, then?' He leaned back in his chair and stared menacingly at the unfortunate Hoskins. 'You know she was the one that was murdered, I suppose.'

'Honest, I'd never seen her before, and I never saw her again,' protested Hoskins.

'All right, lad, but I might need to talk to you again, later on,' said Hardcastle.

*   *   *

'What d'you think, sir?' asked Marriott, after Hoskins had been escorted from the police station.

'He could have done it, Marriott,' said the DDI reflectively, as he felt for his pipe. 'Funnier things have happened. And his answers were a touch too cagey for my liking; pretending that he had a job remembering taking the snap, then saying that he'd thought about asking her out and all that malarkey. For all we know, Hoskins might have put her in the family way a couple of months ago and she came down here to face him with it. But let's make sure it's Fanny Horwood we've got in the mortuary before we start doing too much of Mr Watson's work for him. Heard from Catto, have we?'

'Yes, sir,' said Marriott. 'He'll be here on the eleven fifty from Victoria, along with Mrs Dyer.'

Hardcastle took out his watch, glanced at it and gave it a brief wind before dropping it back into his waistcoat pocket. 'Good,' he said. 'Then we've got time for a sharp walk to this Sussex Street dosshouse to have a chat with Mrs Edwards. A bit of fresh air'll do us good. See if you can find what that PC did with my hat and coat, Marriott – oh, and you'd better ask Mr Watson if he wants to send one of his officers with us. Or even come himself.' The DDI was aware of the proprieties of investigating a crime in someone else's police area.

DI Watson, however, decided against accompanying Hardcastle himself – he had had quite enough of the London detective's acerbic temperament – and sent Detective Sergeant Goodenough, a newly promoted, young and enthusiastic officer.

The weather had undergone one of the mercurial changes that is a feature of the English climate: the snow of the previous day had given way to clear skies, the biting wind had subsided and a watery sun appeared, but with no warmth in it.

'You been to this address before, Goodenough?' asked Hardcastle as the trio set off at a brisk pace, a pace dictated by Hardcastle's desire to finish his enquiries and leave Brighton as soon as possible.

'Yes, sir,' said the Brighton officer. 'I went there with Mr

Watson straight after Mrs Edwards reported her lodger missing and the body had been found.'

'What sort of questions did you ask?'

'Well, I didn't ask any, sir. Mr Watson did all the talking, but he asked when Mrs Horwood had arrived and—'

'We don't know it's Mrs Horwood yet, lad, or for that matter, even *Miss* Horwood,' Hardcastle interrupted sharply. 'That's something we hope to establish later in the day. What else did Mr Watson ask?'

'That was about it, really, sir. We had a look round her room – Mrs, er, Mrs Harris's, that is – and found the photograph and the letters.'

'And Mr Watson only asked when she arrived, did he?'

'As far as I can recall, sir,' said Goodenough. 'But Mrs Edwards did mention that Mrs Harris went out at about two o'clock, I think she said, and came back at around five.'

'I see,' said Hardcastle. His opinion of Watson's investigative abilities was worsening by the hour. 'Well, we'll have to see what she has to say for herself.'

The boarding house in Sussex Street was a forbidding, three-storied, Victorian dwelling with a basement area, and was doubtless filled to capacity during the holiday season.

A small gang of street urchins gathered on the pavement as the detectives mounted the steps. Their more adventurous leader, the proud possessor of a bowling hoop, leaned on the wrought-iron balustrade. 'You come about the murder, mister?' he shouted, doubtless schooled in recognizing policemen by a felonious father.

'Clear off before I take you all down the station and get the matron to wallop your backsides,' said Hardcastle, turning to raise the heavy, brass ram's-head knocker.

The woman who answered the door was in her forties. She wore a hopsack apron, which she quickly removed at the sight of the three police officers on her doorstep, and her hair was pulled back into a tight bun. She was a thin-lipped person, sour of face, and to Hardcastle was typical of seaside landladies. He had spent a miserable week with his wife Alice in

19

a similarly depressing establishment at Southend-on-Sea earlier in the year.

'Clear off, you little buggers,' she shouted at the urchins, and turning to Hardcastle with her hand to her mouth, added, 'Oh, do pardon my French.'

Hardcastle introduced himself, and he and the two sergeants were admitted to what Mrs Edwards called her 'withdrawing room'.

'I understand that Mrs Harris arrived on Saturday morning, Mrs Edwards.' Hardcastle gazed around at the riot of floral furnishings and bric-a-brac that the room contained. A coal fire crackled in the cast-iron grate, around which was a large highly polished brass fender. To one side of it was a stand holding three equally burnished fire irons. Above the mantel-piece was a huge gilt-wood mirror. There was an excess of pictures in heavy frames on the flock wallpaper, and a moulded brass light fitting dominated the centre of the ceiling. All of which, when combined with the brown paintwork, lent the room an overwhelmingly cheerless quality.

'That's right. She said she'd come down on the early train from London. She got 'ere about midday, I suppose. In time for luncheon, any road.' In an attempt to mimic the genteel classes with whom she had once been in service, Mrs Edwards spoke in the sort of strangulated tones that her mother described as a 'cut-glass' accent.

'Did she say what she was doing here? Did she say, for example, that she was here to meet someone?'

'I think she did opine that she was 'oping to meet a gentleman later on,' said Mrs Edwards, 'but it's not my place to pry. I always tell my guests that they're to treat my 'umble abode as if it was their own 'ome.'

'So, she didn't tell you who this man might have been?' asked Hardcastle.

'No, not as such.'

'And what time did she go out that afternoon, Mrs Edwards.'

The landlady folded her hands demurely in her lap and gazed briefly at the heavy lace curtains shrouding the window. 'Straight after luncheon, about two o'clock, I suppose. And she come back again at about five. She insinuated that she'd been for a walk along the front. Certainly 'er cheeks was looking rosier than when she went out.'

'And then she went out again?' asked Hardcastle.

'Yes, at about seven, or maybe 'alf-past. She stayed for 'igh tea. I pride myself on serving one of the best 'igh teas in Brighton, you know, Mr . . . er . . .'

'Hardcastle. Do you happen to know if someone called here with a photograph for Mrs Harris on Saturday afternoon, Mrs Edwards?'

'Oh, yes, come to think of it, I believe they did, Mr 'Ardcastle. That young 'Oskins, a beach photographer, you know . . .' Mrs Edwards tossed her head as though dealing with what she saw as a tradesman was beneath her dignity. 'I understand from my maid – that's Violet Gunn – that 'e delivered a snap at about 'alf past six, saying as 'ow it was for Mrs 'Arris. Violet accepted it, but she never let 'im in. She knows my rules about lady guests not 'aving gentlemen callers. You never know what they might get up to, you see, and I pride myself on running a respectable establishment. Once word gets around that the guests can take liberties, if you knows what I mean, you never knows where it might end. I'm sure you understands, Mr 'Ardcastle, being a policeman, I mean.'

'Are any of the guests who were here on Saturday still here, Mrs Edwards?'

'Only the major, but apart from 'im my terms is strictly Monday to Sunday, otherwise I 'as empty rooms for perhaps 'alf a week.'

'How come you took Mrs Harris in, then? Did she say that she would be staying the week?'

'No. I 'ad an empty room what 'ad not been taken, you see, so I was able to accommodate the young lady, just for the one night, like.'

The door of the room opened and a young man appeared. In his late twenties, he had a moustache and was smoking a pipe. There was a copy of *The Times* folded beneath his left arm.

Mrs Edwards gave him a syrupy smile and touched her hair. 'I'm afraid the withdrawing room is engaged for the moment, Major Springer,' she said. 'I'm talking to these gentlemen about the shocking murder.' She was clearly enjoying the notoriety of being associated with the victim of a killer whom the newspapers were already calling the 'Palace Pier Strangler'.

The young man, unimpressed by a single death after all that he had witnessed in Flanders, nodded and silently departed.

'That'll be the major you mentioned just now, I take it?' Hardcastle queried.

'Oh yes,' said Mrs Edwards. 'Such a nice young gent. Been all through the war, you know. And he 'as medals.'

'I suppose he would have,' said Hardcastle as he stood up. 'We'll just have a dekko round her room, Mrs Edwards, and then we'll be off.'

But the room yielded nothing of interest.

Three

Mrs Kathleen Dyer – again dressed in her customary black – was already at the police station when Hardcastle and the two sergeants returned from Mrs Edwards's boarding house in Sussex Street, and Hardcastle arranged for an office in which to interview her.

'I'm sorry to have brought you all the way down here,' he began gently, 'but I'm afraid that we might have found your friend.'

'She's dead, isn't she?' said Mrs Dyer firmly. Although Hardcastle had warned Catto not to say anything to the woman about the gruesome discovery of a body under Palace Pier, it was obvious that she had guessed. Otherwise, she had thought to herself, why should the police want me to travel to Brighton?

'We're not sure it's her, Mrs Dyer. We're hoping you can help us. You see, the body of a young woman was found here on Sunday morning. She was staying at a boarding house and had given the name of Fanny Harris.'

Mrs Dyer appeared somewhat mollified by this piece of information, and breathed an audible sigh. 'Well, what d'you want with me, then?' she asked bluntly.

'But when the local police searched her room,' Hardcastle continued, 'they found a bundle of letters addressed to your friend Mrs Fanny Horwood at your Davos Street house. And a snap that was taken on the beach last Saturday afternoon.' Without moving his gaze from Mrs Dyer's face, he took the photograph from Marriott and laid it on the table. 'This snap,' he said, pushing it towards the woman with his forefinger.

Slowly, Mrs Dyer looked down, as if loath to study the photograph for fear of what it might tell her. But eventually

23

she did, and her hand went to her mouth. 'Oh, dear God!' she exclaimed. 'The poor child.' She looked up at Hardcastle, accusingly almost. 'Who could have done such a thing?'

'You're certain it's her, Mrs Dyer?' persisted Hardcastle. 'That *is* Fanny Horwood?'

'As God is my witness. It's her, I tell you. And I recognize that necklace. She never went anywhere without it.'

'I'm afraid I'm going to have to ask you to come to the mortuary to identify her,' said Hardcastle reluctantly. It was clear that the woman was upset by the death of her friend, and he guessed that to view the body would distress her even more. But he was surprised by her spirited response.

'Of course,' said Mrs Dyer sharply, and straightened her shoulders. 'I've laid out a few in my time, Inspector. I'm not shy of the sight of a dead body, even though this one's my friend, the poor dear thing.'

'Well, Mr Watson,' said Hardcastle, after he and Marriott had returned from the mortuary, and Mrs Dyer and Detective Constable Catto were on the train back to London, 'Mrs Dyer made a positive identification, so it looks as though my missing person is your murder victim. The corpse is that of Fanny Horwood.'

'I see . . .' said Watson pensively. 'So, what happens now, Mr Hardcastle?'

'What happens now, Mr Watson, is that Marriott and I go back to Cannon Row, where we shall continue our enquiries, in case there's what you might call a London connection.'

'Is there anything you want me to do?' asked the Brighton DI.

'That's a matter for you, Mr Watson. After all, it's your murder enquiry, isn't it?' said Hardcastle. 'But, as I said yesterday, I wouldn't mind putting a wager on the killer being in the Metropolitan Police District. On the other hand, she might have fallen victim to a casual murderer. Like the beach photographer,' he added archly.

'D'you really think so?'

Hardcastle shrugged. 'At the moment, your guess is as good

as mine, but I'd be inclined to give him a bit of a rough going-over,' he said. 'By the way, the jewellery . . .'

'The jewellery?' echoed Watson.

'When she went out, she was wearing a distinctive neck-lace thing, a choker I think they call it. Mrs Edwards said so, and you can see it in the snap that Hoskins took. But you said that, when she was found, she never had it on her. Nor any rings or anything like that. And no handbag, either. If I were you, I'd be looking at robbery as a motive. But no doubt your officers will already have visited the jewellers and pawn shops in Brighton, of which I note there are many, to see if anyone's tried to sell the stuff. I daresay you know the fences on your patch as well as I know them on mine.'

Once again, Watson had been caught out. 'That's in the process of being done now,' he said smoothly, making a mental note to set his officers to the task as soon as Hardcastle had left Brighton.

'I thought that might be the case,' said Hardcastle, certain that Watson had not even thought of it. 'And another thing: you might consider checking on the people who left Mrs Edwards's place on the Sunday. According to her, they all left that day, except for a young chap called Springer – she called him Major – who came in when we were talking to her. I reckon he must have been there from the previous Monday at the very least, if what Mrs Edwards said is true . . . about only taking bookings from Monday to Sunday.'

'Yes, of course,' said Watson, learning more by the moment about the investigation of murder. 'I'll get a man on to it.' And he made yet another note on his pad.

'I'll bid you good afternoon, then.' Hardcastle rose from his chair, put on his hat and coat, seized his umbrella, and made for the door. 'Come along, Marriott.' He gave one last glance at the Brighton inspector. 'No doubt we shall be in touch again, Mr Watson.'

Hardcastle was in a foul mood when he and Marriott arrived back at Cannon Row police station. 'I don't know, Marriott,' he said. 'The Brighton police don't seem to know A from a bull's foot. They could have done everything that we did if they'd got their act together. Bloody waste of two days, that was. And as for that Percy Watson, well, he wouldn't have made detective constable up here, and that's a fact. Talk about having to teach your grandmother to suck eggs.' Although he would never criticize a Metropolitan Police senior officer to a subordinate, Hardcastle had no qualms about airing his views of the incompetent Brighton inspector.

'Yes, sir,' said Marriott, in the absence of a more constructive comment. 'So, what now, sir?'

'Another word with Mrs Dyer, I think, Marriott. She seems to know what's what. First thing tomorrow morning. In the meantime, wetting our whiskers down the Red Lion wouldn't go amiss.'

The houses in Davos Street were huddled together, as though affording each other comfort and protection by their close proximity. Although clearly a poorer class of property, all the windows were sparklingly clean, the curtains freshly washed, the steps newly whitened, and the paths swept.

Mrs Dyer led the two detectives into the parlour of her house at number twenty-seven. 'I've just made a pot of tea, Inspector,' she said. 'Can I offer you a cup?'

'That's very kind of you,' said Hardcastle, gazing round the small room and noting the posed photograph of a sergeant in a khaki uniform with the black buttons of the Rifle Brigade, whom, he presumed, was the late Gerald Dyer.

Mrs Dyer went out to the kitchen, returning minutes later with a tray upon which were a lace doily, a plate of biscuits and what was clearly the best china. 'I'm glad you've come, Inspector,' she said, as she began to pour the tea. 'I've been wondering what to do with poor Fanny's things.'

'Did she have any family that you know of?' asked Hardcastle, as the woman handed him a cup of tea.

'She never mentioned any. Biscuit, Inspector?' Mrs Dyer proffered a plate of home-made ginger snaps.

'Ah, my favourites,' said Hardcastle, and took two. 'Well, it's a bit of a problem, but it would be helpful if you could hold on to them until we . . . That is to say, until . . .' Unusually for him, he found it hard to express what was in his mind.

'Until you've caught the man what did for her, you mean.'

'Yes.' Once again, Hardcastle was surprised by the woman's down-to-earth attitude to the death of her friend.

'If it helps, I don't mind keeping the stuff. There's not much of it.'

'You told Sergeant Marriott here,' said Hardcastle, 'that Mrs Horwood—' He broke off, an earnest expression on his face. 'I suppose she was *Mrs* Horwood, was she?' He had decided that there was little point in prevaricating in his dealings with the late Fanny Horwood's landlady and friend.

'She always called herself that, but as I told Mr Marriott the other day, I never heard nothing about no husband. She never mentioned one.' The woman frowned. 'Come to think of it, though, she did wear a wedding ring. Not that that means much nowadays,' she added dismissively.

'Do you happen to know how old she was, Mrs Dyer?'

'Coming up twenty-one,' said Mrs Dyer, without hesitating. 'Next January was her birthday is what she said. She made a joke of it, saying as how I'd have to give her the key of the door.' She glanced across the room, a sad expression on her face. 'But, of course, she had one already. She'd often be out late in the evening and I told her I wasn't going to wait up for her, so I gave her a key.' A sudden thought crossed her mind. 'I wonder what became of it.'

'Her handbag had been stolen when she was found,' said Hardcastle.

'Oh, glory be,' said Mrs Dyer. 'That means that whoever done for her has got a key to my house. And if her address was in her bag . . .' A worried expression crossed her face as she realized the implications of a murderer having access to her property.

'Might be as well to have the lock changed, then, not that I think you've anything to worry about, but just to be on the safe side.'

'I can't afford things like that,' said Mrs Dyer. 'I'm only a widow, you know.'

'Don't you worry, I'll arrange to have it done and the police will pay for it.' Hardcastle knew that the police fund would not reimburse Mrs Dyer for having her lock changed, but he was determined to put the woman's mind at rest somehow, even if it meant paying for it himself. 'And until it's done, I'll have a constable pay attention to your property. There, how's that?'

'That's very good of you, Inspector,' said a relieved Mrs Dyer. 'More tea?'

'Thank you.' Hardcastle handed over his cup.

'And for you, Sergeant?'

'Thank you, ma'am,' said Marriott.

'Now,' continued Hardcastle, returning to his original question once the teacups had been replenished, 'you said that Mrs Horwood had had a baby called Blanche. When would that have been?'

Mrs Dyer stared into space, calculating. 'About eight months ago, I should think. Like I said, the poor little thing died when it was two months old, from the 'flu it was, and Fanny came here straight after.'

'D'you happen to know where it was born, this child?'

'Westminster Hospital, I suppose, or it might have been the Lying-In in York Road. That's over the river in Lambeth.'

'Yes, I know where the Lying-In Hospital is,' said Hardcastle. 'Just now you said that Fanny would often be out late at night. D'you happen to know where she went on those occasions?'

'No, I don't. I just assumed that she was out enjoying herself, being a young girl.'

'You told Sergeant Marriott that you met Fanny when you were both working on the trams. When would that have been?'

'You do ask a lot of questions, Inspector,' said Mrs Dyer, as though resenting his intrusion into the affairs of her dead friend.

'I'm afraid I have to, Mrs Dyer. I've got to learn as much as I can about this poor young woman. It's the only way we policemen can get to the bottom of a crime like this.'

'Yes, I suppose so.' But Mrs Dyer did not sound wholly

convinced. 'About a year ago, I suppose. After my Gerald was killed at Arras.' She glanced briefly at the photograph on the mantelpiece. 'That was late on in 1917, September. I decided that I'd have to do something, so I got a job as a conductress on the trams out of the Bricklayer's Arms depot, and Fanny was already there. But she left after about three or four months to have the baby.'

'And did she come back? To work on the trams, I mean.'

'No.'

'So, how did you meet up again?'

'She caught up with me one day, after I'd finished the back shift, and said as how she'd been forced to leave her lodgings, and could I put her up for a while. Well, naturally, I said yes, and that's how she came to live with me.' Mrs Dyer looked wistfully at the fireplace and then stood up to poke the embers.

'And in all this time, she never mentioned a husband or a gentleman-friend . . .'

'No, never. Of course, like I said to Mr Marriott here, she might have been wed to a soldier what got himself killed, but she never mentioned no one.'

For a moment or two, Hardcastle stared thoughtfully out of the window. 'Did she pay you rent?' he asked, eventually turning back to face Mrs Dyer.

'Of course. I couldn't afford to let her live here rent-free, and feed her into the bargain.'

'So where did she get her money from? Any idea?'

'No,' said Mrs Dyer primly, 'and I never thought it my place to ask.'

'I see,' said Hardcastle. 'Incidentally, Mrs Dyer, the pathologist told us that Fanny was two months pregnant when she died.'

Kathleen Dyer looked up sharply. 'Well I never,' she said, and after a pause, added, 'Well, the little tart.'

Hardcastle got the distinct impression that Mrs Dyer was about to revise her opinion of her late lodger.

'Perhaps we might just have a look at her room before we leave.'

29

'Of course.' Mrs Dyer led them upstairs to a tiny room at the back of the house.

There was little to see. A few items of cheap clothing in a walnut wardrobe, a solitary hairbrush on the washstand, but nothing that would further the police enquiries into how she met her death.

'Well, thank you, Mrs Dyer,' said Hardcastle, as he and Marriott reached the front door. 'And I'll have someone change the lock for you before you can say—' He broke off, having been about to say 'before you can say Jack the Ripper', but decided that it would be an inapposite comment to make. 'Before you can say knife.'

Hardcastle strode down the corridor to his office, but paused as he passed the CID general office. 'Wilmot.'

'Yes, sir.' Detective Constable Fred Wilmot stood up and walked towards the door.

'You're a bit handy with tools, they tell me.'

'Done a bit of carpentry over the years, sir, yes.'

'Good. Get round to twenty-seven Davos Street and have a dekko at Mrs Dyer's front-door lock. Then get across to that locksmith in Palmer Street, get a replacement and fit it for her. All right?'

'Yes, sir,' said the vaguely mystified Wilmot. 'How shall I pay for it, sir?'

Hardcastle stared cynically at Wilmot for a moment or two before extracting two half crowns from his pocket. 'There's five shillings, lad; that should cover it.' He paused. 'And bring me the change. And a receipt.'

'What's next, sir?' asked Marriott when the two of them were back in Hardcastle's office.

'Hospitals, Marriott. I've a feeling that we might have a bit of luck if we start at the Lying-In. A more likely place for our Fanny Horwood to have had a nipper than if we try the Westminster, I'd've thought. But first, I must get on to the sub-divisional inspector at Rochester Row and ask him to warn the PC on that beat to keep an eye on Mrs Dyer's drum, at least till young Wilmot's got the lock sorted.'

The lady-almoner at the Lying-In, whom, Hardcastle thought, would be the best point of reference, was out making calls, but the matron was in her office. A severe-looking Scotswoman, her appearance, as befitted her exalted rank, was immaculate, and she had a reputation for being the scourge of her nurses, most of whom were, by her high standards, slovenly.

'Well, Inspector, and what can I do for you?' she asked, firmly closing the door of her office. She glanced at the clock over the door. 'Will you take a glass of whisky? I usually have one about now . . . for medicinal purposes,' she added, with a twinkle in her eye. The truth was that the matron had served on the Western Front earlier in the war, and had developed a liking for alcohol – if not a dire need for it – as she cared for the broken bodies of so many young soldiers.

'Thank you, Matron, most welcome,' said Hardcastle with a grin.

'And you, Sergeant?' The matron glanced at Marriott. 'Your inspector allows you the occasional drink on duty, does he?'

'Yes, ma'am,' said Marriott, overawed by the august manner of the woman.

'Well now . . .' The matron took a sip of her whisky and looked directly at Hardcastle. 'This must be an important matter to bring an inspector out.' Having mastered an understanding of the army's rank structure during her war service, she applied it as easily to the police.

'I'm investigating a murder, Matron,' Hardcastle began, and went on to explain the broad circumstances surrounding Fanny Horwood's untimely death. 'I was wondering if you had a record of the birth of a child to the woman some eight months ago.'

'I'll soon tell you.' The matron rose and, crossing to a table upon which rested a large ledger, quickly skimmed through its pages. 'No, there's no record,' she said, turning.

'Perhaps under the name of Fanny Harris, then?'

Again the matron consulted the book. 'Ah, yes, here we are. Born to Fanny Harris on the fourteenth of March 1918, a female child.'

31

'Do you have an address for this Fanny Harris?' asked Hardcastle.

'No, she was shown as of no fixed abode. There's nothing unusual in that, I can assure you. This is a charitable foundation and deals with a lot of what the commissioners euphemistically call "fallen women".' The matron smiled cynically. 'We get a lot of stupid young women here who don't know the meaning of the word "no".'

'Would the child have been named Blanche?'

'I've no idea, Inspector,' said the matron, returning to her chair and picking up her glass. 'But the registrar may be able to help you. The one who deals with births and deaths for this hospital is in the Brixton Road.'

Intent upon wasting as little time as possible, Hardcastle hailed a cab and he and Marriott made for the Lambeth office of the Registrar of Births, Deaths and Marriages.

'Yes, I have it here,' said the registrar, an ill-tempered man in his early sixties, who sounded as though assisting the police in their enquiries was an intolerable interruption in his day's work.

'Did she give an address?'

'Naturally. We insist upon it.' The registrar returned his gaze to the book. 'Number sixteen Sail Street, Lambeth. It's the next turning to Lambeth Walk off the Lambeth Road.'

'And the father's name?'

The registrar afforded Hardcastle a bleak smile. 'I'm afraid there's a blank space in my records where that should have been written, Inspector,' he said.

Four

'A thought's just occurred to me, Marriott,' said Hardcastle, as he took the first bite of a pork pie in the downstairs bar of the Red Lion in Derby Gate, hard by New Scotland Yard.

'And what might that be, sir?' Marriott ordered two pints of bitter, having given up all hope of his DDI ever buying a round of drinks.

'If our Fanny Horwood was in the habit of staying out late of an evening and somehow got herself put up the spout into the bargain, it's possible that she was on the game up West, don't you think? After all, she paid Mrs Dyer rent, and as she wasn't working on the trams any more, she must have got her sausage and mash from somewhere.'

'Sausage and mash, sir?' Sometimes Marriott found difficulty in keeping up with Hardcastle's occasional use of rhyming slang.

'Cash, Marriott, cash,' said Hardcastle.

'Oh, cash. Yes, of course,' said Marriott, finally realizing what the DDI was talking about. 'So, what are you going to do about it, sir?'

'It's a case of what *you're* going to do, Marriott,' said Hardcastle. 'Get down to Vine Street nick and have a look through the station books. See if they've any trace of a Fanny Horwood, or for that matter Fanny Harris, having been nicked for hawking her mutton on their manor. If so, Brighton's ace detective Percy Watson might find that his little murder's a bloody sight more complicated than he thought.' And, as a gloomy afterthought, added, 'Which means that much of the leg-work will doubtless fall on us.'

33

He took the head off his glass of bitter and looked sideways at his sergeant. 'Well, there's no time like the present. I'll see you back at the nick.'

'Right, sir.' Marriott finished his beer at a gulp and made for the door, grumbling quietly to himself, and longing for the day when he would be a DDI, or at the very least a detective inspector second-class.

'Oh, and another thing, Marriott . . .'

Marriott retraced his steps. 'Sir?'

'On your way, call in at Cannon Row and tell Catto to go to the War Office, and see if he can track down whether this Fanny Horwood *was* a war widow and is getting a widow's pension. It's just possible that I'm doing her wrong suggesting she might have been a tom.'

'Right.' Marriott grinned. He very much doubted that Hardcastle was too worried about ascribing prostitution to the dead woman. 'But if she has got a widow's pension, it won't be her old man who put her in the club, will it, sir?'

Unfortunately, Hardcastle's sergeant did find a trace of such an arrest, and very quickly too. He returned from Vine Street police station at three o'clock.

'She was knocked off in Half Moon Street, sir, at a quarter past ten on the evening of . . .' Marriott flicked open his pocket book. 'Of the twenty-second of June 1918, a Saturday, for soliciting prostitution. Appeared at Marlborough Street court in the name of Fanny Harris on the Monday and was fined two and sixpence.'

'Bloody marvellous,' said Hardcastle. 'And we know from the registrar that her kid, Blanche, died on the 31st of May.' He reached forward to the ashtray and picked up his pipe. 'Well, she didn't waste much time getting out on the streets and putting herself about, did she, Marriott?'

'Excuse me, sir.' DC Henry Catto appeared in the doorway.

'Don't tell me you've got good news, too, Catto?' said Hardcastle, a dour expression on his face.

'Yes and no, sir.'

'Well, spit it out, lad, it must be one or the other.'

'The chap I saw at the War Office, sir, said that he can't track down whether Mrs Horwood's got a widow's pension unless he knows what regiment her husband was in.' Catto paused. 'And he asked why we picked the War Office and not the Admiralty, sir, 'cos her old man could have been in the navy.'

'Stone the bloody crows,' muttered Hardcastle, flinging down his box of Swan Vestas matches. 'It strikes me that everyone is trying his best to put the kibosh on this job. If we don't know whether she had a husband, how the blue blazes do we know what regiment he was in? Right, Catto, go to the Ministry of Pensions. They should know . . . even if he was in the navy. Or, for that matter, the bloody marines.'

'Very good, sir,' said Catto, who was getting the impression that Hardcastle thought that the War Office's intransigence was his fault. 'Er, where is the Ministry of Pensions, sir?'

'I don't know, Catto. You're supposed to be a detective. Go and find out.'

'Yes, sir,' said the chastened Catto, rapidly retreating from both his DDI's office and his wrath.

Hardcastle pulled out his watch and examined it. 'Good time to go to Sail Street, Marriott, where our friend the registrar said Fanny Horwood was living when she gave birth.'

Sail Street was in the shadow of the London and South-Western Railway line that ran into Waterloo station, and trains constantly rumbled by, high above the backs of the humble houses. The two detectives doffed their hats as yet another hearse passed by, its occupant doubtless one of the countless victims of the influenza pandemic.

A knife-grinder removed his cloth cap and clutched it to his chest. Pausing, he nodded towards the sad little cortège. 'Another one gawn, guv'nor,' he said to Hardcastle. 'That's two this week out of this street alone. There'll be a third, you mark my words. There always is.' And with that melancholy forecast, he replaced his cap and began whistling a few bars from 'Any Old Iron?' as he carried on with his work.

'Yes, what is it?' The woman who appeared in answer to Hardcastle's knock looked suspiciously at the two men on her doorstep, half guessing what they were.

'We're police officers, madam.' Hardcastle raised his bowler hat and introduced himself. 'And this is Detective Sergeant Marriott.'

'Oh? And what would the busies be wanting with me? Not the missing Ordinary Seaman Grant again, for Gawd's sake?' asked the woman sarcastically, her arms akimbo.

'Er, no,' said Hardcastle, making a mental note to enquire into the mystery of Ordinary Seaman Grant later. 'We'd like to talk to you about Fanny Horwood, Mrs . . . ?'

'It's Mrs Grant, as if you didn't know.' She glanced sideways at a woman in a flowered apron with paper curlers in her hair who had emerged from the neighbouring house and was standing on her doorstep, arms folded, openly examining the two detectives. 'Had your eyeful?' demanded Mrs Grant truculently, and her neighbour promptly disappeared from view. 'You'd better come in, then, because that nosey cow'll have her door on the crack, earwigging, if I know her. Got nothing better to do, some people.'

'I understand that Mrs Fanny Horwood lived here until about eight months ago, Mrs Grant.' Hardcastle kept his overcoat on, and he and Marriott settled themselves in worn armchairs. There was no fire in the grate, but it was the sort of house where a fire was only lit in the parlour on Sundays, if then.

'She calls herself *Mrs* Horwood now, does she?' Mrs Grant scoffed. 'And what's Fanny been up to this time, then?' she asked.

'She's dead,' said Hardcastle bluntly; he thought it unnecessary to soften that stark statement.

'Is she now? Get her throat cut, did she?'

'No, as a matter of fact, she was strangled,' said Hardcastle, 'but you don't seem surprised.'

'No, I'm not.' Mrs Grant gave a knowing nod. 'Them as plays with fire eventually gets their fingers burnt, don't they?'

'What d'you mean by that?' asked Hardcastle, secretly amused by the woman's homespun but acerbic philosophy.

36

'She had it coming, I reckon. Playing fast and loose. She never paid no rent here, you know.'

'You mean she lived here rent-free?'

'That'd be the day,' said Mrs Grant with a mocking laugh. 'I'm not running a charity, you know. It's hard enough making ends meet now me husband's gone.'

'I'm sorry to hear that,' said Hardcastle, thinking that Mrs Grant was yet another war widow.

'Well, you needn't be, and that's a fact,' said Mrs Grant. 'Got conscripted for the navy in 1916 by Lord Derby, Gawd bless him. Nine months later he cut and run the first time his ship was back in Portsmouth. Haven't heard hair nor hide on him since. Had the police and the shore patrols round here practically every other day, but I'm hoping they'll leave it be now the war's over. Left me without a brass farthing, he did. Good riddance to bad rubbish, I say.'

'What did you mean, then, Mrs Grant, when you said that Mrs Horwood didn't pay any rent?'

'Had it paid for her, didn't she? Some fancy man come round here once a month, right up till she went into the Lying-In to have her bastard.'

'And she didn't come back?'

'Only to collect her belongings. Well, that's how it turned out, anyway. She said something about her beau – that's what she called him, toffee-nosed little cow – having come on hard times and couldn't afford to pay no more. Welcome to Queer Street, I says. First off, she asked me if she could stay on till she'd got herself fixed up, so I showed her the door. Damned cheek, I called it.'

Hardcastle, who had been trying to pose a question during this tirade, eventually managed to ask, 'D'you happen to know the name of this man who paid the rent for Mrs Horwood?'

'Yes, I do. He was called Jack Foster and he fair gave me the creeps. Right smarmy, he was, if you know what I mean. A bit of a dandy. All togged up like a dog's dinner. Curly-brimmed bowler hat, fancy waistcoat and them co-respondent shoes.'

'D'you happen to know where he lived, Mrs Grant?' asked Marriott, who, until then, had been making notes. Not that it had been worth his recording much of what the woman had said.

Mrs Grant glared at him, as if resenting a mere sergeant's intrusion into the conversation she was having with the inspector. 'No, I can't say as how I did. Although she did mention something about him being in a good way of business down Clapham Common once or twice. Said something about him being a brush maker. Well, I reckon he must have gone bottoms up, and that's why the money stopped. Course, he was married, you know.'

'Did she tell you that?' asked Hardcastle.

'No, she never. Didn't have to. You can tell, can't you?'

'And what age would this Jack Foster have been?'

'About thirty, I'd've thought,' said Mrs Grant without hesitation.

'I think we learned as much about the errant Ordinary Seaman Grant as we did about Fanny Horwood,' said Hardcastle, as he and Marriott strode into the Lambeth Road in search of a cab.

'I can't say I blame her old man for slinging his hook, sir,' said Marriott. 'A right tartar, she was.'

'No, nor me, Marriott, but we're going to have to do some searching to track down this Jack Foster merchant.' Hardcastle waved his umbrella at a cab and directed the driver to Scotland Yard. 'Half the time you tell 'em Cannon Row, you finish up at Cannon Street in the City,' he muttered.

'Yes, sir,' said Marriott, who had received this piece of advice from his DDI on almost every occasion that they had taken a cab back to the police station.

Hardcastle strode down the corridor, pausing only to summon Detective Sergeant Herbert Wood from the general office.

Taking off his hat and coat, Hardcastle settled behind his desk and lit his pipe. 'I've got a job for you, Wood,' he said. 'You and Wilmot.'

'Yes, sir.'

'Get out to Clapham Common and put yourself about, the pair of you. I'm wanting to have words with a certain Jack Foster who seems to have been Fanny Horwood's fancy man. See what you can find out.'

'Is that all we know about him, sir?' asked Wood, horrified that he had been set the task of finding a man with so ordinary a name in so large an area as Clapham Common.

'We know he's about thirty, probably married, and was in business as a brush maker,' said Hardcastle.

'D'you want him nicked, sir?' asked Wood, by no means certain that he would even find the man.

'No, I don't. I just want to know where he is, so's Marriott and me can have a chat with him. Now, off you go. No time like the present.' Hardcastle took a file from the corner of his desk. 'Now then, Marriott, what's Catto been doing about this sticky-fingered scullery maid down the Army and Navy Club in Pall Mall?'

It wasn't until Monday the eighteenth of November that Detective Sergeant Wood reported having traced Jack Foster. But during that time, Hardcastle received a telegraph from Detective Inspector Watson at Brighton, who reported that Danny Hoskins, the beach photographer, had not only been interviewed again, but that a search warrant had been executed at his mother's house in Victoria Road.

'Well, I'm buggered,' said Hardcastle, when Marriott brought him this news. 'The bold Mr Watson must have got up early that morning. Did he find anything?'

'Another photograph of Fanny Horwood, sir. This time with a man. Seems it was taken on the beach some time in August. At least, he thinks it was about then.'

'That would have been after she moved in with Mrs Dyer, then,' mused Hardcastle.

'And Hoskins said he'd never seen her before the Saturday she was done in, sir,' said Marriott.

'Oh, it hadn't slipped my memory,' said Hardcastle in a voice full of menace. 'So, are we to be allowed a sight of this

photograph, Marriott? Did the ace Inspector Watson vouch-
safe that information?'

'Yes, sir,' said Marriott. 'It arrived by this morning's post.
Mr Watson did find some other snaps as well, sir.'

Hardcastle nodded. 'Any of 'em our victim?'

'Mr Watson didn't say, sir.'

'Well, let's have a look at it, then,' said Hardcastle, taking
the photograph. 'That's Fanny Horwood right enough, Marriott,'
he said, studying the poor-quality print through a magnifying
glass, 'but the man she's with could be just about anyone. Be
interesting to see whether it's this mysterious Jack Foster.'

'We should know pretty soon, sir,' said Marriott. 'Bert
Wood's just back. He thinks he's found him.'

'Fetch him in here, then, Marriott. This is a murder enquiry,
you know. What's he doing? Swilling tea?'

Detective Sergeant Wood entered the office wiping his lips
with the back of his hand. 'You wanted me, sir?'

Hardcastle handed Wood the photograph that had just arrived
from Brighton. 'Have a look at this, Wood. Is that the Jack
Foster you've tracked down?'

'I wouldn't know, sir,' said Wood. 'I haven't actually seen
him. Me and Wilmot eventually found a boarded-up premises
in Acre Lane that had a sign saying "J. Foster, Brush Maker",
so I made a few local enquiries. Seems that Foster went bust a
couple of months back. The last they heard of him was that he
was living in Combermere Road, Stockwell. So I took a chance
and knocked on a door at random, like. They knew him all right
– they thought I was a debt collector, so I didn't put 'em wise
– and they told me he lives at number five. I never called there,
sir, because I didn't want to put my foot in it, so to speak.'

'Good work, Wood,' said Hardcastle. That grudging
acknowledgement was praise indeed from the DDI. 'Remind
me to buy you a pint some time.'

'Yes, sir, thank you, sir,' said Wood, knowing that the like-
lihood of his ever getting a drink out of Hardcastle was remote
to say the least. Not unless there was another war . . . and
another Armistice.

* * *

Hardcastle decided to waste as little time as possible, and he and Marriott called at 5 Combermere Road at four o'clock that afternoon.

The door opened cautiously and a face appeared round it. 'Yes?'

'You Jack Foster?' asked Hardcastle.

'Who wants to know?' The man peered nervously at Hardcastle and then at Marriott before returning his gaze to the inspector.

'Police,' said Hardcastle, pushing the door wide, 'and I want a few words with you, my lad.'

'Yeah, I'm Jack Foster, and if it's about them debts, well I can't pay and that's an end of it,' said the man, as he retreated into the dingy hallway.

'I'm not interested in any debts,' said Hardcastle, following Foster into a poorly furnished sitting room. 'At least, not yet. I want to know what you know about Fanny Horwood.'

'What about her?' Foster looked distinctly apprehensive.

Hardcastle wondered if the man's nervousness was a result of what the police call 'guilty knowledge', but the reason for his anxiety became obvious a moment later when a young woman entered the room.

'Er, this is my wife Lily,' said Foster.

'Mrs Foster,' murmured Hardcastle, nodding in the woman's direction.

'What's going on, Jack?' Perhaps no more than twenty-five, Lily Foster was a pretty woman who had clearly made the best of herself in the face of the Fosters' straitened circumstances; her clothing, though neat and clean, was obviously of poor quality.

'It's nothing, love,' said Foster. 'These gentlemen have come about the business. Nothing for you to worry your pretty head about. You'd best make a start on getting the tea ready.'

Lily Foster glanced suspiciously at the two detectives and then left the room. Moments later she could be heard singing in the kitchen.

'Right then, Mr Foster,' said Hardcastle, 'let's get back to Fanny Horwood, shall we?'

41

'I don't know what you want from me,' said Foster, 'I've never heard of her.'

'Is that a fact? Well, how come you paid her rent at sixteen Sail Street, Lambeth for a few months, eh?'

'Oh, you know about that, do you?'

'And a few other things besides,' said Hardcastle as he studied the man. Foster was wearing neither jacket nor collar and tie, but the neckband of his shirt was still fastened with a stud, and there was a tear in one of the sleeves. There was little now of the dandy that Mrs Grant had described, and it was obvious that Foster had indeed fallen on hard times. 'When did you last see Fanny Horwood, then?'

'Months ago.' Foster licked his lips nervously. 'She threw me over for another.'

'When exactly?'

Foster, his mind working feverishly, glanced across the room at a print of a sailing ship that adorned the wall above the fireplace. 'August Bank Holiday Monday, it was. That's when she told me she'd found someone else.'

'Did she say why she'd had enough of you? Find out you was married, did she?'

'No, nothing like that. She knew already.'

'I see,' said Hardcastle. 'And were you the father of her child, the one she called Blanche?'

Foster nodded. 'Yes, I was. We was going to get wed, see.'

'But you're married already,' said Hardcastle accusingly. 'You just introduced me to your wife Lily.'

'Well, we're not really married,' said Foster, licking his lips once again. 'Not in church, if you take my meaning.'

'Let me get this straight,' said Hardcastle. 'You're not married to Lily, but you're living with her. Nevertheless, you proposed marriage to Fanny and, on August Bank Holiday Monday, she gave you the heave-ho. Got that right, have I?'

'Yeah, that's about the strength of it. Anyway, why are you asking me all these questions about Fanny Horwood?'

'Because she's been murdered.'

'Oh, my oath!' exclaimed Foster. 'When did that happen?'

'Saturday the ninth of November . . . or Sunday the tenth, in Brighton. So, for a start, you can tell me where you were the night of Saturday the ninth.'

'Oh Gawd!' said Foster, and sank into a rexine-covered armchair, his head in his hands. 'Who could have done a thing like that to such a sweet girl?'

Hardcastle unbuttoned his overcoat and took out his pipe. 'Don't mind if I smoke, do you, Mr Foster?'

Foster looked up and shook his head. 'No, it's Liberty Hall here,' he said, appearing to collect his thoughts.

Hardcastle was convinced that the man was making up a story, but waited nevertheless. 'Well?' he said eventually.

'I was out with a woman,' said Foster at last, lowering his voice.

'A woman who was not your, er, wife Lily, I take it?'

'That's right.' Foster was looking quite wretched now.

'So, who was this woman?'

'What d'you want to know that for?' Foster looked up at Hardcastle, now leaning nonchalantly against the mantelpiece and puffing contentedly at his pipe.

'Because I want to satisfy myself that you weren't the one what murdered Fanny Horwood, Foster. There, that simple enough for you?'

'Oh, yes, I see. Can this be kept between us? I wouldn't want Lily to find out.'

'Who was she, this woman you say you spent the evening with?' demanded Hardcastle firmly, unwilling to give any undertakings of confidentiality.

'Her name's Dolly Hancock.'

'And you say you were out with her on Saturday the ninth of November. Is that right?'

'Yes.'

'And how did you explain that away to Lily?'

'I told her I had to meet someone about the business,' said Foster.

'Ah, yes, the business,' said Hardcastle, who always believed in gathering as much information as possible, whether it was relevant at the time or not. 'What about this business of yours? I'm told you went bust.'

'It was the bloody war,' said Foster savagely.

'What's the war got to do with it?'

'When it started, in 1914, I landed a contract for the army, making brushes. Boot brushes, scrubbing brushes and brooms, see. Well, that all went along tickety-boo until about last July. Then some stuck-up War Office bloke – from Hounslow, he said he was – come down to Acre Lane and said they didn't want no more brushes. He said the war was coming to an end and that the army had more brushes than you could shake a stick at. Well, I never had no other outlets, 'cos everything I made went to the army, and they was selling off their surplus, cheap like, so that was me done for.' Foster let out a loud sigh at the unfairness of the world in general and the War Office in particular.

'Bad luck,' said Hardcastle.

'And where did you go on Saturday the ninth, Mr Foster?' Marriott looked up from his pocket book.

'Eh?' Foster was clearly surprised at the sergeant's intervention. 'Er, we was down the King's Arms in Stockwell Road, Dolly and me. Often in there. The guv'nor knows me well. Ask him.'

'We shall, Mr Foster,' said Hardcastle. 'Don't you worry about that. And while you're about it, you can tell me where this Dolly Hancock lives.'

'I don't rightly know, and that's the truth,' said Foster. 'We always meets at the pub, see.'

'That's all right, then,' said Hardcastle. 'Well, we won't keep you any longer.' But at the door, he paused. 'Why weren't you in the army, Foster?'

'I was exempt, being a brush maker an' all. Anyhow, I've got a dickey heart.'

Hardcastle nodded. 'Yes,' he said, 'I can believe that.'

The two detectives walked back up Combermere Road, Hardcastle swinging his umbrella in a quite jocular fashion.

'Well, sir, d'you believe him?'

'You know me, Marriott,' said Hardcastle. 'I never believe anyone, but I think he's probably a cut-price stage-door johnny, and a white-feather man to boot. But we'll see.'

Five

Walking out into Stockwell Road, Hardcastle took out his treasured hunter and clicked open the cover. 'Just gone six o'clock, Marriott. About the right time to go across to the King's Arms and have a chat with the landlord, I think. See if this alibi of Foster's holds water. Doubtless the beer at the King's Arms will. It ain't much of a stride down there, so we'll walk it. Do us good.'

The street was full of people hurrying home from work before another of London's acrid fogs descended on the capital. Paperboys cried their usual headlines of doom – although people were not so interested in the news now that the war was over – and a one-legged man with a row of medals on his chest leaned heavily on his crutches and offered matches for sale.

Pausing to avoid a passing tram, the two detectives crossed the road, and Hardcastle took out the photograph that DI Watson had sent from Brighton. 'It's definitely him, Marriott,' he said. 'That's Jack Foster right enough. When did Mr Watson say that Hoskins claims to have taken it?'

'He said August this year, sir, but he wasn't too sure.'

'Not too sure of anything, that one,' muttered Hardcastle. 'When we get back to the nick, be so good as to send a telegraph to Brighton, and suggest to Mr Watson that now we've tracked down Fanny's fancy man in the shape of Jack Foster, he might like to come up to the Smoke and have a chat with him. After all, Fanny Horwood got topped on his manor, not ours. I don't mind giving him a handout, but there's a limit, you know.'

'I'll get that sent off as soon as we get back, sir.'

46

'Foster said that it was August Bank Holiday that Fanny Horwood told him she'd found someone else,' mused Hardcastle, examining the photograph once more. 'You'd better mention that to Mr Watson, otherwise he won't see the relevance of the date that Hoskins said he took this. She's looking a bit too lovey-dovey in this here snap for a woman who's just told Foster she was throwing him over. There's something amiss here, Marriott. Either Foster's lying or Hoskins is. And Hoskins reckoned that November was the first time he'd seen her. Now, if he liked the look of her in November, he must have remembered seeing her in August, don't you think? Put a bit in that telegraph suggesting that Mr Watson asks Hoskins how many other photographs he took on the ninth of November. I think Master Hoskins may know more than he's telling,' he added reflectively. 'He's already admitted taking a shine to Fanny the last time he snapped her, and if the killing *was* down to him, he might just have realized that he'd said too much already. We've only his word for it that he didn't take her for a drink after all. Could be that they had an argument at some stage and he did for her in a rage. And it might have had something to do with her being pregnant. Maybe by Danny Hoskins.'

'Anything else, sir?' asked Marriott.

'Not for the telegraph, no.' Hardcastle took out the other photograph, the one that Hoskins said he had taken in November. 'Frankly, I can't see a beach photographer being out looking for trade on a cold November day, Marriott. Supposing he'd arranged to meet Fanny on the beach. He takes her picture – he probably always takes his camera, just in case – and then they goes off together. We still don't know why she decided to go to Brighton all on her own, do we? There's something a bit fishy about all this, Marriott. Something very fishy indeed.'

As they reached the gloomy Victorian public house where Foster said that he had spent the evening of the ninth of November in the company of Dolly Hancock, they heard the sound of a piano accompanying a raucous chorus of 'It's a Long Way to Tipperary'.

47

'Sounds like they're still celebrating the Armistice, Marriott,' said Hardcastle, pushing open the door of the saloon bar and sweeping aside the red velour curtain. A thick pall of tobacco smoke hung beneath the brown-stained ceiling. 'And I reckon that joanna needs a bit of tuning, an' all.'

To Marriott's surprise, Hardcastle not only ordered two pints of best bitter but paid for them.

The landlord himself served the two detectives. He was a large man with a flowing moustache and a ruddy complexion, and his shirtsleeves were rolled to the elbow.

'Sounds as though they're enjoying themselves,' said Hardcastle, nodding towards the public bar, which was crowded with singing soldiers and sailors and their women-folk.

'They won't be so cheerful when they finds there ain't no jobs for them, guv'nor,' said the landlord. 'And there'll be hundreds more coming out of the munitions factories looking for work, too. I get about three a day in here, looking for a barman's job.'

'I'm Divisional Detective Inspector Hardcastle,' said the DDI, leaning closer to the landlord.

'What's happened to George Lambert, then?' The landlord expressed no surprise at being visited by the police.

'Know him, do you?'

'Comes in from time to time,' said the landlord, folding his arms and leaning on a mahogany-topped bar that was scarred with cigarette burns.

'He's still there.' Hardcastle knew the DDI of L Division, whose headquarters were at Brixton. 'I'm from Cannon Row, across the river.'

'So, what brings you down here, then, guv'nor?' The landlord pulled two more pints and placed them on the bar in front of the policemen. 'On the house,' he murmured.

'Thanks,' said Hardcastle. 'As a matter of fact, I'm interested in a man called Jack Foster—'

'That reckons.' The landlord let out a derisive hoot of laughter. 'Don't tell me he owes you money as well.'

'Not a chance,' said Hardcastle. Beside him, Marriott silently
agreed. 'Come in here often, does he?'

'Aye, as and when he's got cash, which ain't often now, I
can tell you. What's he been up to, then, thieving?'

'Not that I know of, although it wouldn't surprise me,' said
Hardcastle.

'No, nor me, neither.'

'He claims he was in here the night of Saturday the ninth
of November with a doxy called Dolly Hancock.'

'Hold on.' The landlord turned and took a small book from
behind the till. 'Yes, he was,' he said. 'He put half a dollar
on his slate that night and I always gets them what does to
sign me book just in case they try coming the artful later on.'

'And this Dolly Hancock was with him, was she?'

'He had a woman with him, but I don't know who she was.
Looked like a tart, but it's a bit difficult when they come in
with a bloke, see. I reckon she was on the game all right, and
you know the rules about licensees harbouring prostitutes better
than I do, guv'nor.'

'Yes, well, I'm not too worried about that,' said Hardcastle.
'Right now, I've got bigger fish to fry.'

'What's he been up to, then?' the landlord asked again as
he gave the bar a cursory wipe with a cloth and then glanced
left and right to make sure his barmaids were not idling and
gossiping.

'It may be nothing,' said Hardcastle, unwilling to tell the
landlord that Foster was one of a number of suspects for
murder. 'D'you happen to remember what time he left?'

The landlord folded his arms again and leaned back slightly,
sucking through his teeth. 'It must have been about half-past
six that he went. Least, that's when I served him, and I don't
recall having seen him after.'

Hardcastle glanced at his sergeant. 'Got the photograph
there, Marriott?'

'Yes, sir.' Marriott produced the November photograph and
showed it to the landlord. 'Was that the woman Foster was
with?' he asked.

If Fanny Horwood was the girl that Foster had been with,

49

it would have meant that she had travelled up from Brighton and returned there that evening. And if that was the case, Foster would have a lot of questions to answer. But Hardcastle realized, straight away, that if that was what had happened, then both Danny Hoskins and Mrs Edwards had been lying. With Hoskins it was likely, but Mrs Edwards would not profit by failing to tell the truth.

The landlord took the print and studied it closely. 'No,' he said eventually, 'nothing like her.' He handed it back. 'D'you want me to ask around, guv'nor? See if anyone knows who she was.'

'No thanks,' said Hardcastle, downing his second pint. 'I think I know where I can find her.' He had decided that Foster had not been telling the truth when he had told the detectives that he did not know where Dolly Hancock lived, and determined to have another talk with the bankrupt brush maker.

Marriott had sent off Hardcastle's telegraph the moment they had returned to Cannon Row police station, and the Brighton inspector's reply arrived during the night.

'Mr Watson says he's too tied up with other matters to come himself, sir,' said Marriott, proffering the telegraph form.

'I wouldn't've thought that Brighton was the murder capital of the world somehow, Marriott,' said Hardcastle mildly. 'So, what *did* he say?'

'He's sent Detective Sergeant Goodenough, sir. He's the chap who came with us to Mrs Edwards's place.'

'That'll probably serve us better,' said Hardcastle. 'Has the makings, does that lad.'

'He asks if we can find some accommodation for him, sir.'

'Yes, all right. Get him fixed up in Ambrosden section house,' said Hardcastle, referring to the single policemen's quarters in the shadow of Westminster Cathedral. 'When's he arriving?'

'He's here already, sir. Arrived first thing this morning.'

'Did Mr Watson say anything about the other matters, Marriott?'

'Yes, sir. He says that the other matters are being looked into.'

'And he won't be doing that in a hurry,' muttered Hardcastle. 'Where's Goodenough now?'

'Outside, sir.' Marriott opened the door and beckoned to the Brighton sergeant to come in.

'Ah, Goodenough,' said Hardcastle, as the young detective nervously entered the DDI's office, 'now's your chance to shine. Sergeant Marriott here will tell you what's happened so far, then you can decide what you want to do next. It's the Brighton force's murder, after all.'

Goodenough was already overawed at being so close to New Scotland Yard, and was honest enough to admit that he had a lot to learn about murder. 'I've not been long promoted, sir,' he said, 'so, if it's all right, I'd rather be guided by you. Charlie Marriott was just telling me how many murders you've investigated.'

Hardcastle gazed at the young detective, wondering whether he was trying to flatter him into doing the work of the Brighton police for them. Eventually he decided that the young sergeant opposite him was more naïve than cunning. 'You stick by me, lad,' he said, 'and you'll learn a thing or two, and that's a fact.' He turned his attention to Marriott. 'I think it might be a good idea if you and Goodenough went across to Stockwell and brought Foster in here for a chat, Marriott. We'll give him a bit of a hard going-over, because I'm not too sure he's coming across.'

'Right, sir,' said Marriott, accustomed to the ways of his DDI.

Goodenough was quite startled at this course of action – and the way in which Hardcastle had ordered it – but had been assured by Marriott that the DDI was a very astute detective and knew what he was doing. He certainly found it a refreshing change from the vacillating ways of Detective Inspector Watson of the Brighton Borough Police.

When the two sergeants had departed, Hardcastle sent for DC Catto. 'What have you found out from the Ministry of Pensions, then, Catto?' he asked.

'There's no record of a Mrs Fanny Horwood or a Mrs Fanny Harris being in receipt of a war-widow's pension, sir.'

'Well, that blows that,' said Hardcastle phlegmatically, 'although I can't say it comes as a surprise. Right, then, I've got another job for you. Get across to Somerset House, as fast as you like – in fact, take a cab – and find out if Jack Foster is married to a Lily Foster. He's about thirty and she's about twenty-five. Well, don't dally, lad, get on with it.'

'Right, sir.'

Catto might have been surprised at being given authority to take a cab, but Hardcastle was even more surprised to receive another telegram from Brighton, or more particularly, at what that telegram contained. He put on his spectacles and skimmed through it:

TO DDI HARDCASTLE A DIV METROPOLITAN
FROM DI WATSON A DIV BRIGHTON BOROUGH
POLICE
A WITNESS HAS COME FORWARD STATING
THAT SHE SAW DANNY HOSKINS WHOM SHE
KNOWS TALKING TO A WOMAN BELIEVED
FANNY HORWOOD AT ABOUT 5 PM ON
SATURDAY 9 NOVEMBER IN KINGS RD JUST
ABOVE BEACH NEAR WEST ST + STOP + THEY
APPEARED TO BE ARGUING + STOP + END

'Yes, well, that's all very interesting, but what does he want me to do about it?' asked Hardcastle of Detective Constable Wilmot, who had brought him the telegraph form.

'I don't rightly know, sir,' said Wilmot, unsure whether Hardcastle was actually seeking his advice or just thinking aloud.

'Well, I do, lad. Send him a wire asking him what Hoskins had to say about it all. He's a carney little bastard is that beach photographer, and I reckon he knows something.' But, as Wilmot reached the door, Hardcastle called him back. 'Before you do that, lad, get across to records office in the Yard and see if you can find any previous convictions for Foster. And while you're about it, do a check on Danny Hoskins of Brighton. Don't know why I didn't think of it sooner,' he added, half to himself.

Marriott returned at half past ten. 'Jack Foster's downstairs in the interview room, sir,' he said, 'and Wilmot says to tell you that he was convicted of larceny at the end of 1917. Got a carpet.' He handed the DDI a file.

'If he was in the nick for three months, that probably explains why his business went bust,' said Hardcastle. 'I don't reckon it had anything to do with this toff from the War Office he was on about.'

'And Catto found a record of Foster having got wed,' Marriott continued. 'Seems he married a Lily Morgan on the thirteenth of April 1918.'

'Well, well. So, what's he playing at?' Hardcastle opened Foster's criminal record file and glanced briefly at the photograph before standing up. 'Get hold of young Goodenough and we'll go and have another chat with our Mr Foster. The sooner we get this Brighton job sorted out the better. We're wasting too much time on it.'

Jack Foster was clearly apprehensive at having been brought peremptorily to Cannon Row police station. He was sitting huddled in the austere room where the police usually carried out their initial interrogations prior to the suspect being charged and placed in a cell, as he knew only too well.

'You told me yesterday that you were in the King's Arms on Saturday the ninth of November.' Hardcastle sat down on the hard wooden chair opposite Foster and lit his pipe. 'What time would that have been?'

'Er, I'll have to think about that.' Foster rubbed his forehead just above his right eyebrow with the knuckle of his thumb.

'Well, don't waste too much time thinking about it, cully,' said Hardcastle, filling the small room with tobacco smoke.

'I think I left there about nine, guv'nor. Maybe half past.'

'Did you put anything on the slate that night?'

'Yes, I did, as a matter of fact,' said Foster, licking his lips. 'Half a dollar.'

'And what time would that have been?'

Again Foster paused. 'About then, I think. About nine.'

Hardcastle recalled that the landlord had told him that he had last seen Foster at about half past six, at which time Foster had signed his book for the two shillings and sixpence credit he had been granted. But he did not tell Foster that. 'And where did you go from the King's Arms?'

'I went home.'

'Did you now? And your Lily will vouch for that, will she?'

'You don't have to ask her, do you?' Foster was clearly alarmed by that question.

'I hope you haven't forgotten that I'm investigating the murder of Fanny Horwood, the woman whose child you fathered, Foster, and I'll ask any questions I like of who I like. And if it buggers up your love life, well, that's hard luck, ain't it?'

'I don't know nothing about poor Fanny getting herself murdered, guv'nor, I swear it. In fact, when we split up, back in August, she give me a letter from a bloke called Sidney Mason.'

'And what did this letter have to say?' asked Hardcastle, tamping down his tobacco with a finger and cursing as he burned it.

'It said that he and Fanny had decided to get married and they was moving to the continent – France, it said – and they was going to set up house there.'

'Is that a fact? And have you still got this letter?'

'It's at home.'

'Why didn't you tell me about it yesterday when I called at Combermere Road?'

'It was a bit awkward, what with my Lily being there, guv'nor, and I forgot I'd got it, so help me.'

'So, if I send Sergeant Marriott to collect it, he'll be able to find it, will he?'

'I'd rather you didn't do that,' said Foster hurriedly. 'If my Lily—'

'Your Lily's not daft,' said Hardcastle. 'If I know women, she'll have cottoned on to your capers. All right, when Sergeant Marriott takes you back to Combermere Road, you'll be able to find this letter, will you?'

'Yes,' said Foster. 'Then you'll see I'm telling you the truth.'

'And who is this . . . what did you say his name was?'

Hardcastle had not forgotten the name, but from time to time found it useful to give suspects the impression that he was not too bright.

'Sidney Mason,' said Foster promptly.

'And where does he live?'

'I don't know,' whined Foster. 'I never met him. I asked Fanny but she wouldn't tell me. I think she thought I'd go round and duff him up.'

'And would you have done?' asked Hardcastle, an amused expression on his face. In his opinion, the puny Foster would not have been able to fight his way out of a paper bag. 'What with you having a dickey heart an' all.'

'Well, I was pretty cut up about Fanny giving me the elbow, I can tell you.'

'You ever been in trouble with the police before, Foster?' asked Hardcastle.

'No, never.' Foster looked around the interview room, at its forbidding, brown-painted walls and its high, barred windows, as though it was all new territory to him.

'Now then,' said Hardcastle, reverting to his earlier line of questioning, 'you said you went straight home from the King's Arms on the night of the ninth of November, but you didn't want me to ask your Lily. Having said you'd told her you were out on business, I find that a bit of a puzzle.'

Foster raised his hands in an attitude of surrender. 'I spent the night with Dolly Hancock,' he said, finally admitting defeat.

'In that case, it'd be in your interests to tell me where she lives, so I can check your story.'

Foster let out a long sigh of resignation and gave Hardcastle an address in Clapham.

'That's all right, then,' said Hardcastle, standing up. 'Looks to me like it's just bad luck, you having got mixed up in all this. I'll get Sergeant Marriott to take you back to Stockwell and you can give him this letter from . . .'

'Sidney Mason, guv'nor,' said Foster.

'Ah, yes . . . Sidney Mason,' said Hardcastle slowly, and took a moment to rekindle his pipe. 'And that should be that. I daresay this is the last we'll be seeing of each other.' He glanced at the Brighton sergeant, who, throughout Hardcastle's questioning, had remained silent in the corner. 'Come along, Goodenough, there's work to be done.'

A relieved Foster was escorted out of the station by Marriott, whom Hardcastle had told to take a cab, and Hardcastle and Goodenough mounted the stairs to the DDI's office.

'Well, lad, and what did you make of that?' asked Hardcastle.

'Looks like Foster's a victim of circumstance, sir.'

'Circumstance be buggered,' said Hardcastle vehemently. 'It's all my eye and Betty Martin. The lying little bugger's got a previous for thieving *and* he's married and churched to the woman he claims he's only living with, both of which he's denied.'

'But why didn't you tell him you knew, sir?' asked the mystified Goodenough.

'Don't do to let on too much about what you know, Goodenough. Helps to catch 'em wrong-footed, if you take my drift.'

'Oh!' said Goodenough, who was learning more of crime detection in the Metropolis by the moment. 'But what about this Sidney Mason, sir?'

'Yes, Goodenough, what indeed? Looks as though we're going to have to find him, don't it?'

'But where do we start looking, sir?'

'There's ways and means, Goodenough, ways and means.' In truth, Hardcastle had no idea where to begin such a search. But, on reflection, he added, 'Maybe the shipping offices at

Dover might be a start. For all we know, Sidney Mason might have been the one who topped Fanny Horwood and then ran.'

Six

'Is that it, then, Marriott?' Hardcastle fingered the single sheet of paper that comprised the letter Foster claimed Fanny Horwood had received from Sidney Mason. 'No envelope?'

'No, sir. Foster said that Fanny hadn't given it to him.'

'How convenient,' said Hardcastle. 'So, we've only got his word for it when he says that she showed it to him in August. If we had an envelope, we'd've had a postmark.' He put on his spectacles and unfolded the paper. 'And there's no date on the letter itself, let alone an address.' Putting it to his nose, he sniffed. 'No scent, neither. A bit unusual when a woman's handled it. Anyway, let's see what it says. "My dearest Fanny,"' he began, '"I know that parting from Jack was a wrench, particularly as he was poor little Blanche's father. But I understand your feelings when you say that you couldn't go on after her death, what with Jack saying that he wasn't going to leave Lily after all. Some men can be so selfish, but I'm not one of them, Fanny, dearest. You'll be pleased to know that I've been across to the Continent and found us a lovely little place not far from Calais. I'm sure we'll be very happy there and out of Jack Foster's way for good. Your ever loving Sidney."' Hardcastle placed the letter in the centre of his desk. 'Well, that don't mean much, at least not until we find this Sidney Mason. Not that we even know it's Mason, being signed just Sidney.'

'Goodenough said you were thinking of the shipping offices at Dover, sir,' said Marriott.

'Yes, I did. But on second thoughts, Victoria station will do as well. Get Catto to go down there and have a word with the continental booking office people. See if a Sidney Mason's ever booked a passage, say from the beginning of the year.'

'I'll get him on to that right now, sir.' Marriott turned to leave and then paused. 'By the way, sir, Wilmot eventually came up with a record for Hoskins.'

'Did he now? And?'

'Middle of 1916, he was done for false pretences. He'd pretend to take photographs of couples on the beach or in the town, usually of soldiers and their girls, and promise to post them on. He'd take their money but they never got the pictures.' Marriott looked up from the file he was holding and grinned. 'Probably on account of his not having any film in the camera. Seems he reckoned on them being over the other side and either dead and buried, or too busy to bother. Well, a couple did bother and the town magistrates weighed him off six months. They said it was scurrilous, him taking advantage of brave fighting men like that.'

Hardcastle laughed. 'Serve the little bugger right,' he said. 'Come to think of it, why wasn't he in the army himself? Seemed a fit enough young fellow.'

'There was something about that in his antecedent history, sir,' said Marriott. 'Seems he got called for enlistment just before he went into clink, but he told the Brighton investigating officer that they'd turned him down on the medical because he had flat feet.'

'Yes, and Kaiser Bill's my uncle,' said Hardcastle. 'I reckon that Brighton lot'd believe anything Hoskins told 'em.' He picked up Sidney Mason's letter again. 'I'll tell you what, Marriott, get Goodenough to talk to his guv'nor at Brighton and ask him if any of the letters that were found among Fanny Horwood's effects were from Foster. If so, get him to send one up here and we'll have a look at the handwriting. See if they match. I think there's a bloke across at the Yard who's a dab hand at that sort of thing.' He put the letter in the drawer of his desk. 'Pity we can't get fingerprints off of paper,' he mused wistfully. He stood up and donned his Chesterfield overcoat and bowler hat. 'Time to have a chat with Dolly Hancock, I reckon, Marriott.'

*   *   *

The woman with whom Jack Foster claimed to have spent the night of the ninth of November lived in a seedy street off Clapham Common.

'You'd better come in, then,' said Dolly, when Hardcastle announced that they were police officers, and walked back into the sitting room, leaving him to close the front door and follow.

'You know Jack Foster, I believe?' said Hardcastle.

'No law against it, is there?' Surly of manner and probably no more than twenty-one years of age, Dolly Hancock was dressed in a loose-fitting peignoir of artificial silk with a V-neck so deep that if Hardcastle's daughter Kitty had appeared in such a garment, Mrs Hardcastle would have had a few strong words to say to her.

'Do you recall the Saturday night before Armistice Day?' asked Hardcastle. 'That'd be the ninth.' He noticed that a half bottle of Gordon's gin was standing on the sideboard along with a dirty glass.

'What about it?' Although it was two o'clock in the afternoon, Dolly Hancock looked as though she had just tumbled out of bed.

'Can you remember where you spent that evening?'

'What business is it of yours?' demanded Dolly.

'I'm investigating a murder and that *makes* it my business,' said Hardcastle.

'Oh!' Dolly did not seem in the least surprised by this revelation, and Hardcastle was certain that Foster had warned her that she would be receiving a visit from the police. 'Matter of fact, I was out with Jack that night. Down the King's Arms in Stockwell.'

'And what time did you leave there?'

Dolly affected a thoughtful expression, as though she had difficulty in recalling exactly what had happened that night. 'About nine, maybe half past,' she said eventually. 'What's this all about? Is Jack in some sort of trouble?'

'And where did you go from there?'

'Come home here, of course.' Dolly cast a longing glance at the gin bottle.

'Alone?'

'Of course. What d'you take me for?'

'I see.' Hardcastle made a point of looking at Marriott. 'You are noting all this down, Marriott, aren't you?' he asked. 'Because it's evidence.'

'Yes, sir.' Marriott glanced up from his pocket book. He and his DDI had played this game before.

'Good.' Hardcastle switched his gaze back to Dolly. 'And you're sure about that, are you, Miss Hancock?'

'Why? What did Jack say?'

'He said he spent the night in your bed. With you.'

'Oh, that's nice, ain't it? I've got a reputation to think about, you know.'

Hardcastle thought that it was a little late for Dolly to be thinking about her reputation. 'Well?'

'Yes, as a matter of fact, he did, but he don't have to go about shouting it from the rooftops, do he?'

'And would you be prepared to swear to that in court?'

'Now just you hold on, mister,' said Dolly, giving a credible impression of being alarmed at the prospect, and Hardcastle wondered whether the girl had had any acting experience. 'What's all this about court? I ain't going to no court.'

'If I have a witness summons served on you, then you'll go to court,' said Hardcastle mildly.

'Do what you like, but you can't make me say nothin', even if I'm there. I knows me rights, you know.'

'So, what you're really saying is that you can't be certain whether you did spend the night with Jack Foster. As you're not prepared to swear to it.'

'Oh, I'm certain all right. When a girl's had that Jack Foster in her bed, she won't easily forget what he—' But Dolly obviously thought better of completing the sentence, and the two detectives were never to discover her opinion of Jack Foster's merit, or otherwise, as a lover, or what perversions he might have practised.

'Very well,' said Hardcastle, 'I think that's all.' He paused. 'For the moment.'

Back in the street, the two detectives strode swiftly along Old Town and into The Pavement. 'We'll get the underground, Marriott,' said Hardcastle. 'It'll be quicker.'

'That Dolly seemed a right tart, sir,' said Marriott.

'Yes, and I wouldn't mind wagering they know her at Clapham nick, too. Be as well if you found out, when you've got time. What's more, there's no doubt in my mind that Jack Foster's spoken to her and told her what to say when we turned up. Still, no more than I expected.'

As the two men reached Clapham Common station, Hardcastle tossed a halfpenny at a newsvendor and picked up a copy of the early edition of the *Star*. 'I wondered how long it'd be before Fleet Street got a hold of it, Marriott.' Hardcastle half turned the newspaper so that his sergeant could see the headlines:

**BRIGHTON MURDER: YARD CALLED IN.
ENQUIRIES SWITCH TO LONDON.**

'Is that going to help us, d'you think, sir?' asked Marriott.

'Your guess is as good as mine, Marriott. But it's all here. They obviously know we've seen Jack Foster and they'll have sent a stringer down to Brighton, because there's a bit about us having had a go at Danny Hoskins, and there's a photograph of him taking photographs.' Hardcastle chuckled at the irony of that. 'It's an old snap, too, because the beach is crowded. Got that from the local rag most likely.' He folded the paper and tucked it under his arm. 'Which reminds me. When we get back to the nick, get on to Mr Watson at Brighton and ask him if he's interviewed Hoskins about that witness who said she'd seen him having an argument with a woman on the seafront the day before Fanny's body was found.'

But later that evening there occurred an incident that was to take Hardcastle's mind off the murder of Fanny Horwood. For the moment.

Marriott had been summoned to the front office of Cannon

Row police station to interview a man who wished to complain that he had been the victim of a crime.

The man was tall, well dressed, and was about fifty years of age. His appearance implied that he was from the monied strata of society.

'Good evening, sir. Please sit down. How can I help you?'

The man remained standing. 'Are you the officer in charge of the CID here?' he asked.

'No, I'm Detective Sergeant Marriott.'

'I see. Well, I'd rather talk to the man in charge. It is a serious matter.'

'I can assure you that I—'

'The officer in charge, please.' The man's haughty demeanour made it obvious that he was not going to make do with a mere underling.

'Very well, sir. If you'd care to wait a moment, I'll see if he's available.' Marriott was quite accustomed to this attitude among people of substance who thought that the crimes they had suffered were so important that only the top man could deal adequately with them. But he derived some pleasure from being fairly certain that the man thought he was at Scotland Yard, a mistake frequently made by callers at the police station immediately opposite the headquarters of the Metropolitan Police.

Hardcastle came down from his office and walked into the interview room. 'I'm Divisional Detective Inspector Hardcastle,' he said. 'I understand that you wish to report a crime.'

'You *are* the officer in charge of the CID, are you?'

'Yes, I am. Won't you sit down, Mr . . . ?'

'Stevenson. Alderman Richard Stevenson.'

'And where do you sit as an alderman?' Hardcastle sat down and took out a pen.

Stevenson hesitated, as though the question was irrelevant. 'The City of Westminster,' he said eventually.

'And your profession, Alderman?' Hardcastle asked as he began to make notes.

'I'm a stockbroker.'

63

Hardcastle put down his pen and looked up. 'And what exactly d'you wish to tell me, Alderman?'

Stevenson produced a copy of that morning's *Daily Chronicle* and pointed to a photograph on the front page. It was a photograph of Dolly Hancock, taken at her front door in Clapham. 'I'm fairly certain that this is the woman who was with the man who blackmailed me, Inspector,' he said.

'I see,' said Hardcastle. 'Can you be sure?'

'As sure as one can be, given the poor quality of this photograph.'

'Perhaps you'd tell me the circumstances, then.'

For the first time since his arrival at the police station, some of the man's hauteur ebbed away. 'I'm afraid I've been rather foolish, Inspector.' Stevenson paused, as though wondering, even now, whether he could bring himself to recount the whole sordid tale.

'It happens to everyone at some time or another,' said Hardcastle, in an attempt to encourage the man to speak out. Anything concerning Dolly Hancock was of great interest to him.

'I got embroiled with this woman, I'm afraid. She's a prostitute.'

'Yes, I know,' said Hardcastle, certain that his statement was not too wide of the truth.

'You know?' Stevenson raised his eyebrows.

'I've had dealings with her.'

'Oh, of course, this Brighton murder. It's all here in the paper, how you interviewed her and so on.'

'Shall we concentrate on *your* problem, Alderman?' Hardcastle was irritated that the press seemed to be dogging his every footstep.

'Yes, of course. I'm afraid I, er, allowed myself to be picked up by her one night. I'd been to a lodge meeting in St James's Street and foolishly decided to walk across St James's Park to Victoria station. I usually take a cab all the way, but I'd had a few drinks, you see, and I thought it'd clear my head. If only I'd taken a cab *that* night, none of this would have happened.' Stevenson looked ruefully at Hardcastle, as though trying to invoke his sympathy.

'Yes, go on,' said Hardcastle, who was never surprised at the stupidity of otherwise quite sensible and respectable men.

'I went with her to her rooms – they were somewhere off Victoria Street – and, well, I, er—'

'You bedded her,' said Hardcastle, determined not to let the man down too lightly.

'Well, yes.'

'And then she found out that you were an alderman, a freemason and a stockbroker.'

'That was silly of me,' said Stevenson, staring at the scarred surface of the table, 'but I'm afraid I let it slip.'

Hardcastle briefly wondered how it was that Stevenson had let slip all three elements of his status. 'So, she decided to put the squeeze on you or she'd tell your wife. You are married, I take it?' To Hardcastle it was a familiar tale.

'Yes, I am, but that wasn't quite what happened. Actually it was worse than that. Just as we had, well, just as we'd finished, the door burst open and this man appeared. He was in a frightful rage and said that he was the woman's husband.' Stevenson was clearly embarrassed at relating the story.

'Oh dear,' said Hardcastle, resisting the urge to smile. 'So, what happened then?'

'He was a rough sort of fellow, her husband, and he said that unless I stumped up fifty pounds, he'd take me to court. He said that he'd sue his wife for divorce and cite me as co-respondent. Then the wretched woman burst into tears and said that she hadn't been willing. It was a nightmare, Inspector, I can tell you.'

'And so you paid him?'

'I didn't see that I had any alternative. The scandal would have destroyed me completely. I mean to say, being cited by a man of one's own class is one thing, but for the husband of a prostitute to do so would be ruinous, especially as the damned woman was then suggesting that I'd, er, more or less raped her. Anyhow, he arranged to meet me the following day, outside my bank in Piccadilly, to collect the money.'

'And when did all this happen, Alderman?'

'Last July.'

'Why, then, have you waited so long to report it to the police?'

'I didn't know who she was.'

'But you just told me that you'd been to her house.'

'Yes, I know,' said Stevenson, 'but as I said, I was slightly tipsy and it was dark. I had a walk round the area a few days later and I couldn't find the house where she'd taken me.'

'Did she give you her name?'

'Only that it was Dolly, but there are thousands of women called Dolly in London, probably in Victoria, too. It wasn't until I saw the paper this morning that I realized that she was the woman.'

'I see. Well, the position is this, Alderman. It would seem, from what you tell me, that this woman has committed an offence under the Larceny Act of 1916. I can arrest her and charge her with conspiring with another to demand money with menaces. I can also make an attempt to find her husband – if, in fact, he is her husband – and charge him similarly. However, that would mean that you'd probably have to attend an identification parade, and you'd certainly have to give evidence at the Old Bailey.'

'But I couldn't possibly do that,' said the alarmed alderman.

'Your identity would be protected, Alderman. These cases are always dealt with sympathetically. You'd be known as Mr X.' Hardcastle sat back and awaited the man's decision.

Stevenson lapsed into deep thought for a few moments. 'All right,' he said eventually. 'If you can guarantee my anonymity.'

'I can certainly guarantee *that*,' said Hardcastle, 'although I can't guarantee that nothing will appear in the newspapers. But you can rest assured that they won't name you. Otherwise they'd be guilty of contempt of court, for which there is a heavy penalty, and it's always possible that in serious cases the editor would be sent to prison. It's not a chance they're prepared to take.' Although Stevenson had already agreed to give evidence, Hardcastle felt that he had to point out the pitfalls.

'Very well, then, Inspector,' said Stevenson. 'I'll have to put my trust in you.'

'Good.' Hardcastle stood up. 'I'll have my sergeant take a statement from you, then.'

'But I thought that you'd be dealing with this,' said Stevenson.

'Alderman,' said Hardcastle, gazing down at the still-seated Stevenson. 'I am the officer *in charge* of the CID on this division. Be so good as to allow me to direct which of my officers should do what.'

Fanny Horwood's bundle of letters – there were six of them – arrived by first post the following day and Hardcastle spread them out on his desk. Each appeared to have been written by Jack Foster and contained the sort of trite declarations of undying love so often found in such missives.

Hardcastle opened his drawer and, taking out Sidney Mason's letter, laid it beside the others. 'Well, Marriott,' he said, 'you don't have to be an expert to see that this is in a different hand from all those written by Foster.'

'It's still possible he might have written it, sir, and disguised his writing,' said Marriott.

'You're a Job's comforter and no mistake, Marriott. But I suppose we'd better be on the safe side and send them across the Yard for this sergeant to have a look at. What's he call himself?'

'A graphologist, sir.'

Hardcastle shook his head. 'I don't know what the job's coming to, Marriott,' he said. 'Everyone seems to want to call himself by some fancy name these days. God knows what it'll be like in fifty years' time.' He sighed. 'Well, at least I shan't be here to see it. Any news from Catto?'

'No, sir, he's still down at Victoria. Apparently there's a lot of paper and booking slips, and the like, to go through.'

'Well, that can sweat for a bit. First thing is to get off to Bow Street and get a warrant for Dolly Hancock's arrest. Come along, Marriott.'

Seven

Just before the day's proceedings began at Bow Street police court, Hardcastle and Marriott were shown in to the chief magistrate's chambers.

'A delicate matter, sir,' said Hardcastle, producing his 'information', to which was attached a copy of the statement that Marriott had taken from Alderman Stevenson.

The chief magistrate read through the documents with the accomplished speed of an experienced lawyer, and then handed Hardcastle a New Testament and a card bearing the oath.

Hardcastle took the book in his right hand, but having sworn this particular oath many times, rattled it off without a glance at the aide-memoire: 'I swear by Almighty God that I shall true answer make to all such questions as the court may demand of me. Ernest Hardcastle, Divisional Detective Inspector, A or Whitehall Division, Metropolitan Police.'

'Is this your information, Inspector?'

'It is, sir.'

'And is this your signature?'

'It is, sir.'

'And is this information true?'

'It is, sir.' Hardcastle hoped it was. Stevenson's identification of Dolly Hancock from a newspaper photograph was less positive than he would have liked, but he was sure enough of his own persuasive detective abilities to be certain that, if she was the woman who had blackmailed the alderman, a confession would be forthcoming.

The chief magistrate took out his fountain pen, slowly unscrewed the cap and with a flourish signed the warrant for Dolly Hancock's arrest. 'A nasty business, Mr Hardcastle,' he said, as he handed the document to the DDI. 'Some men can be very foolish.'

'Indeed, sir.'

Hardcastle really had no need of a warrant for Dolly Hancock's arrest. The offence alleged against her was one for which he could have used his common-law powers. But Hardcastle was a cautious man. If it was later held that the arrest was an unlawful one – which it might prove to be, should Dolly Hancock turn out *not* to be the woman involved – the responsibility would rest not with Hardcastle, but with the chief metropolitan magistrate, whose signature was on the document now in the DDI's pocket.

Determined to deal with the arrest as quickly as possible, Hardcastle and Marriott took a cab from Bow Street to Clapham.

It was some time before Dolly Hancock answered the door, and then only after what the police are prone to call 'repeated knockings'.

If anything, the woman appeared even more dishevelled than the last time Hardcastle had called on her. Rubbing sleep from her eyes and flicking her untamed, long hair back over her shoulders, she stared at the two policemen. 'Oh, it's you,' she said. 'I thought it was more of them hacks that's been plaguing the life out of me. What d'you want this time, then?' she asked, as she retreated into the hall. 'I told you all I know.'

'Dolly Hancock, I have a warrant for your arrest on charges of conspiring with another to demand money with menaces on a date between the nineteenth of July 1918 and now.'

By this time, Dolly had reached the sitting room. She turned suddenly, her mouth open in shock. 'You what?' she demanded.

'You heard,' said Hardcastle. He turned to Marriott. 'What's that new fiddle-faddle we're supposed to tell 'em now, Marriott?'

Marriott smiled. 'Dolly Hancock, you're not obliged to say anything, but anything you do say will be taken down in writing and may be used against you.'

'I ain't saying nothing if it can only be used against me.' Dolly sank into a worn armchair and thrust out her legs.

'All it means,' explained Marriott, realizing that the woman was sharper than she at first appeared, 'is that what *you* say can't be used against any *other* person.' The sergeant had been obliged to clarify the final phrase several times since the introduction of the Judges' Rules by their lordships of the King's Bench Division earlier that year, and who were soon to remove its ambiguity.

'What are you going on about?' Dolly stood up again and walked to the sideboard. Pouring herself a hefty measure of gin, she drank it down at a gulp.

'Complaint has been made by one Alderman Stevenson . . .' began Hardcastle, and went on to outline the charge that would be brought against the woman.

'It's a bloody lie.' Dolly had, by this time, sat down again. 'He had his way with me and he paid for it. What's wrong with that? It ain't against the law. Only soliciting is. And I don't know nothing about anyone asking him for no fifty quid.'

'So, you did have sexual intercourse with Alderman Stevenson, then?' asked Hardcastle.

''Course I bloody did. And I give him a good tumble for his money, an' all.'

Hardcastle nodded with satisfaction. At least Stevenson had got the right woman. 'Who was the man who claimed to be your husband, Miss Hancock?' he asked hopefully.

'I don't know nothing about no man.'

Hardcastle shrugged. 'Very well,' he said. 'If you want to take it on your own, that's your business. We shall now take you to Cannon Row police station, where you'll be charged.'

'Well, that's bloody right and no error,' said Dolly. 'I'd better put some clothes on, then.' She seemed resigned to her arrest. 'If it hadn't been for them bleedin' reporters, that toff wouldn't never have found out where I was,' she added disgustedly. 'I s'pose he was ashamed of hisself after, and decided to take it out on me, just because I'm a working girl. Well, that weren't my fault. Good job I made him pay in advance, selfish bugger. Men!' She spat the word. 'All the bleedin' same deep down.'

It was a sentiment that Mrs Hardcastle would have found difficult to dispute.

By the time that Dolly Hancock had been charged at Cannon Row police station, DC Catto was waiting to see Hardcastle, but his information was of little help to the DDI's investigation.

'There's no record of a Sidney Mason having made a booking to go to France from Dover any time this year, sir. We went through the lists of all the passengers, but all we came up with was a Michael Mason who lives in Stoke Newington.'

'Be worth having a word with him, I suppose,' said Hardcastle, making a note in his day book. 'Might be a relative.'

'The clerk down at Victoria said that it's always possible that a passenger could book at Dover or even walk on the ferry at Western Docks and pay his fare on board. If that happened, there wouldn't be a record at Victoria. And like as not, sir, the clerk said, in that case there'd be no record at Dover either.'

'Thank you, Catto, that's a great help,' said Hardcastle drily. 'But get down to Dover tomorrow and make enquiries just the same.'

That same afternoon, Hardcastle was back at Bow Street court, giving evidence of Dolly Hancock's arrest and securing her remand in custody. As he had promised Stevenson, no mention was made of the alderman's name.

The court reporters were fully conversant with the finer points of the law and they knew that there was nothing to stop them printing an account of Dolly Hancock's appearance in the dock. Consequently, above a brief article and a copy of the previous day's photograph of the woman, the early editions of the evening papers proclaimed:

BRIGHTON MURDER
LONDON WOMAN ARRESTED

Even though there was mention of the charge of blackmailing the mysterious Mr X, it was evident that the press had assumed that Dolly's arrest had something to do with the body found under Palace Pier.

Hardcastle was irritated, yet again, at Fleet Street's intrusion, but it so happened that the newspaper report was to be of some value to him in solving the murder of Fanny Horwood.

But further irritation was to follow. When Hardcastle returned to Cannon Row, there was yet another telegraph message from Detective Inspector Watson awaiting him.

In his message, Watson said that when an officer had called at Danny Hoskins's house to take him to the police station for questioning about his argument on the seafront with a woman, he was not there. The beach photographer's mother had told the police that he was away on holiday, but she claimed that she did not know where he had gone or when he would return.

Hardcastle was unconvinced. 'He's run,' he said phlegmatically. 'He knows something, Marriott, I'll wager. Anyway, people don't leave Brighton to go on holiday, do they? Brighton's where they *go* for a holiday. Something's up and no mistake.'

'Well, it's possible they might go somewhere else, sir. After all, if you live in Brighton, you'd get fed up with it eventually, I suppose.'

'I'm fed up with it already, Marriott,' said Hardcastle, 'and I *don't* live there. I'll tell you this much, if I ever commit a crime, I'll make for Brighton.' He picked up his pipe and teased the ash with his letter opener. 'Mr Watson said nothing about Springer, then.'

'Springer, sir?' At times Marriott found it hard to keep up with Hardcastle's mercurial changes of direction.

'Major Springer's the fellow who came into what Mrs

72

Edwards called her "withdrawing room" when we was talking to her. I suggested to Watson that he had a few words with him, to see if he'd been there when Fanny Horwood arrived on the Saturday.'

'Yes, of course.' Marriott nodded. 'Shall I send him a message, sir?'

'Yes, do that, Marriott. See if we can't get him moving.' Hardcastle was becoming increasingly frustrated by what he saw as the indolence of the Brighton police, and decided that he would go there the very next morning 'to chivvy them up a bit'. 'Otherwise,' he told Marriott, 'we'll be tied up with this damned murder for ever more.'

But, unbeknown to Hardcastle, a decision had already been made that would involve him in the murder of Fanny Horwood to a far greater extent than hitherto.

'Excuse me, sir.' Detective Sergeant Wood tapped lightly on Hardcastle's open office door.

'What is it, Wood?'

'A message from Commissioner's Office, sir. You're to see the superintendent CID immediately.'

'God help us, will I never be allowed to get on with this damned enquiry?' Hardcastle muttered, as he donned his Chesterfield and bowler hat, prior to crossing the courtyard to the forbidding edifice of New Scotland Yard.

The head of the Central Office of the CID laughed as Hardcastle entered his office. 'I've got some good news for you, Ernie,' he said.

'I could do with some, sir,' said Hardcastle.

'The chief constable of the Brighton Borough Police has asked officially for assistance from the Yard in connection with the murder of Fanny Horwood.'

'About time,' mumbled Hardcastle. 'So, who are you sending, sir?' When such requests were received from provincial forces, it was invariably an officer from the Yard who was sent.

'You, Ernie. The assistant commissioner said that, as you'd got involved already, it'd make more sense to send you rather than an officer from Central Office who'd have to start from scratch.'

'Am I to be in charge of the enquiry, sir?' Hardcastle had worked out of London before and there was always a problem about who was really overseeing the case. If the enquiry was successful, the local officers wanted to share the glory; if it failed to secure a conviction, they tended to shy away from any responsibility.

'Yes. The chief constable was adamant about that. I got the impression, from what Mr Thomson said, that the CC hasn't got much faith in this DI of his . . .' The superintendent paused and glanced at a sheet of paper on his desk. 'Watson?' He looked up.

'I'm not surprised, sir,' said Hardcastle. 'Needs a squib up his arse, does that one.'

The superintendent grinned. 'Well, I reckon you're just the chap to do it, Ernie.'

If Detective Inspector Watson was surprised to see the two London detectives, he did not immediately show it. But then Hardcastle had long ago come to the conclusion that Watson would not be surprised by anything.

'You'll have heard that I've been officially assigned to take charge of this murder of yours, I suppose,' said Hardcastle, the moment he and Marriott were shown into the DI's office.

'Yes. The chief told me last night.' Watson was clearly unhappy at his chief constable's decision and felt, rightly, that his professional expertise had been called into question.

'Perhaps you'd show me to his office, then,' said Hardcastle.

'Yes, of course.' Watson stood up and led the way down the corridor to an office even more ornate than his own.

'Ah, Mr Hardcastle, it's good to see you.' The chief constable leaned back in his leather-bound chair and linked his hands across his belly. 'Naturally, we'll give you all the assistance we can. You have only to ask. Mr Watson here will act as your deputy for—'

'I have a deputy, sir,' said Hardcastle. 'Detective Sergeant Marriott is highly experienced in the investigation of murder.'

'Yes, of course,' said the chief constable. 'What I meant

was that Mr Watson will act as liaison between my force and you.'

'No doubt there's an office that's been made available for me here, sir.' Hardcastle had no intention of allowing Watson to treat him like some resented incomer.

'Certainly.' The chief constable glanced at his DI. 'Watson, make sure that there is a suitable office for Mr Hardcastle to use, will you.'

'I'm not sure that we have any spare offices, sir,' said Watson unwisely.

'Really? Better give him yours, then. You can move into the main CID office, what?'

Hardcastle did not intend to waste any time, and back in the DI's office, he asked, 'Any sign of Hoskins the photographer, Mr Watson?'

'Not as yet, but enquiries are continuing.' Watson's surly response was probably the result of being peremptorily ejected from his office by the chief constable.

'I should hope so,' growled Hardcastle.

'However, one of my officers asked Major Springer to call in this morning. He's downstairs now. You suggested that he might have some information.'

'Not exactly.' Hardcastle was irritated by the casual, almost foppish, manner of the Brighton officer, an opinion that was reinforced when he noticed that Watson kept his handkerchief tucked into his sleeve. 'I suggested that he be spoken to *in case* he had any information.'

Major Dudley Springer was twenty-eight years of age, but had the eyes and drawn face of a man much older. However, given the experiences he had undergone on the Western Front, that was hardly surprising.

'I understand you wanted to see me?' he asked, taking off his British warm overcoat and laying it over a chair in the interview room.

'I'm obliged to you for taking the trouble to come in, Major Springer,' said Hardcastle.

'I really don't know how I can help you,' said Springer.

'Were you staying at Mrs Edwards's boarding house on the

75

week leading up to the murder?' Hardcastle did not have to
say which murder; there had been only the one and the local
newspapers were full of it.

'Yes, I was.'

'I'm particularly interested in the young woman's move-
ments on the ninth of November, Major Springer. I was
wondering if you saw her at all.'

'We exchanged a few words at high tea on that Saturday.'
Springer touched his moustache.

'Did she say anything about why she was in Brighton, or
did she mention that she was meeting someone?' asked
Hardcastle, pulling his pipe from his pocket.

'Ah,' said Springer, taking out his own pipe, 'd'you mind
if I do?'

'Not at all.'

'She did, as a matter of fact, but only because I'd mentioned
it first.'

'And why did you do that?' Hardcastle's eyes narrowed.

'A man called at the house asking for her.'

'Did he now?' Hardcastle paused in the act of filling his
pipe and looked up. 'What time would that have been?' he
asked, wondering if the mysterious caller had been Hoskins
delivering the photograph he had taken earlier.

Springer's fingers played a brief tattoo on the table top.
Hardcastle had noticed earlier that he seemed to be suffering
from some sort of nervous complaint. 'About half past four,
I suppose.'

'Who was he, d'you know?'

'No, not if you mean do I know his name. I'd just come
down the stairs on my way to the sitting room' – Springer
was obviously having no truck with Mrs Edwards's description of it as the 'withdrawing room' – 'and just as I reached
the front door, there was a knock, so I opened it.'

'Yes, go on.'

'There was this fellow there asking for Mrs Harris. It is her
you're talking about, isn't it?'

'Yes, it is.' Hardcastle nodded. 'But her real name's Fanny
Horwood.'

'I told him that she'd gone for a walk on the beach, so he thanked me and said that if he didn't meet her, he'd call again.'

Hardcastle was furious that the local police had not discovered this vital piece of evidence before. 'Can you describe this man?' he asked.

Springer lit his pipe and then blew out the match before dropping it into a tin ashtray. 'Apart from his face, not really, Inspector. It was beginning to get dark and there wasn't a lot of light in the porch. He was probably my height – I'm five feet nine – and he was wearing a belted raincoat and one of those new felt hats, a trilby I think they call them.'

'Any facial hair? A beard or a moustache?'

'No. In fact, I'm sure he was clean-shaven.'

'Was he wearing glasses, or carrying an attaché-case? Anything like that?'

'I don't think so. I'm sorry, but I didn't really pay much attention to him. He was just someone who'd called at the door.' Springer paused. 'I'm sure I'd recognize him again though.'

'And did this man come back?'

'Not as far as I know. I went out myself a bit later on, after high tea.'

'But Mrs Harris came back for high tea, didn't she? You said you'd engaged her in conversation at that time.'

Springer put his pipe down on the table, thrust his hands into his trouser pockets and leaned back in his chair. 'Yes, of course,' he said thoughtfully. 'I told her that this man had called, asking for her, and she said that she hadn't seen him. I remember now that she left the rest of her tea and said that it was all right, she knew where to meet him. Said something about having arranged to meet him at a hotel, somewhere in the town.'

'Mmm! Could have been a hotel or a public house, I suppose,' mused Hardcastle. 'Did she mention the name of it, by any chance?'

'No, no she didn't. I'm sorry I can't help you any further, Inspector. It's a terrible business, isn't it?'

'Yes, Major Springer, it is, but nothing, I suppose, compared with what you've seen.'

'That's true,' said Springer, 'but the murder of an innocent young girl in Brighton, after the war's over, seems different somehow.'

Hardcastle nodded in agreement. 'Are you staying in Brighton long?' he asked.

'I'm not sure. Why?'

'It's just that if this man is found, I may need you to identify him.'

'I'll probably be here for a bit,' said Springer. 'You see, my wife died while I was in Arras, so I'm at a bit of a loose end. Not sure what I'm doing, really.'

Hardcastle watched the sorrowful figure of Springer walk aimlessly out of the police station and felt a momentary wave of sympathy for the man. 'He ain't got much to look forward to,' he said gruffly, as he and Marriott made their way back to the office that had been allocated to the London DDI. 'On the other hand, he ain't entirely out of the wood as far as I'm concerned.'

'D'you think he might have had something to do with it, sir?' asked Marriott.

'You should know my methods by now, Marriott. Everyone's a suspect until they're eliminated. And so far, Major Springer's not been.' Hardcastle paused as he touched the handle of Watson's office door. 'Get on to the nick and tell Catto to make some enquiries at the War Office about Major Springer. See what they know about him.'

'Any luck?' Watson asked imprudently, as Hardcastle entered his office. He was packing up a few of his belongings prior to transferring them to the room next door that he would be sharing with the junior detectives until the enquiry was over.

'There's no luck attached to a murder enquiry, Mr Watson,' said Hardcastle sharply. 'It's all hard work and leaving no stone unturned. It might interest you to know that Major Springer's just given me a description of a man who called at Sussex Street on the ninth, and who may well be Fanny Horwood's murderer. If your officers had done their job, they'd've turned that up straight after the killing instead of leaving it to me to find out days later.'

Watson was clearly taken aback by this latest attack on his professional competence, but did his best to recover. 'We tend to operate in a different way from the Metropolitan Police,' he said churlishly. He had never been spoken to in so direct a manner, even by his own chief constable, a man not noted for his courtesy.

'Yes, I can see that,' said Hardcastle. 'However, I'd be obliged if you would arrange for enquiries to be made to see if Mrs Horwood, alias Mrs Harris, was seen in any hotel – or for that matter public house – in the area in the company of this man whose description I've just obtained from Major Springer.'

'Good heavens!' The suggestion clearly shocked Watson. 'But there are literally hundreds of public houses in the Brighton area.'

'Yes,' said Hardcastle, 'I daresay there are.'

Eight

The information that Detective Constable Henry Catto had gleaned from his enquiries at the War Office regarding Major Dudley Springer did nothing to dispel Hardcastle's innate suspicion of anyone and everyone connected with a murder enquiry, no matter how tenuous that connection appeared to be.

'It seems, sir,' said Marriott, reading slowly through the latest telegraph message to arrive from London, 'that Major Springer was not widowed, not according to the regimental records office of the Royal Engineers. At least, not when he said he was.'

'Oh?' Hardcastle looked up from the pile of mostly useless statements he was reading and took off his spectacles. 'What do they know about him, then?'

'He was discharged from the army on the seventh of July 1918, suffering from "wounds received"—'

'Wounds? What wounds? He seemed healthy enough to me, Marriott.'

'That's how the War Office described it, sir,' said Marriott. 'I suppose it's a general term to cover just about everything, but apparently he had some sort of nervous breakdown.'

'Nervous breakdown!' exclaimed Hardcastle. 'What was he, a scrimshanker?' Despite being a police officer of long standing, Hardcastle, in common with others who lacked first-hand experience of the war, did not know that an increasing number of soldiers were suffering from what was now being called neurasthenia, a description that embraced any nervous condition brought on by the fighting, and known colloquially as shell-shock.

'I doubt it. He got a Military Cross,' said Marriott. 'He was a tunneller apparently, and working underground for months on end affected his mind.'

'What the devil was he doing down a tunnel if he was a major?'

'D'you remember the mining of the Messines Ridge, sir, the middle of last year?'

'Yes, of course I remember it. What about it?'

Hardcastle clearly recalled reading the account in the *Daily Mail* of the huge mines that had been set by the British and Empire armies under the Messines-Wytschaete Ridge in Flanders. Nineteen of them had been detonated at three o'clock in the morning of the seventh of June 1917, killing thousands of Germans. But sadly the British high command had failed to capitalize – to any great extent – on this brilliant and imaginative assault.

'Well, according to the War Office, sir, Springer was involved in that from start to finish. I remember reading in the papers that sometimes there was fighting underground between our lads and the Huns.'

'So, they threw him out, did they?' muttered Hardcastle.

'Yes, sir. The point about it all, though, is that his wife – Harriet, her name was – was being paid an allowance right up until he was discharged. There's nothing in the records about him having been widowed. And he was only in Arras the once, for about three weeks in 1915. That's where he said he was when she died. But according to the army, she was still alive up to July this year.'

Hardcastle scratched thoughtfully at his moustache with the stem of his pipe. 'There's something a bit awry here, Marriott. Why's he going about making up tales like that?' He peered into the bowl of his pipe and then put it in the ashtray.

Marriott shrugged. 'That's supposing the War Office got it right, sir.' He grinned at the DDI. 'I have known them make a dog's dinner of things before.'

'Yes, like the Battle of the Somme, for instance,' growled Hardcastle. 'I think we'll have to have another word with the bold major. And while we're about it, we'll have another little chat with Mrs Edwards. See if she knows aught about this mystery man that Major Springer said called at the house on the Saturday afternoon. After all, we've only got his word for it.'

'But he did say that he told Fanny Horwood about the man and that she went off, leaving her tea.'

'That's what he said, Marriott, but if he's told lies about his wife dying, he might have told them about this here chap who supposedly called at the door. For all we know, he might have done Fanny in and made up that yarn to cover hisself.' Hardcastle had no intention of accepting Major Springer's uncorroborated statement. 'And we haven't been able to ask Fanny herself, because she's in the mortuary awaiting a decent Christian burial. Even though she's turned out to have been a whore like Dolly Hancock.' He picked up his pipe, looked at it and put it down yet again. 'By the way, is there anything in that telegraph message about Catto's trip to Dover?'

'Yes, sir, he said there was no trace of a Sidney Mason having gone to France this year, nor Fanny Horwood or Harris, neither.'

Phyllis Edwards seemed almost pleased at the arrival of the two detectives, as if she were relishing the notoriety of having known the victim of the 'Brighton Strangler'.

'Come into the withdrawing room, gents,' she said. 'I daresay you could do with a cup of tea.'

'Thank you,' murmured Hardcastle, dismissing any thoughts of smoking his pipe in such pristine surroundings.

Mrs Edwards rang a small brass bell, and when a nervous young girl appeared, ordered tea for three. 'In the best china, mind, girl,' she added. She turned to Hardcastle. 'I'm afraid there's no biscuits,' she said, 'not with the rationing being still on an' all.'

'I suppose not,' said Hardcastle. Nevertheless he thought that Mrs Edwards probably managed to obtain them – at a price – without bothering about coupons, but obviously thought it unwise to admit as much to the police.

'Now then, 'ow can I 'elp you?' asked Mrs Edwards.

Hardcastle repeated Major Springer's account of the man who had called on the Saturday enquiring for Fanny Harris. 'Did you know anything about this man, Mrs Edwards?'

'No, I'm afraid I 'ad no knowledge of no gentlemen callers. As I opined the last time you was 'ere, Inspector, it's not a thing I encourage.'

'Did you know anything about a conversation between Major Springer and Mrs Harris?' In order to avoid confusion in Mrs Edwards's mind – not an easy thing to do – Hardcastle deliberately kept to the name that Fanny Horwood had used when she took a room at the boarding house. 'Apparently he told her about this man when they were having tea together.'

'No, I can't say as 'ow I did.' Mrs Edwards turned as the young woman brought in the tea. 'Just put it down there, girl,' she said, indicating an occasional table. 'And careful, mind.'

'Shall I pour it, ma'am?' asked the girl.

'No, you leave it be,' said Mrs Edwards. 'I'm 'aving a confidential talk to these two gents. From Scotland Yard, they is,' she added, seeking to enhance her own importance in the matter of Fanny Harris's murder by exaggerating the status of her visitors.

As the young servant girl bobbed briefly and left the room, Mrs Edwards faced Hardcastle once more. 'You can't be too careful, you know, Inspector,' she said. 'The servants 'as this shocking propensity for gossip, and you won't want your business to be the talk of the town, will you now?' She smiled beatifically and folded her hands demurely in her lap. But then realizing that the tea was standing, she turned her attention to pouring it.

Hardcastle forbore from mentioning that the murder was already the talk of the town. 'I was asking if you had heard any part of this conversation,' he said.

'Oh, no,' said Mrs Edwards, handing Hardcastle and Marriott their tea in fine porcelain cups. 'I 'as a maid for serving at table.'

'Is that the young woman who just brought in the tea?'

'The same,' said Mrs Edwards.

83

'Perhaps I can have a word with her before I go, then,' said Hardcastle, picking up his teacup.

Mrs Edwards frowned slightly at the thought that her maid might have more information to offer the police than she had herself. 'If you think she can 'elp. She's a bit dizzy-'eaded, though.'

'And would Major Springer happen to be in, d'you know?'

'I shall ascertain, Inspector.' Mrs Edwards reached for the bell again. 'Find out if the major's in 'is room, girl,' she said when the young maid reappeared. Then, glancing at Hardcastle, she asked, 'Would you wish to converse with 'im, Inspector?'

'If he's there, yes,' said Hardcastle.

'Well, you 'eard the inspector, girl. Off you go.'

A minute or two later, Major Springer sauntered into the room. Regardless of Mrs Edwards's deep frown, he continued to smoke his pipe. 'I understand you wanted to speak to me again, Inspector,' he said.

'Yes, Major.' Hardcastle looked at Phyllis Edwards. 'Well, thank you for your assistance,' he said, 'and for the tea. Perhaps you wouldn't mind if my sergeant and I spoke to the major in private.'

'As you wish.' Mrs Edwards rose imperiously from her chair and flounced towards the door, irritated that she was not to be privy to whatever it was that Hardcastle wished to discuss with Springer.

'Thank you, and I'll have a chat with your young girl before I go. What's her name, by the way?' Hardcastle knew it was Violet Gunn – Hoskins had told him previously, and Mrs Edwards had confirmed it the last time he had called at Sussex Street – but he found it profitable to feign forgetfulness from time to time.

Pausing at the door, Mrs Edwards appeared to give the question some thought, as if knowing the names of her staff was something that was beneath her dignity. 'It's Violet,' she said eventually. 'Violet Gunn.'

'You told me that your wife had died while you were in Arras, Major Springer,' said Hardcastle, when the door was finally and firmly closed behind Mrs Edwards.

'Yes, that's right.' Springer leaned down to knock out his pipe on the front of the fire basket before sitting down opposite Hardcastle and Marriott. Unlike his demeanour at the police station that morning, he appeared now to be quite relaxed.

'But that's not true, is it? The only time that you were in Arras was in 1915, which is where you said you were when she died. However, the War Office have told me that your wife continued to receive an officers' marriage allowance until your discharge from the army in July this year.' Hardcastle sat back in his chair and waited to see what Springer would say to that.

A tic started beneath Springer's left eye and he pressed a finger to it. 'She left me, Inspector,' he said, but then regaining some of the boldness that must have won him his Military Cross, asked, 'But what the hell's that got to do with you?' He leaned forward, elbows on knees, and held his head between his hands. He sat like that for a few seconds and then looked up again. 'I'm sorry. That was uncalled-for. I do apologize.'

Hardcastle assumed that Springer regarded the desertion of a wife as having some sort of social stigma attached to it. 'I have a job to do, Major,' he said mildly. 'And right now that job is finding out who murdered Mrs Horwood. That means asking questions, and when I don't get straight answers, I get suspicious.'

'I never thought you'd check,' said Springer, appearing to recover himself. 'I'd forgotten that it was 1915 when I was in Arras. I just said the first thing that came into my head. I had a pretty bad time of it—'

'My sergeant tells me it was the tunnelling,' said Hardcastle. 'The Messines mines and all that.'

'Only partly. Actually it was the whole bloody war.' There was a strained expression on Springer's face now. 'I got a spot of furlough in about August 1917, not long after the Messines show. Needed it, too.' He smiled ruefully at what he imagined to be a weakness. 'But when I got home, unexpectedly, I found her in bed with some white-feather johnny.

She was quite brazen about it. Said she no longer loved me and wanted a divorce. I can tell you, Inspector, that just about finished me.'

Hardcastle nodded sympathetically. It was a familiar tale. Hundreds, if not thousands, of soldiers and sailors had discovered that their wives had been unfaithful while they were in the trenches or serving at sea. 'And are you divorced?'

'No. Harriet moved to Nottingham almost immediately, and I've not seen her since.'

'But she continued to draw marriage allowance?'

'Yes. We're still married, you see. Legally, that is.'

It crossed Hardcastle's mind briefly that there might be some element of fraud about that, but he had no intention of pursuing it. It was obvious that Springer had had enough to contend with, what with the war and an unfaithful wife. 'Getting back to this man who called at the door, Major,' he said, 'you're quite sure that neither he nor Mrs Horwood made mention of where they proposed to meet?'

'Absolutely, Inspector. He just said that he knew where he could find her – something like that – or he'd come back. As far as I know, he didn't return. And when I told – Mrs Harris . . . ? That was her name, was it? I thought you called her something else before.'

'Her real name was Fanny Horwood,' said Hardcastle, 'but that needn't bother you.'

'Yes, well, anyway, when I told her, she seemed to know who he was and where to meet him.'

'Well, thank you, Major, and as I said last time we spoke, when we do find this fellow, I may need you to take a look at him, just to see if he's the same man.'

'Anything I can do, Inspector, just say,' said Springer, rising from his chair.

As Springer left the room, the young servant girl appeared in the doorway and bobbed. 'May I take the tea things, sir?' she asked.

'You'll be Violet Gunn, I imagine?' Hardcastle smiled benevolently.

'Yes, sir.' Violet was a comely young woman with red

86

cheeks, and a white cap sitting neatly on top of her upswept hair.

'Well, sit down, Violet. I want to talk to you.' And when the girl appeared uncomfortable at the thought of taking a seat in the 'withdrawing room', Hardcastle said, 'It's all right, lass, Mrs Edwards knows I'm going to speak to you.'

'Yes, sir.' Violet sat down, perching on the edge of the chair and twisting her fingers nervously in her aproned lap.

'How old are you, Violet?'

'Seventeen, sir.'

'And you've always lived in Brighton?'

'Yes, sir.'

'And how long have you worked for Mrs Edwards?'

'Six months, sir.'

'I see. Now, Violet, do you remember the Saturday that Mrs Harris was here?'

'Yes, sir. The ninth of November, that'd be.'

'That's correct.' Hardcastle nodded approvingly; Mrs Edwards's assessment of the girl as dizzy-headed did not seem quite accurate. 'And you do know who I'm talking about when I mention Mrs Harris?'

'Oh yes, sir. A pretty woman, she was, and very, er . . . refined . . . ?' Violet hesitated, wondering whether she had used the right word.

Hardcastle smiled. The London-born-and-bred Fanny Horwood, although only twenty herself, must have appeared worldly to a girl who had spent all her short life in Brighton. 'And did you serve her with high tea on that day?' he asked.

'Yes, sir.'

'And was Major Springer there, too?'

Violet looked wistfully across the room. 'Oh yes, sir.' It was obvious that she was greatly taken with the war hero.

'Did you hear them talking, in particular about a man who had called at the door asking for Mrs Harris?'

'I never listen to what the guests is saying, sir.' Violet appeared horrified that Hardcastle might have thought her to be an eavesdropper.

'I know that you wouldn't do so intentionally, Violet. But

87

this is important. You see, the man who called, and who was seen by Major Springer, may have been the man who murdered her.'

Violet's hand shot to her mouth. 'Oh, my goodness,' she said, and, appalled that the murderer might have been to the house where she worked, she immediately crossed herself.

'Well, did you hear anything?'

Violet shook her head. 'No, sir, apart from when the major asked for some more bread.'

'But you heard nothing about Mrs Harris saying that she had to meet someone? Or the major telling her that someone had called asking for her?'

'No, sir, nothing like that.'

'Tell me, Violet, did Mrs Harris finish her tea, or did she go out halfway through the meal?'

'I don't know about that, sir. Her plate was empty, but I never knew how much she'd ate. But she did leave half a cup of tea.' Violet smiled and looked round nervously. 'But I don't blame her for that,' she whispered. 'It's not very good tea. Only cheap stuff that Mrs Edwards gets from the market.'

'Really?' Hardcastle chuckled. 'The tea you served this afternoon tasted all right.'

'Well, it would be, sir. Mrs Edwards keeps some Assam, special like, for visitors. Costs sevenpence ha'penny a quarter an' all.'

'So, Marriott, after all that, we've only got Springer's word that this fellow turned up at Mrs Edwards's Sussex Street boarding house. Mrs E never knew he'd come, and young Violet, who's a sight brighter than Mrs E thinks she is, didn't hear anything at the table.' Hardcastle leaned back in Detective Inspector Watson's chair, folded his arms and gazed around the office. 'These provincial Dogberrys do all right for themselves, don't they, Marriott?'

'But that doesn't mean that Springer had anything to do with it, does it, sir?'

'No, it doesn't.' Hardcastle leaned forward again, and picking up his matches, lit his pipe and filled the office with the aroma of St Bruno. 'Mr Watson doesn't smoke, does he?' he said with a chuckle. 'No, Marriott, it doesn't mean that Major Springer had anything to do with it, but it doesn't mean that he hadn't, either.'

'So, what happens next, sir?'

'Sit down, m'boy,' said Hardcastle. 'I'm thinking.'

Marriott took a seat, realizing that his governor was about to descend into one of his more loquacious moods. 'D'you mind if I smoke, sir?'

'Feel free, m'boy, feel free,' said Hardcastle, waving a hand distractedly in the air. For a moment or two he savoured his tobacco before continuing. 'I think we'll have a further look at Major Springer and his vanishing missus. Send to Catto and tell him to go back to the War Office and find out where they were sending Mrs Springer's allowance. Then perhaps we'll see what this is all about.'

'What's the point of that, guv'nor?' asked Marriott.

'The point, m'boy, is that we'll find out whether the tale the major told us is the true one, or whether the boot was on the other foot.'

'I'm sorry, guv'nor, I don't quite—'

'Supposing that Springer was the one who was entertaining a fancy woman and that's why Mrs Springer pushed off. And supposing that fancy woman happened to be Fanny Horwood. After all, the leading question is what is Major Springer doing languishing in a Brighton boarding house and killing time by wandering about the town every day.'

Nine

'Mrs Hoskins is it?' Hardcastle, accompanied by Good-enough, stood on the doorstep of the terraced house in Victoria Road. Marriott had been left at the police station attempting to get some semblance of order into the mounting pile of paperwork that always accompanies a murder enquiry.

'Yes.' The woman was clearly in the midst of housework, and her attitude was one of resentful impatience at having been interrupted. She wore an ankle-length grey cotton dress with sleeves rolled to the elbow and an apron that looked as though it had not seen the washtub for many a long day.

'I'm Divisional Detective Inspector Hardcastle of the Metropolitan Police, and this is Detective Sergeant Goodenough of the local force.'

'Is that so? Well, if you're looking for my Danny, you won't find him here. I don't know why you police keeps hounding him, mister. He ain't done nothing wrong.'

'I'll be the judge of that, Mrs Hoskins,' said Hardcastle, still standing on the doorstep. 'But if he's done nothing wrong, why's he run?'

Mrs Hoskins stood four-square in the doorway. 'Who said he's run?' Having pushed her long, lank hair away from her eyes, she placed her reddened hands firmly on her hips, making it obvious that she had no intention of admitting the detectives. 'What's more, we don't want coppers nosing round here every five minutes. This is a respectable neighbourhood, this is.' But the dirty windows, and the overgrown front garden, with its long grass and weeds, tended to belie such a claim of respectability.

'Well, that's easily settled, then,' said Hardcastle. 'You just tell me where he's gone and that'll be that.'

'Like I told that other D – the one what come the other day – he's on holiday.' But then Mrs Hoskins relented, although she did not move her position. 'Well, it's a working holiday, like.'

'And what's that supposed to mean?' demanded Hardcastle.

'He's up London somewhere. There's certainly bugger-all for him on Brighton beach in November, and he said he'd be best off up there, what with the Armistice and all them folk celebrating. Wouldn't be surprised if you didn't find him taking photos on Trafalgar Square.' The trace of a smile appeared on Mrs Hoskins's face.

'I doubt it,' said Hardcastle, 'not unless he's got a licence, and they're hard to come by.' He wondered whether Danny Hoskins had put his mother up to such a story as a joke, but promptly dismissed that thought. Hoskins was unlikely to know that the area covered by Hardcastle's police station at Cannon Row included Nelson's Column and the square that surrounded it. And in any event, it was doubtful that he would risk antagonizing the London policeman even if he had the wit to do so. 'But I can tell you this much, missus, anyone obstructing the police in a murder enquiry is likely to finish up in Queer Street, and that's a fact.'

Mrs Hoskins scooped up the front of her apron and wiped her brow with it. 'What d'you mean, a murder enquiry? My Danny's had nothin' to do with no murder.'

'Don't tell me you know nothing about the murder of Mrs Fanny Horwood, alias Harris, Mrs Hoskins – it's been in all the papers – and you know as well as I do that your Danny's been interviewed in regard to that matter. And furthermore, the Brighton police have been here searching his room, which you must also know about. What's more, he took a photograph of Mrs Horwood on the beach on the afternoon of Saturday the ninth of November. So, he's probably the last person to have seen her alive, other than her killer.' Hardcastle paused to give his next statement some effect. 'Unless he was the one what did for her. In which case, they'll hang him.'

91

Mrs Hoskins was visibly shaken by the prospect of her son going to the gallows, and reached out to the doorpost for support. 'He's a good boy is my Danny,' she said, a measure of desperation creeping into her voice. 'He wouldn't hurt a fly.'

'You know exactly where he is, don't you, Mrs Hoskins? And I don't suppose you want me to send for a Black Maria and have you taken down to the nick for questioning. The neighbours would enjoy that, wouldn't they?' Standing beside Hardcastle, Goodenough attempted to contain his surprise at the blunt and uncompromising attitude of the Metropolitan officer, a startling contrast to the easy-going methods of his own inspector.

Danny Hoskins's mother stared malevolently at Hardcastle for some seconds. 'You wait there, mister,' she said, and turned abruptly on her heel. Seconds later she returned, clutching a piece of paper. 'There, that's where you'll find him.'

Hardcastle took the proffered paper and glanced at it. 'So, what's he doing in Tooting?'

'Looking for work. There's no money to talk of in the photo-taking business down here, even in the summer,' said Mrs Hoskins. 'There's too many of them at it, see.' And recovering her former arrogance, she added, 'Satisfied?'

'Thank you,' said Hardcastle, pocketing the piece of paper and raising his hat.

'I tell you, he never had nothing to do with that floozy's murder,' Mrs Hoskins shouted as Hardcastle and Goodenough walked down the short path to the street. 'Go on, you ask him.'

Back at the police station, Hardcastle told Goodenough to send a message to Cannon Row.

'Mark it for DS Wood and instruct him to apprehend Danny Hoskins at this Tooting address his mother gave us' – Hardcastle handed the sergeant the piece of paper bearing Hoskins's present whereabouts – 'and bring him back here to Brighton, *tout de suite*.'

'Yes, sir.' Goodenough looked up from the pad on which he was writing. 'What's he to be apprehended for, sir?'

'Heavens above, Goodenough, Sergeant Wood's been at the game long enough. He'll think of something.'

'Very good, sir.' Goodenough started to write again.

'The truth is, lad, I rather fancy Hoskins for this murder,' said Hardcastle. 'You can put that in the message, but tell Wood not to mention it. Put in some fanny about me wanting him to identify some more photographs.' He stood up, a satisfied expression on his face. 'And when you've sent it, come back here. You and me's going to have a chat with this witness who said she saw Hoskins arguing with a young woman on the seafront, the day before Fanny Horwood's body was found under Palace Pier.'

'Yes, sir.' Goodenough grinned. Things had never moved this fast under the lethargic Detective Inspector Watson. He moved rapidly towards the door and collided with a chair.

'And Goodenough . . .'

'Yes, sir?' The enthusiastic young sergeant turned.

'Don't run before you can walk, lad.'

Mavis Brandon worked as an assistant in a drapery and haberdashery store on Grand Parade, owned by her father, and lived with her parents over the shop. She was a tall, attractive young woman with Titian hair and laughing, brown eyes, and it was obvious that any man would set his cap at her. In fact, many had, but most had failed to capture her attention for any length of time. And that, Hardcastle was at once to learn, included Danny Hoskins.

'Yes, we walked out for a week or so,' she said, as she sat primly in the centre of the sofa in the front room on the first floor. A wire-haired terrier, greying at the muzzle, settled itself at the girl's feet and eyed the two detectives suspiciously. 'But he was rather a silly young fellow, common too. And my father didn't approve of him. Not that I take much notice of what my father says,' she added, and laughed infectiously.

'I understand from Detective Inspector Watson, Miss

Brandon, that you saw Danny Hoskins talking to a young woman on the seafront during the afternoon of Saturday the ninth of November.'

'Yes, I did. At about four o'clock, maybe a little before. It was my afternoon off and I'd been for a walk with Kitchener.' Mavis leaned down and tickled the dog's ear. 'My father named him after the general.'

'Field marshal,' murmured Hardcastle, a stickler for accuracy in such matters. 'And where was this meeting, exactly?'

'About halfway between West Pier and Palace Pier, I suppose.'

'Did Mr Watson show you a photograph?'

'There was no need, Inspector,' said Mavis. 'I know Danny Hoskins when I see him.'

Hardcastle smiled. 'I've no doubt you do, Miss Brandon,' he said. 'I meant a photograph of a woman who may have been the woman you saw with him.'

'No, he didn't.' Mavis inclined her head and smiled at Goodenough.

Hardcastle sighed and held out his hand to the Brighton sergeant. 'Got the photograph there that Hoskins took of Mrs Horwood on the beach, Goodenough?'

'Sorry, sir, what was that?' Goodenough was clearly taken with the winsome Miss Brandon and could hardly bear to take his gaze from her face.

'The photograph, Goodenough. For heaven's sake concentrate.'

'Yes, sir. Sorry, sir.' Goodenough withdrew the photograph from his pocket and stood up to hand it to Mavis. The dog raised its head and growled, deep in its throat.

'Quiet, Kitchener.' Mavis touched the dog's head and then smiled at Goodenough. 'He's very protective of me, you know,' she said.

'Is that the woman you saw, Miss Brandon?' Hardcastle asked.

Mavis studied the photograph carefully, moving it slightly to catch the light from the lace-curtained window. 'It could be,' she said eventually. 'That gold neck-chain she's wearing looks familiar. I remember thinking at the time how nice it was.'

'You told the other officer that she and Hoskins appeared to be arguing, Miss Brandon.'

'I wouldn't go that far,' said Mavis. 'You see, Danny thinks he's God's gift to women and he takes it hard when they turn him down. Just won't take no for an answer sometimes.'

'So, what happened?'

'I couldn't hear what they were saying,' said Mavis. 'It was just an impression, if you know what I mean. I think that he'd probably asked her out, or to go for a drink or something, but she didn't seem to want to go with him. Eventually she turned and walked away, as though she couldn't be bothered with him any more.'

'And Hoskins? What did he do?'

'Well, he stood there, watching her for a bit, sort of sulking. It's an expression I know well. Then he turned and walked away too.'

'In the opposite direction?'

'Yes, towards West Pier. The woman had gone towards Palace Pier.'

'Did you talk to Hoskins at all?'

'Certainly not,' replied Mavis spiritedly.

'And was that the last you saw of either of them?'

'Yes, at least then.'

'What d'you mean by that?'

'I didn't see the woman again, but I saw Danny the following day, the Sunday,' said Mavis. 'I was out early, taking the dog for a walk, as a matter of fact, when I saw the crowd down by Palace Pier. It was when they found the body, and there were policemen everywhere. That would have been about seven in the morning – I've always been an early riser – and I saw Danny there. Taking photographs, he was. I suppose it was one of those that appeared in the *Evening Argus*, but not until the Monday.' That seemed to amuse her and she chuckled, and glanced at Goodenough again.

'Would you be prepared to come to the mortuary, Miss

Brandon, and view the body of Mrs Horwood? I'd like to know whether it was the same woman that you saw with Hoskins.'

Mavis hesitated briefly. 'Well, I must admit that I don't much care for the idea, but I suppose it's my duty.'

Hardcastle nodded. 'It's not very pleasant, I must agree,' he said, 'but I'll send Detective Sergeant Goodenough with you.'

It was an arrangement that appeared to please both Mavis Brandon and Douglas Goodenough.

Hardcastle stood in the doorway of the CID general office at the police station and looked around. His eyes eventually lighted upon Detective Inspector Watson, who had rearranged the furniture so that he occupied an oasis at the far end, thus separating himself from the lesser members of the department.

'A moment of your time, Mr Watson, if you please,' said Hardcastle, and walked back to the office that, until recently, had been occupied by the Brighton inspector.

When Watson arrived, Hardcastle was already seated behind the desk. 'About the enquiries at the hotels, public houses and pawnbrokers, Mr Watson . . .' he began.

Watson closed the door and advanced on the DDI. 'I'm a little irritated at being treated as though I'm a nobody, Mr Hardcastle,' he said angrily, and remained standing in front of the desk. 'I *am* the detective inspector in charge of the CID in this part of Brighton, and what's more I—'

'Why don't you sit down, Mr Watson,' said Hardcastle mildly, and withdrew his pipe from his pocket. 'The situation is this: I've been appointed by your chief constable to investigate this murder and, as you heard when I saw him, he has placed me in charge. Now, I am a first-class detective inspector, and you are a second-class detective inspector. So, there you have it. If you don't like the arrangement, I suggest we both go and see the chief now.' He struck a match and lit his pipe, puffing clouds of smoke into the air.

Watson frowned, wondering how long it would take to rid

his office of the smell of tobacco once Hardcastle had returned to London.

As if reading the Brighton man's mind, Hardcastle said, 'The sooner we resolve this enquiry, the sooner I'll be gone. I don't want to stay here any longer than I have to, Mr Watson. Now, what about the pubs and the hock shops?'

'As I said before, there are a lot of hotels and public houses in Brighton,' said Watson, at last deigning to take a seat, 'but my officers are working their way through them. As for pawn-brokers, we have circulated them all with a description of the missing jewellery, but so far there has been no response.'

'And how many of these pawnbrokers d'you know to be receivers of stolen property, Mr Watson?'

'A few,' said Watson grudgingly, 'but we are capable of leaning on them when the occasion demands. We do know our own toby, Mr Hardcastle.'

'I'm pleased to hear it,' said Hardcastle. 'Perhaps you'd be so good as to keep me informed.'

It was late afternoon when Goodenough returned to the police station, and he reported immediately to Hardcastle.

'She was a bit taken aback by the sight of a stiff, sir—' he began eagerly.

'Who was, lad?'

'Er, Miss Brandon, sir.' Goodenough sounded a little surprised that Hardcastle seemed not to know what he was talking about.

'Well, say so, then. I'm overseeing this enquiry, Goodenough, not just a bit of it, and there's more than one woman's name in my index, so when you report, you report fully, d'you understand?' Although Hardcastle knew who Goodenough was talking about – and suspected that the young officer was somewhat smitten by the comely Miss Brandon – he had decided to make a gentle point about exactness, something that seemed to be lacking locally.

'Yes, sir.' Goodenough looked a little crestfallen at the DDI's rebuke.

'Carry on, then.'

'I escorted Miss Brandon to the mortuary, sir, and she was about ninety per cent certain that Mrs Horwood was the woman she saw in conversation with Danny Hoskins, the beach photographer, during the afternoon of the—'

'All right, lad, no need to overdo it.' Hardcastle laughed and held up his hand. 'But just remember that when you and I get to court with this case, you'll likely be up against one of the finest silks in the country, so you can't afford to be slipshod. And what's more, you need to make notes of everything you do.'

'Yes, sir. Sorry, sir.'

'And don't keep apologizing, Goodenough. I'm only telling you these things for your own good. Now then . . .' Hardcastle stood up and reached for his coat. 'Being a resourceful detective sergeant who knows his manor, you'll likely be familiar with a good pub where we can get a half-decent glass of ale.'

'Yes, sir,' said Goodenough.

'Right then, lad. Lead on, and you can have the privilege of buying me a pint.'

When the two detectives returned to the police station, there was a telegraph message from Detective Sergeant Wood awaiting them. It said that Danny Hoskins had been arrested in Tooting and would be returned to Brighton the following morning, escorted by Detective Constables Catto and Wilmot.

'That's a bit more like it,' said Hardcastle, rubbing his hands together. 'Now all we've got to do, Goodenough, is think up some questions to ask him.'

'D'you reckon he did it, then, sir?'

'I never count my chickens before they're hatched, Goodenough,' said Hardcastle. 'The important thing about a murder is that you treat everyone as a suspect to start with. Then you eliminate them, one by one, until you're left with the one who did it.'

'Like Sherlock Holmes, you mean, sir,' said Goodenough enthusiastically. Three pints of best bitter had boosted the young detective's confidence.

'No,' said Hardcastle, 'not like Sherlock Holmes. Like a professional police officer who bases his work on hard evidence. And that's what we're looking for.'

Ten

Hardcastle was not very taken with the dingy hotel in which he and Marriott were staying during their sojourn in Brighton. The rooms were small and, far from looking out over the sea, the only view Hardcastle had from his window was a backyard containing a number of dustbins. But the allowances afforded to detective officers – even of the DDI's rank – when working away from their usual place of duty were such that it was the best he could afford; he had no intention of subsidizing his stint in Brighton from his own pocket.

Consequently, as on every other morning since their arrival in the south-coast resort, he and Marriott walked briskly to the police station and arrived by eight o'clock, a habit that had, at first, somewhat alarmed both the CID and the Uniform Branch; DI Watson was rarely seen before about nine-thirty, and the chief constable even later.

On this particular morning, Catto and Wilmot were already there, having caught the early train from Victoria station in London.

'Well, Catto, where is he?'

'In the cells down below, sir.'

'Good. Say anything on the way down, did he? Or say anything to Sergeant Wood when he felt his collar?'

'Not a dicky bird, sir, apart from telling me that he didn't have anything to do with Fanny Horwood's death.'

'Now why should he say that, I wonder?' Hardcastle settled himself in DI Watson's chair and selected one of the three pipes that lay on the desk. 'You never said anything to him about me fancying him for this murder, did you?'

'No, sir,' said Catto, 'and neither did Sergeant Wood. He

told Hoskins what you said to say, in the message, that is, about wanting him to have a look at some more photographs. But on the way down in the train, he suddenly said something along the lines of, "I know your guv'nor thinks I did for that girl, but I swear I never."'

'Did he now? And you hadn't put it to him?' Hardcastle's eyes narrowed suspiciously.

'Certainly not, sir, no. Up till then we'd been talking about last Saturday's Arsenal match, and then he just come out with it, like it'd been playing on his mind.'

Hardcastle grunted. 'Well, we'll have to see if we can't play on the young bugger's mind a bit more, Catto. Bit of guilty knowledge there, by the looks of it. And have you found out anything about Mrs Springer, or have you all been sitting on your backsides up there just because I'm down here?'

Catto grinned. 'Wouldn't dare, sir. Not with Mr Rhodes in charge.'

'Cheeky young sod,' growled Hardcastle, but he was confident that, in his absence, his deputy, Detective Inspector Edgar Rhodes, was more than capable of keeping an eye on things on A Division. 'Well, you haven't answered my question.'

'According to the Royal Engineers records office, sir, Mrs Springer was living at an address in Chelsea right through the war, and was still living there when Major Springer was discharged from the army.'

'Well, well,' mused Hardcastle. 'So much for her having gone to live in Nottingham in 1917. Was she ever in Nottingham, Catto? Did they tell you that?'

'Not according to the army, sir, no.'

'And is she still at the Chelsea address?' asked Hardcastle.

Catto knew that the DDI would have expected him to check that information and he had done so. 'Yes, sir. I made a few discreet enquiries in the vicinity and she was last seen there on Tuesday morning.'

'Interesting.' Hardcastle made a note in his day book, a record of things that had to be done. 'I think we'll have a word with her, when we have a minute. But in the meantime, Marriott,' he said, glancing at his sergeant, 'we'll go down and see if we can't put a bit of a fright into Master Hoskins.' He led the way out of the office, but stopped at the open door of the general office. 'Mr Watson about, is he?' he enquired.

Detective Sergeant Goodenough, whose desk was nearest the door, stood up. 'He's not in yet, sir.'

Hardcastle took out his watch and stared at it pointedly. 'I see,' he said. 'Perhaps you'd ask him to see me when he does arrive, Goodenough.'

'Certainly, sir.' And when Hardcastle had left, Goodenough raised his eyebrows and grinned at another sergeant.

Danny Hoskins proved to be possessed of more mettle than Hardcastle had given him credit for, and went on the offensive the moment the London detective stepped into the interview room. 'What's this all about?' he demanded aggressively. 'All I did was to take a photograph of that girl, and the next thing that happens is that two busies turn up at my place in London and nick me.' He remained lounging in his chair, a half sneer on his face.

But Hardcastle had years of experience dealing with hardened criminals, let alone with suspects of the third-rate calibre of Hoskins. 'On the afternoon of the ninth of November, Hoskins, you were seen arguing with Fanny Horwood, otherwise known as Harris, on the seafront somewhere between Palace Pier and West Pier.' It wasn't quite what Mavis Brandon had said, but it would do for a start.

Hoskins adjusted his position slightly. 'No, you've got that wrong,' he said, but his original confidence had ebbed slightly.

'A reliable witness will come to court to testify to that,' said Hardcastle mildly.

'Court? What's a court got to do with it?' Hoskins now began to look downright disconcerted by Hardcastle's line of questioning.

'Now then . . .' Hardcastle reached out for the sheaf of notes that Marriott had made at the time of the first interview with Hoskins. 'You said previously that you had seen Mrs Horwood sitting on the beach, alone, at about half past three that afternoon, and you took a photograph of her.' He held out his hand

102

again and took the photograph from Marriott. 'This photo-graph.' He laid the print on the table and pushed it towards Hoskins.

'Yeah, so what? I never denied it. In fact, it was me what told you.' But Hoskins was starting to look shifty, his eyes everywhere but on Hardcastle.

'Not until the local police found you and faced you with it,' said Hardcastle, his voice almost a whisper. 'However, you then went on to say that you considered asking her to join you for a drink, but thought better of it.' He glanced briefly at the notes, the relevant parts of which he had under-lined with a red pen in advance of the interview. 'You then said that you returned at about five o'clock but she'd gone. And later on, you said that you'd not seen her again.'

Once again, Hoskins shifted his position on his chair and avoided looking at the detective. 'So, I made a mistake. It don't mean I killed her.'

Hardcastle laid the notes on the table. 'Did I or any of my officers suggest that you'd killed her?' he asked quietly.

That appeared to take Hoskins by surprise. 'Well, what am I doing here, then? I mean, why did you have me nicked and brought all the way back here?'

'Quite simply this, Hoskins. When I came looking for you a second time, you'd vamoosed, and your dear mother claimed that she didn't know where you'd gone. Why did you tell her not to let on, eh?'

'I never.'

'Really? Well, she was very backward when it come to telling us your address, and it wasn't until I threatened to arrest her that she came across.' Hardcastle thought he knew the answer, but was not going to give Hoskins a convenient opening.

'Look, guv'nor . . .' Hoskins ran his tongue round his lips; the fact that his mother had come close to being arrested did nothing for his own hope of an early release from the police station. 'It's this geezer, see.'

'What geezer?'

'I owe money, see. And this bloke, a bookie up Wilson

103

Road racecourse he is, has been after me. That's why I took off, and why I told Ma not to let on.'

Hardcastle glanced at his sergeant. 'Have you ever noticed, Marriott,' he asked, a marked element of sarcasm in his voice, 'that every conversation with a criminal somehow ends up at the races? If they've suddenly come into money they can't explain, they won it on a horse. And if this same criminal happens to run, it's because a bookmaker's after him.'

'I'm not a criminal,' protested Hoskins.

Hardcastle stared at the prisoner for a few moments. 'Was this another Danny Hoskins, beach photographer of this parish, who got half a stretch in 1916 for false pretences, then, lad?'

Hoskins sat back, deflated. 'Oh, you know about that, do you? Well, I can tell you, it was a fix. I sent them photos. They must have got lost in the post, what with the war and everything.'

'Of course they did, Hoskins. This country's prisons are full of innocent men, aren't they? Even them as takes pictures with no film in their camera. Now then, let's stop buggering about and get on with it. How come you was seen talking to Fanny Horwood at about four o'clock on King's Road? And more to the point, why did you tell me you hadn't talked to her at all?'

'After what had happened, I thought you might think as how I'd had something to do with it.'

'Well, you're right about that, Hoskins. Go on.'

'That's it, really.'

'Oh no it's not. And I'm getting a little fed up with this cat-and-mouse palaver of yours. So, you met Fanny Horwood again. What happened?'

Again Hoskins licked his lips. 'Like I said before, I fancied her, so after I took her photo, I asked her if she'd care to have a wet with me.'

'And this was at about four o'clock?'

'Yeah, about then.'

'Go on.'

'Well, she said she couldn't, because she had an appointment. But they always say that. It's like stringing you along,

104

like they want to go with you but don't want to seem to give in too easy.'

'Did she say who she had this appointment with?' asked Hardcastle, casting a quick glance in Marriott's direction to ensure that he was taking notes.

'No, she never, and I never asked, because I thought she was making it up. I reckoned there never was no man.'

'Did she say it was a man, then?' asked Marriott, looking up from his note-taking.

Hoskins seemed dismayed not only by the question, but that it had come from the other detective, and hesitated before replying. 'Er, come to think of it, I don't think she did.' He paused. 'But I guessed it must be a bloke.'

'And how long were you talking to her, Hoskins?' asked Hardcastle.

'No longer than three or four minutes, I s'pose.'

'And had she left the beach by this time?' Hardcastle knew, from Mavis Brandon's account, that Hoskins and Fanny had been speaking to each other on King's Road, the main thoroughfare that runs along the seafront.

'Yeah, she had. She was walking towards Palace Pier when I caught up with her.'

'And that was the last time you saw her?' Again it was Marriott who posed the question.

'Yeah, it was, not counting the Sunday morning.' Hoskins was beginning to get flustered now.

'What d'you mean, not counting the Sunday morning?' asked Hardcastle, taking back the questioning again. He and Marriott were well versed in interrogating suspects and had often found that by posing their questions alternately they gave themselves time to think of the next question, but gave the suspect no time to fabricate an answer.

'I was out early and I see all this fuss going on down the beach, by Palace Pier. It was when they found the body, so I took a few photos, hoping I might sell 'em.'

'And did you?'

'Yeah, the *Evening Argus* took one from me. Only give me half a dollar for it, an' all.'

105

'Bit of luck you had a film in your camera that time,' commented Hardcastle. 'Anyhow, let's go back to August.'

'What?' For a brief moment Hoskins had looked relieved, believing the interview to be over, but was startled to find that Hardcastle had yet more questions for him. 'What about August?'

Hardcastle took the other photograph from Marriott. 'You took this photograph in August.' He pushed it across the table.

Hoskins stared at it. 'I ain't never seen it before,' he said.

'Detective Inspector Watson executed a search warrant on your premises and discovered this print among your collection, Hoskins. And you told him that you'd taken it in August. So, don't tell me you haven't seen it before.'

Hoskins picked up the photograph and examined it afresh. 'Oh, maybe I did take it, then,' he said lamely.

'D'you recognize anyone in it?'

'Yeah, it's her what got killed.'

'Yes, it is. Now then . . .' Hardcastle paused, picked up Marriott's notes again and turned a few pages. 'When I interviewed you last, I asked if you had ever seen Mrs Horwood before. Your answer was' – he peered more closely at the notes and spoke slowly to emphasize Hoskins's previous answer – '"Honest, I'd never seen her before."' The DDI put the notes back on the table and gazed at the beach photographer. 'So, what have you got to say to that, my lad?'

'Blimey, guv'nor, I can't remember all the people I took photos of. I've taken hundreds over the years.'

'Some of which were actually received by the people who paid for them,' said Hardcastle drily.

'Yeah, well . . .' said Hoskins, and lapsed into silence.

'I suggest to you, Hoskins, that you knew Mrs Horwood quite well. I suggest that you met her at least in August – maybe after that, even – and probably put her in the family way, and when she came back in November to tell you that she was expecting, you murdered her.'

The blood drained from Hoskins's face and he stared at Hardcastle, tears welling up in his eyes. 'God help me, guv'nor, I never had nothing to do with it,' he said, his voice breaking.

'I wouldn't do nothing like that. She was a lovely girl.'

Hardcastle gazed unemotionally at the distraught young man opposite him. 'Well, I'm far from satisfied as to your innocence, Hoskins, and I shall have you detained here for further enquiries.'

Hoskins looked up. 'I want a solicitor,' he said.

Hardcastle smiled. 'You can't afford one, lad, not if what you say about being hounded by this bookie is true. And apart from that, you'll only see a solicitor when I say you can. It might interfere with my enquiries, see.' He turned to Marriott. 'Put him down,' he said.

'Well, sir, what d'you think?' asked Marriott when they were back upstairs in Watson's office.

'He's a carney little bugger, Marriott,' said Hardcastle, 'but I'm not all that sure about him. He's certainly a tuppenny-ha'penny con man and I wouldn't be surprised if he wasn't up to all sorts of mischief, but quite frankly, I don't think he's up to murder. But we'll see. Let him stew for a few hours – maybe till tomorrow – and then we'll have another word with him.' He opened his tobacco pouch. 'Bugger it, I'm out of baccy.' With a sigh, he put his pipe back on the desk and took out his watch. 'Just gone ten. Right, Marriott, I think we'll go to London.'

'London, sir?' Once again, Marriott was surprised by Hardcastle's sudden decisions. 'What for?'

'I think it's time we had a word with Mrs Major Springer, as the army likes to call the wives of officers. For all we know, Marriott, while we've got Hoskins locked up downstairs, it might be Dudley Springer we ought to be looking at.'

'D'you really think so, sir?'

'Just because he's an army officer, and a hero to boot, don't mean he can't kill someone, Marriott. After all, it's been his trade for the last four years. And we've seen one or two of his sort take the eight o'clock walk since 1914.'

But Hardcastle's journey to London was set to be delayed on two counts, though not for long.

DI Watson entered the office just as Hardcastle was donning his overcoat. 'I'm told you wished to see me, Mr Hardcastle,'

he said, only thinly veiling his resentment that such a dicta-
torial summons should have been conveyed by way of a
sergeant.

'Wait downstairs, Marriott, and close the door.' Once the
sergeant had departed, Hardcastle glared at Watson. 'Mr
Watson, I am conducting a murder enquiry. *Your* murder
enquiry. I've already interviewed Hoskins, who might or might
not have murdered Fanny Horwood, and I'm about to go to
London to make further enquiries regarding the matter. If I
can get here at eight in the morning, I expect you – who your
chief constable has assigned to assist me – to be here at the
same time.' Without giving Watson a chance to reply, he
added, 'That's all.' And with that he swept out of the office,
leaving Watson impotent with fury.

The further delay occurred as Hardcastle and Marriott left
the police station and were confronted by a trio of reporters.
One, a local man named Hargreaves, stepped forward.

'Inspector, is this right that you've arrested Danny Hoskins,
the beach photographer, for the murder of Fanny Horwood?'

'No,' said Hardcastle, who was quite accustomed to fencing
with the press. 'Mr Hoskins kindly came to the station to
volunteer some information. You see, lads,' he continued,
surveying all three reporters and adopting a benevolent tone,
'Mr Hoskins is a vital witness. He took a photograph of the
dead woman on the Saturday afternoon, and quite possibly is
the last person to have seen her alive – apart from her killer,
of course.' That was not true; Major Springer had certainly
seen her later on, when he had high tea with her at Mrs
Edwards's boarding house, but Hardcastle saw no profit in
giving the press more information than they already possessed.
At least, not until he could turn it to his advantage.

'I'm Charlie Simpson, London *Daily Chronicle*, Mr
Hardcastle. Is Dolly Hancock a suspect for the murder?'

Hardcastle laughed. 'Now, whatever gave you that idea?'

'Well, you arrested her. We had it on our front page.'

'It may come as a surprise to you, Mr Simpson, but the
Metropolitan Police has more than one crime to investigate,
you know. And so have I.'

'But our readers are particularly interested in this murder, Mr Hardcastle,' persisted Simpson. 'D'you anticipate arresting someone for it soon?'

'When I'm investigating a murder, my lad, I always anticipate arresting someone for it.' Hardcastle stepped between the reporters. 'Come along, Marriott.'

Eleven

It was just past two o'clock on the Saturday afternoon when Hardcastle and Marriott mounted the steps to the front door of Harriet Springer's house in Elm Park Gardens, Chelsea, a square of elegant residences lying between King's Road and the Fulham Road, nearer to World's End than to Sloane Square. The road outside the houses was covered in straw to deaden the sound of carriage wheels that might disturb the seriously ill.

'Another one near snuffing it, Marriott,' commented Hardcastle, nodding at the straw. 'I hope it ain't Mrs Springer.'

A maid showed them into the drawing room and invited them to take a seat. 'The mistress won't be long, sir,' she said to Hardcastle.

The woman who entered a few moments later was tall and slender. She wore a ruched afternoon gown of limpet-grey taffeta with Magyar sleeves and a lace collar. Even to Hardcastle's eye the dress appeared expensive; Mrs Hardcastle – had she seen it – would have told him that seven guineas was the very least it would have cost.

'Gentlemen?' Harriet Springer gazed confidently but quizzically at the two policemen as they rose from their chairs. In her mid-twenties, she was the sort of woman that *The Tatler* would have described as 'a society beauty'.

Hardcastle introduced himself and Marriott.

'Do sit down,' said Mrs Springer. 'I'm intrigued to know why two detectives should be calling on me.' She inclined her head in a questioning attitude.

'I understand that you were married to Major Dudley Springer, ma'am,' Hardcastle began.

'I still am,' said the woman.

'But I understood from the major that you had separated,' said Hardcastle, somewhat taken aback.

'I wonder whatever gave you that idea,' said Mrs Springer, half to herself. She smiled. 'But more to the point, Inspector, perhaps you would be so good as to tell me why you are taking an interest in my marital status.'

Hardcastle explained, as briefly as he could, how Springer came to be a vital witness in the Brighton murder case.

'Yes, that's all very interesting, Inspector,' said Harriet, 'but I still don't see what our private life has to do with it.' She smiled again, this time directly at Hardcastle, mocking him.

'Quite simply, Mrs Springer, I don't know whether your husband's lying or not.' Hardcastle, with little time to waste on social banter, somewhat brutally ended the woman's teasing approach to his enquiries. 'You see, he told me that you had died while he was in Arras in 1915. I now know that to be untrue, obviously, and I am obliged to test the truthfulness of a witness. It'd be no good me putting him in front of a jury at the Old Bailey, or Lewes Assizes for that matter, if he was going to change his story.'

'I see, and do you think he murdered this poor girl?' Harriet Springer inclined her head once more. Although Hardcastle had been careful to avoid any suggestion that he regarded the major as a suspect, she thought she had detected the real reason for his questions.

'It is police practice to regard everyone as a suspect,' said Hardcastle stiffly, 'but not particularly so in your husband's case.'

'If I am to help you, then perhaps you'd better tell me what he said to you. About our marriage, I mean.'

'When we had proved by reference to the War Office that he was lying about your, er, death,' said Hardcastle, 'he then told me that he had come home on leave and found you in bed with a man, and that you had told him that you wanted a divorce. Then he said that you had gone to live in Nottingham.'

Harriet Springer threw back her head and laughed, a tinkling, girlish laugh. 'Oh, poor Dudley,' she said. 'I've never been to Nottingham in my life.'

'It's not true, then? That you are separated, I mean.'

'No, it most certainly is not.' Harriet's face assumed a serious expression. 'You see, Inspector, Dudley suffered a breakdown of some sort, due entirely to the war. He was engaged in tunnelling – he was with the Sappers, you know – and I suppose it got to him. It's only just coming out now, the sort of strain that our men underwent. We at home knew little of it, although I saw some of the tragic results, nursing at Charing Cross. I was a VAD during the war.'

'I see.'

'I'm not sure you do,' said Harriet. 'He was discharged from the army in July of this year, as a result of a nervous condition, doubtless brought on by his experiences, but he had come home on leave in August last year, just after the mines went up at Messines. He was an absolute wreck, Inspector. It was awful to see him. He was drinking heavily and had no interest in me at all. He went back after his leave, although he was clearly in no fit state to do so – even my limited training enabled me to see that – and I think they posted him to some base camp in Boulogne until eventually he was sent home. I've been at my wits' end, not knowing where he is half the time. I didn't even know he was in Brighton. He started by going out for long walks, then he'd stay away for a night or two, then a week at a time. This time, he's been away for a fortnight or more. I spoke to a consultant I know and he said that the only way was to let him get over it in his own time, but I doubt he ever will.' The teasing had vanished now and Harriet Springer was obviously moved, and concerned for her husband's welfare. 'Is there any way you can persuade him to come home?'

Hardcastle shook his head. 'He's a grown man, Mrs Springer, and he's committed no offence. He's a free agent and if he wishes to stay in Brighton, there's nothing I can do.'

'Do you really think he may have killed this girl, Inspector?'

'As I said before, Mrs Springer—'

112

'Yes, I know what you said, Inspector, but . . .' Harriet paused, momentarily. 'I shouldn't say this about my own husband, I suppose, but you mustn't overlook the fact that, like all soldiers, Dudley's a trained killer. It's what he and thousands of others have been doing for the past four years.' There was a trace of a tear and she turned quickly as she brought a handkerchief to her eye.

'Thank you for being so frank, Mrs Springer,' said Hardcastle as he and Marriott stood up. 'I'm sorry that you have had so much to bear.'

'What d'you make of that, sir?' asked Marriott as the two policemen strode towards King's Road.

'Less happy than before we came, Marriott,' said Hardcastle. 'Mrs Springer is more shrewd than she makes out. She more or less suggested that her husband could have done it. Now, I wonder why she should have done that, planting the seed, so to speak. Or is there another man after all, like the major said? If there is, and the major gets himself hanged, that'd solve all her problems, wouldn't it?' He shook his head. 'I don't know. We started off with a simple strangling and now we're into all sorts of complications. But one thing's obvious, we'll have to have another go at Major Springer.'

Reluctantly, Hardcastle returned to Brighton.

On Monday morning, having despatched Marriott to Mrs Edwards's boarding house first thing, with a request that Major Springer call, once more, at the police station, Hardcastle spent an unprofitable hour or so examining statements and writing reports. At noon, he made his way to the detectives' office. 'Where is Detective Inspector Watson, Goodenough?'

'Out on enquiries, sir,' said the Brighton sergeant.

'What sort of enquiries?'

'He's up at Preston, sir, looking into a burglary. One of the town councillors has had his house broken into.'

'Oh, well, I suppose that's pretty important in this part of the world.' At best, Hardcastle would have sent a sergeant to deal with such a crime. 'Is the chief constable in his office?'

'I don't know, sir.' Goodenough had no need to concern

himself with the whereabouts of so lofty an officer as the chief constable.

Hardcastle turned on his heel and made directly for the chief's office.

'As a matter of fact, Mr Hardcastle, Mr Watson is a little distressed that he's being made use of,' said the chief constable, when Hardcastle had finished complaining about the professional indifference of the Brighton inspector. 'He's a very good officer and he does have other enquiries to attend to.' Almost apologetically, he added, 'And the councillor whose house has been broken into is a member of the watch committee.'

'Be that as it may, sir, Mr Watson doesn't strike me as being great shakes at a murder enquiry. Now, if he's not going to do the job, perhaps I should ask Mr Thomson to send me a DI from London.'

'I don't think that will be necessary, Mr Hardcastle.' The mention of Scotland Yard's assistant commissioner for crime, and the prospect that he would learn of the shortcomings of the Brighton force and its officers, did not please the chief constable. Added to which, he would have to explain to a parsimonious watch committee why he had incurred the additional expense of asking for another officer from London when he had plenty of his own.

'On the other hand, sir,' said Hardcastle smoothly, 'perhaps it might suit all round if Mr Watson was to get on with his own work and you were to give me DS Goodenough, fulltime like. He's got the makings has that young man. Not that I'd let on to him, of course.'

Although jealous of his authority and its implicit right to deploy his own officers as he saw fit, the chief constable was also aware that to have an unsolved murder on his books would not bode well for the force's reputation, and in turn his own. 'Very well, Mr Hardcastle. If you think Goodenough's up to it, I'll assign him to you for the duration of the enquiry. Now . . .' The chief brushed a hand across a desk devoid of paperwork and glanced at the clock, conscious that he had a civic luncheon to attend, a luncheon at which questions might be asked about Brighton's most serious crime of the moment. 'Perhaps you'd be so good as to advise me of the progress of your enquiries.'

Hardcastle gave the chief constable a succinct appreciation of what he had discovered so far and, without waiting for comment, turned to go. But at the door he paused. 'Shall I tell Goodenough, sir, or do you wish to do so yourself?'

'I'm afraid I'm lunching with the mayor, Mr Hardcastle,' said the chief constable, 'so perhaps you'd be so kind as to tell Goodenough that he's attached to you until further notice. Oh, and tell him to hand over his work to someone else.' Dismissing the matter from his mind, he crossed the office and buckled on the Sam Browne belt he affected.

Satisfied that he had got rid of Watson, a man not greatly interested in the murder of Fanny Horwood – or perhaps aware of his own inability to investigate it – Hardcastle returned to the detectives' office. 'Goodenough, come with me,' he said.

Douglas Goodenough followed Hardcastle along the corridor and into the office from which Watson had been evicted. 'Yes, sir?'

'Sit down, lad.'

Apprehensively, Goodenough perched himself on a chair; he had never been allowed to sit down in the presence of Detective Inspector Watson, a man at pains to guard his own petty authority, and was surprised that Hardcastle had invited him to do so.

'I have just spoken to the chief constable, Goodenough, and he has assigned you to this murder enquiry full-time. From now on, you work to me and no one else. Understood?'

'Yes, sir. But I do have other cases that have been given to me. What shall I do about—?'

'The chief says you're to hand them over to another officer,' said Hardcastle. 'Your only concern now is to assist me and Sergeant Marriott to find the murderer of Fanny Horwood.'

Twenty minutes after Goodenough's departure, Watson stormed into Hardcastle's office. 'What is the meaning of this?' he demanded furiously.

'What is the meaning of what, Mr Watson?' asked Hardcastle mildly.

'How dare you take one of my sergeants without consulting me. Sergeant Goodenough has other cases to deal with and I am his superior officer.'

'*Senior* maybe, but *superior* I doubt,' said Hardcastle, further enraging the Brighton DI. 'But since you ask, I have just spoken to the chief constable and he saw fit to assign Goodenough to this murder enquiry full-time. His enquiries are to be given to another of your officers. The chief also expressed the view that you should be allowed to carry on with your own onerous duties. How's your serious burglary getting along, by the way?'

'Why didn't the chief tell me himself?' demanded Watson, by no means placated that the direction had come from his own chief officer, and even further annoyed that he had not waited for Goodenough to tell him so before launching his vitriolic attack on Hardcastle.

'Apparently, he's having lunch with the mayor,' said Hardcastle, thoroughly enjoying the local politics of which he was, thankfully, no part. 'I gather that was more important.'

Watson plucked a handkerchief from his sleeve and held it to his nose before casting a final look of disdain in Hardcastle's direction. Striding swiftly from the office, he almost collided with Marriott, who was on the way in.

'Mr Watson seems a bit upset about something, sir.'

'The chief constable's taken him off the enquiry, Marriott, at my request, and replaced him with Goodenough.'

Marriott realized that further questions about a disagreement between two detective inspectors would be impolitic, and made no comment. Apart from which, he had more important news to impart. 'Major Springer's upped and gone, sir.'

'Gone? Gone where?'

'Mrs Edwards doesn't know, sir. Apparently he packed his bags on Saturday afternoon and said that he was going. Being the nosey woman she is, Mrs Edwards asked him where he was off to, but he said he hadn't made up his mind.'

'What time did he go?'

116

'Mrs Edwards reckoned it was about a quarter past three, sir.' Marriott knew that Hardcastle would want to know, and had questioned the landlady accordingly.

For a moment or two, Hardcastle sat deep in thought. 'Is Mrs Edwards connected to the telephone, Marriott?' he asked eventually.

'Yes, sir, she is. I noticed it in the hall.'

'Yes . . .' said Hardcastle reflectively. 'And so is Mrs Springer. And a quarter past three would be just after we left her place in Chelsea. I wonder . . .'

Violet Gunn, Mrs Edwards's maid, bobbed briefly as she answered the door of the Sussex Street boarding house. 'The mistress is upstairs, sir,' she said. 'I'll tell her you're here.'

'I understand that Major Springer's left, Mrs Edwards,' said Hardcastle, the moment the landlady entered the room.

'Indeed 'e 'as, Mr 'Ardcastle, as I told your Mr Marriott 'ere.' Phyllis Edwards gave the impression that it was quite unnecessary to have to repeat what she had already told the sergeant.

'At about a quarter past three on Saturday, I understand.'

'Exactly so.'

'Tell me, Mrs Edwards, did he receive a telephone call on Saturday, perhaps just before he decided to leave?'

Mrs Edwards took off her glasses and wiped the lenses on her apron, which she had not bothered to remove on this occasion. 'I really can't say, Inspector. I don't 'ave no recollection of 'im using the instrument.'

'What's the procedure when the telephone rings?' asked Hardcastle.

'If I'm not in earshot, so to speak, my maid Violet answers it and then finds the person what the call's for. Guests wishing to make calls 'ave to seek my permission first . . . and pay. The cost of trunk calls is quite atrocious, and if I don't keep a check on it, they runs up my bill something chronic.'

'I imagine so,' said Hardcastle. 'Then perhaps I could have a word with Violet.'

Mrs Edwards turned to the small brass bell she used to

summon the sole member of her staff, and rang it sharply.

'Yes, ma'am?' Violet hovered in the doorway of the sitting room.

'The inspector wishes to ask you some questions, girl. Mind you be truthful now.'

'Sit down, Violet,' said Hardcastle.

The maid glanced nervously at her employer and, receiving a grudging nod of approval, took a seat.

'Major Springer left here on Saturday afternoon, Violet. Is that right?'

'Yes, sir.'

'Did he say where he might be going?'

'I told the sergeant this morning—' began Mrs Edwards.

'If you don't mind, Mrs Edwards, I'm questioning *this* witness. Kindly allow her to answer.'

Mrs Edwards tossed her head and took a sudden interest in a horse-drawn dray that was passing the window.

'Well?' Hardcastle looked at the maid again.

'No, sir, he never said nothing. Only that he was going.'

'Did he receive a telephone call just before he went, or at any other time during the day?'

Once more, Violet glanced apprehensively at the landlady. 'Yes, sir, he did. At about three o'clock, I suppose it was.'

'And you answered the telephone, did you?'

'Yes, sir.'

'And was the caller a man or a woman?'

'It was a lady, sir.'

'And did this lady identify herself?'

'Pardon, sir?'

'Did the lady say who she was? Did she, for example, say that it was his wife? Or did she say something like "tell him it's Mrs Springer"?'

'Oh no, sir, nothing like that. She just asked if she could speak to Major Springer. I asked her to hold on and I went upstairs to his room and told him.'

'And was the major packing his bags when you told him?'

'No, sir. He was sitting in his armchair, smoking his pipe and reading a book.'

Mrs Edwards frowned, presumably at the grave affront of a guest smoking in his room, but said nothing.

'And it was after this telephone call that he said he was leaving, is that right?'

'Yes, sir. He said he had to leave straight away and that he was in a bit of a hurry. I asked him if I could help him to pack, but he said he hadn't got much stuff and it would only take him a few minutes.'

'And he went at about a quarter past three?'

'Yes, sir. He used the telephone to call a taxi.'

Mrs Edwards finally broke her silence. 'And did 'e pay for the call?' she demanded.

'I don't know, ma'am,' said Violet, glancing at the landlady.

'You know the rules, girl. If anyone uses the instrument—'

'Perhaps you'd wait until I'm finished, Mrs Edwards,' snapped Hardcastle. 'The matter I'm dealing with is considerably more important than the price of a local telephone call.'

'If it *was* local,' said Mrs Edwards with a sniff.

'He's hardly likely to summon a taxi from Newcastle, is he?' Hardcastle was becoming increasingly irritated, both by Mrs Edwards's interruptions and her browbeating of the young girl who had the misfortune to be in her employment. 'Incidentally' – the DDI now turned to face Mrs Edwards fully – 'which taxi company would he be likely to call from here?'

'Central Cabs, I imagine,' said Mrs Edwards, with yet another toss of her head. 'It's the only reliable one in the town.'

'As a matter of interest, Mrs Edwards, where were you while all this was going on?'

The landlady hesitated for some time before replying. 'I was upstairs, making the beds,' she said at last, clearly distressed at having to admit that she undertook some of the domestic work involved in running her boarding house.

Hardcastle smiled. 'I see,' he said.

'But I came down in time for 'im to settle 'is bill. That's not a thing I can entrust to the staff.'

'And that, presumably, is when you asked him where he was going?'

'It was. But as I told the sergeant 'ere, 'e never vouchsafed no opinion about that.'

Goodenough was despatched to the office of Central Cabs, but the driver who had picked up Major Springer from Mrs Edwards's boarding house was able to say only that he had taken him to the railway station. His passenger, said the driver, did not say where he intended going from there.

'No more than I expected,' muttered Hardcastle.

Twelve

'Well, Marriott, it looks like we've a couple of things spoiling here. First off, we've got Hoskins locked up with not much to go on, except that he's got a bit of form. And second, Major Springer goes adrift, and I'd put money on his missus having warned him off, but Lord alone knows why. Unless he's mixed up in all this.'

'If he was, sir, I doubt that he'd've waited for us to go knocking on Mrs E's door. He'd've run straight off. 'Course, it might be that this mental trouble of his is what causes him to roam about, like Mrs Springer said.'

'Yes, maybe, Marriott, but there again, she claimed not to know where he was.'

'But we don't know for sure that it was her who telephoned him, sir.'

'True. Perhaps he's got a lady friend on the side that Mrs Major Springer don't know anything about. Even so, I think we'll have him circulated in the *Police Gazette*. See to it, will you.'

'Want him arrested, sir?'

'No, Marriott, just want to find out where he is. I want to know why he ran off like that. Meantime, I'm not too sure that Mr Watson did a half-decent job on searching Hoskins's rooms. I think the time's come to get a brief and do it properly. Where's the magistrates' court?'

'No idea, sir, but why don't we send young Goodenough to get the warrant. He'll know where it is . . . maybe, and it'll be a bit of experience for him.'

'Yes, that it would, Marriott. See to it, will you. And tell him to be quick about it.'

*　　*　　*

121

'Oh, it's you again.' Arms akimbo, Danny Hoskins's battleaxe of a mother stood on the doorstep of her house in Victoria Road. 'And what d'you want this time?'

'I have a warrant to search these premises, Mrs Hoskins,' said Hardcastle, 'and I'd advise you that any obstruction on your part would land you in serious trouble. So be so good as to direct me to your son's room.'

'How many times do I have to tell you lot that my Danny's a good boy. Anyhow, the place has been turned over before. By you and that toffee-nosed inspector from Bartholomews nick,' she said, recognizing Goodenough and pointing a finger at him. 'My Danny wouldn't do no murder and that's a fact.'

'I'll be the judge of that,' said Hardcastle. 'But you won't object to us proving that he didn't do it, will you?'

'Please yourself.' Mrs Hoskins, resigned to having her house rummaged by the police, stepped aside. 'Up the stairs and first door on the right. That's where he sleeps, but he does his developing down the cellar. He's got it rigged up as a studio.' Then, as an afterthought, she added, 'And don't go messing the place up.'

'You were with Mr Watson the last time he came here, Goodenough,' said Hardcastle, opening the door of Hoskins's bedroom, 'so what did he look for?'

'Well, he didn't actually search, sir,' said the young Brighton sergeant. 'He just asked Hoskins where he kept his photographs. Hoskins turned up a couple of shoe boxes and that was that.'

'You mean he didn't do a *proper* search?' demanded the incredulous Hardcastle.

'Not as such, sir, no.'

'Well, bless my soul.' Hardcastle restricted himself to that mild comment, deeming it unprofessional to criticize Goodenough's inspector in the presence of one of his own subordinates. 'Well, this time, lad, I'll show you how a search is done proper like. Get to it, Marriott. And don't get in his way, Goodenough, or we'll finish up in a right bugger's muddle.'

Marriott began meticulously to search the room. He took

the bedclothes off the narrow iron-framed bed, and searched beneath it. He emptied the chest of drawers, one drawer at a time, and thoroughly examined the wardrobe and its meagre contents. But he found nothing of any significance.

'Right, now we'll take a gander at the cellar,' said Hardcastle as he began to descend the stairs to the ground floor.

Mrs Hoskins was in the hall, hands on hips. 'Well?' she demanded.

'Well, nothing,' said Hardcastle. 'Where's the door to the cellar?'

'There,' said the woman, pointing.

Hardcastle led the two sergeants down a set of open wooden stairs. 'Well, I must say he's got this fixed up handsome. Electric light an' all.' Covering one wall was a sheet of black twill, and in front of it a dilapidated couch covered with a few yards of red velvet.

For the moment ignoring the photographic equipment and the floodlights, Marriott made for another chest of drawers. In the bottom drawer, he found a wooden box, secured with a padlocked hasp and staple.

'Did you see that last time you was here, Goodenough?' asked Hardcastle as Marriott placed the box on a bench.

'No, sir. We didn't come down to the cellar at all.'

'Thought as much,' muttered Hardcastle. 'You got that Boy Scout knife of yours, Marriott, the one with the thing for getting stones out of horses' hooves on it?'

'Yes, sir,' said Marriott with a grin.

'Well, don't stand there. See if you can do some damage with it.'

It took but a moment for Marriott to prise off the hasp and staple. 'More photographs, sir,' he said, handing them to the DDI. 'And the negatives, by the look of it.'

'I don't wonder he kept these locked up,' said Hardcastle, grunting as he shuffled the thirty or so prints through his fingers. 'I'm not sure we ought to let young Goodenough here have a sight of them, though. Might upset his blood pressure something cruel.'

'Bit tasty are they, sir?' Marriott asked.

123

'You could say that, yes. Blimey, now we're getting some-where. Have a look at these, Marriott.'

The London sergeant took the photographs and whistled as he studied them. 'Well, I'm blowed,' he said. There were at least six photographs of a naked Fanny Horwood in extremely provocative poses. 'And I reckon they was taken there, sir.' He pointed to the couch.

'Oh, it gets better,' said Hardcastle. 'Here's some of Dolly Hancock, likewise unclothed, and one of her and . . . oh my sainted aunt! Here, Marriott, see if you recognize this man, but keep the name to yourself.'

Marriott's eyes opened wide in disbelief as he recognized Alderman Richard Stevenson, an expression of horror on his face, naked on a bed with an equally naked Dolly Hancock. 'He never said anything about photographs being taken, sir. And he'll have known, because they must have been taken with a flashlight.'

Hardcastle sighed. 'It never rains but it pours, Marriott,' he said, 'but anyway, that makes Hoskins good for a charge under the Obscene Publications Act, to say nothing of blackmail.'

'So, are you going to charge him, sir?'

Hardcastle tapped the side of his nose. 'Not yet,' he said. 'For the moment we'll use it as a stick to beat him with, if you take my meaning. Right now, we've bigger fish to fry.'

'Can I have a look, sir?' asked Goodenough, who had been standing behind Hardcastle, slightly bemused by the exchange between the DDI and his sergeant.

'Yes, all right,' said Hardcastle. 'You'll have to learn about the wicked ways of the world sometime, I suppose. But don't show him the one of the man, Marriott, that's evidence in another case. Perhaps.'

Goodenough took the photographs eagerly and skimmed through them, blushing slightly as he did so. 'Oh no!' he exclaimed suddenly.

'Now what?' Hardcastle demanded.

'This one, sir.' Goodenough, an expression that combined shock and disappointment etched clear on his face, handed the DDI one of the prints. 'It's Mavis Brandon.'

Hardcastle studied the photograph. 'Mmm! I must have missed that one,' he said. 'I wonder what a demure young lady like Miss Brandon was doing with all her clothes off while Hoskins took pictures of her. Still, Goodenough,' he added, with a rare display of sensitivity, 'at least they're not obscene like the others. I suppose that's what you'd call a tasteful artistic pose.' He put the photograph of Alderman Stevenson and Dolly Hancock in his pocket. 'I think we'll leave that one out, Marriott. At least, for the time being.'

'What now, sir?' asked Marriott, once he and Hardcastle were satisfied that there was nothing else to be found.

'Back to the nick and front Hoskins with this little lot.' Hardcastle took the photographs from Goodenough and replaced them in the box. 'Be interesting to hear what he's got to say about 'em.'

'How much longer are you going to keep me here?' Hoskins had partially recovered from his last bruising encounter with the London DDI and was on the offensive once more, lounging in his chair with a half sneer on his face.

By way of a reply, Hardcastle threw the photographs of the naked women on the table that separated him from his prisoner. 'We found these in your cellar at Victoria Road, Hoskins.'

'Oh!' said Hoskins, visibly stunned by this latest revelation.

'Is that all you can say?' Hardcastle spread the prints with his forefinger. 'Fanny Horwood, Dolly Hancock and Mavis Brandon.'

'Yeah, well, they asked me to.'

'Really? All rushed down your place, tearing off their clothes, begging you to take pictures of 'em. Is that it?'

'Well, not exactly.'

'No, Hoskins, not exactly at all. And what does your dear mother think about your little sideline, eh?'

'Gawd blimey, she don't know nothing about it, guv'nor. I only ever took 'em when Ma was out. She goes out a lot.'

'I thought she might.' Hardcastle chuckled. 'And where did you flog 'em? And for how much?'

'Up the Smoke,' Hoskins admitted miserably. 'A shilling apiece.'

'Where in London?'

'Round and about. Pubs mainly.'

'I see.' Hardcastle glanced at Goodenough. 'I'm going to ask the prisoner another question about a certain person, Sergeant, and I don't want you mentioning it to anyone. And that includes Mr Watson. Got it?'

'Yes, sir,' said the mystified Goodenough, who had not seen the photograph of Alderman Richard Stevenson and Dolly Hancock.

'We also found this photograph, Hoskins.' Hardcastle withdrew the print from his pocket and tossed it on to the table.

'I don't know nothing about that,' said Hoskins, his alarm failing to disguise his lie.

'You'll have to do better than that, lad, because we found it in your cellar. And it so happens that the individual in this photograph is what you might call a person of substance, and, as a result of his information to police, certain charges of blackmail have been brought.' Hardcastle paused. 'Now, it seems to me as though you're well involved, and that could cost you fourteen years in chokey,' he added, by no means sure that he was right about the sentence.

Hoskins went as white as freshly fallen snow and began sweating. 'I never knew it was anything like that, guv'nor, so help me. I done it for a mate.'

'And what was this mate's name?'

Hoskins ran his tongue round his lips. 'Jack Foster,' he said in a whisper.

'Ah, I thought as much, and where did you take this revealing portrait, eh?'

'Up the Smoke.'

'Where up the Smoke?'

'It was a room over a shop in some place called Perkins Rents. That's the name of the street. It's down Victoria way.'

'Yes, I know Perkins Rents,' said Hardcastle, sighing inwardly that this crime was firmly located in the area for

126

which he had responsibility. 'And how did you come to be there taking photographs?'

Hoskins remained silent. Suddenly Hardcastle slapped the top of the table with the flat of his hand so sharply that not only did Hoskins start up in alarm, but so did Marriott and Goodenough. 'I'm waiting,' he thundered.

'It was Jack's idea,' said Hoskins hurriedly. 'He said as how he wanted proof that his missus was cheating on him. He reckoned that she'd gone on the game and took men to this flat what she'd got down this Perkins Rents place. It was dark, see, and him and me hid behind a curtain and I set up me camera and the flood. I took the picture when Jack give me the nod. I never knew there was nothing wrong about it, guv'nor, honest.'

'Is that a fact?' said Hardcastle. 'Well, you might like to know, Hoskins, that Jack Foster's lawfully wed to someone called Lily. The woman in this picture of yours, who you also took these other nude pictures of, is Dolly Hancock. And she's currently banged up in Holloway awaiting trial for blackmail. This blackmail.' The DDI tapped the photograph with a forefinger. 'But he was right about Dolly Hancock being on the game. And her and Foster have got a nice little racket going, earning a few sovereigns out of putting the screws on the likes of that gent in your photograph, see.'

'Oh Gawd!' said Hoskins.

'Yes, that about sums it up,' said Hardcastle drily. 'And how many other times did you oblige Jack Foster in this room in Perkins Rents?'

'There weren't no more, guv'nor, honest. I only done it the once.'

'So, what did he pay you?'

Hoskins fidgeted with the edge of the table. 'Ten bob . . . and me train fare.'

'Slave labour,' said Hardcastle in an aside to Marriott. 'So, how did you meet this Jack Foster, Hoskins?'

'It was when he come down here one weekend. Must have been back in June, I reckon.'

'And what happened? Just stroll up and ask you if you

127

wanted to take a photo of his missus doing the business? That it, was it?'

'Not exactly. I met him in a pub and sold him some of them.' Hoskins pointed a grubby finger at the pile of photographs on the table. 'He said his wife – I s'pose he meant Dolly – wouldn't mind me taking a few of her if I'd share the profits with him. And he said he'd show me where to flog 'em up the Smoke. Well, trade was a bit slack, has been for the past year or more, so I said yes. The next weekend he brung her down and I took 'em. Then he told me, on the QT like, that she was putting herself about, and would I go up the Smoke and take a picture of her at it.'

'There's also a photograph of Mavis Brandon among that lot.' Hardcastle gestured at the small pile of photographs. 'How did that come about?'

'She was up for it an' all,' replied Hoskins casually. 'We was walking out for a bit and I told her I was doing some artistic work. She asked what sort and when I told her, she said she didn't mind having a go.'

'And you sold those as well, did you?'

Hoskins hesitated. 'Yeah, one or two,' he whispered.

Hardcastle glanced sideways at Goodenough and noted the look of utter contempt on the young sergeant's face. Facing Hoskins again, he said, 'Well, I wouldn't like to be in your shoes when her old man gets to hear of it. Mind you, he'll probably have to wait a few years till you get out of the nick. Anyway, that's all very interesting, but now tell me about Fanny Horwood, her what was murdered.'

'What about her?' Hoskins was constantly licking his lips now.

Hardcastle sighed and leaned back in his chair. 'First off, you lying little toerag, you told me that you'd never seen her before the ninth of November, that's the Saturday she got topped, or at least the day before. And you gave me some eyewash about not having spoken to her, but later on you changed your tune and told me you'd had a chat with her about four o'clock. But when we fronted you with another photograph, you said you'd taken it in August. And now it seems you've taken a few of her in the altogether. When was that?'

'That was June an' all, maybe July. Jack Foster come down again and this time he had Fanny with him. We had a few drinks down the Feathers, up Preston way, and he said as how she'd be willing for me to take a few snaps of her the same as them I'd took of his Dolly. Except she wasn't his Dolly, so you say.'

'No, she wasn't, Hoskins, and that's a fact.' Hardcastle leaned forward and studied the miserable figure of the beach photographer. 'And when did you put Fanny Horwood in the family way? After one of these little photographing sessions of yours, was it? There was Fanny, naked as the day she was born, and you took a fancy to her. Is that it? Quick tumble on that couch in the cellar. Then, in November, down she comes and tells you the sorry tale that she's up the spout. Oh dear, you think, I can't have that, so, late that Saturday night, you take her for a walk down on the beach, all romantic like, and you strangled her under Palace Pier.'

Hardcastle knew that the post-mortem examination had shown Fanny to be only two months pregnant, but she might well have had intercourse with Hoskins and, unaware of the identity of the real father, she had persuaded the photographer that the child was his.

'I never, guv'nor, honest,' pleaded the anguished Hoskins. 'I'd never do a thing like that. She was a sweet girl, was Fanny.'

'Save it for the jury, Hoskins,' said Hardcastle. 'And while you're tucked up nice and safe in your comfortable little cell down below, you can think about telling me the truth.'

Hardcastle stood up and moved towards the door. But then he paused. 'When did you last see Jack Foster?' he asked.

'Weekend of the Armistice – well, the Saturday before, I mean.'

'That'd be the ninth, then. The night Fanny was murdered.'

'Yeah, but I tell you, guv'nor, I never had nothing to do with it.'

'So, Marriott,' said Hardcastle, once Hoskins had been

returned to his cell, 'Foster was down here that weekend after all. And he reckoned he was drinking with Dolly Hancock in the King's Arms till nine o'clock. Time we had another word with him. And that leery landlord. But they'll wait.'

Hardcastle had sent a message to Mavis Brandon asking her to call at the police station, and now she was seated in the same room recently occupied by Hoskins. But Hardcastle, appreciating that Goodenough had taken a shine to the girl, excluded him from the interview. For both their sakes.

'When I last spoke to you, Miss Brandon,' Hardcastle began, 'you told me that you'd walked out with Danny Hoskins for a week or so.'

'That's right.' Mavis, elegantly attired in a high-necked tweed costume with buttons up one side of the jacket, high boots and a fetching tricorn hat, surveyed the detective with a demure half-smile on her face.

'And you just walked out with him? Nothing else?'

'No, of course not.' But Mavis, unable to disguise her anxiety as she made the denial, was sure that something else was about to come out.

Without comment, Hardcastle produced the photograph of the girl and placed it on the table between them.

Mavis leaned forward only slightly before blushing scarlet and putting her hand to her mouth. 'Where did you get that from?' she asked in barely a whisper.

'From Danny Hoskins's so-called studio.'

Opening her handbag, Mavis took a handkerchief from it and carefully dabbed at her eyes. 'It was a mistake,' she mumbled.

'So I imagine,' said Hardcastle. 'Perhaps you'd care to explain it?'

'I'd been going out with him for about ten days, on and off, and I'd already decided that I was going to end it. But one evening, just before that, he took me to a pub in Montpelier Road and I, er, well, I'm afraid I got a little tipsy. Then he suggested that I went back to his house in Victoria Road – it was only round the corner from the pub – to have a look at

130

some of the photographs he'd taken of all the old buildings in Brighton.'

Hardcastle raised his eyes to the ceiling, but forbore from asking if Hoskins had mentioned etchings. 'And what happened next?'

'He said he was applying to become a member of the Royal Photographic Society and that, as well as the snaps of old buildings, he needed to submit a photograph of a beautiful girl, unclothed. Anyway, as I said, I was a bit tipsy and I went ahead and did it for him. I know I said that I didn't much care for him, but at the same time I wanted to help him. He said he was hoping to get out of the rut of taking photographs on the beach, move to London and become a society photographer.'

'I rather think he was spinning you a yarn there, Miss Brandon,' said Hardcastle mildly. The prospect of a swindling little tuppenny-ha'penny beach photographer like Hoskins aspiring to membership of so eminent an association as the Royal Photographic Society was equalled only by Mavis Brandon's gullibility in believing it.

'I realize that now.' Mavis, her tears flowing quite freely, was clearly very distressed. Looking up and pointing at the photograph, she asked, 'What's going to happen to that?'

'I'm afraid we're going to have to hold on to it for the moment, Miss Brandon. It may be required as evidence. But once we've done with it, I shall make sure you get it back, together with the negative.'

'D'you think anyone else has seen it?'

'I doubt it,' said Hardcastle, not wishing to distress the girl further by telling her that Hoskins had admitted to hawking copies around London pubs.

'I don't know what my father would say if he found out,' said Mavis.

'I shouldn't tell him if I were you, Miss Brandon. We can do without having another murder in Brighton.' Hardcastle cast a fatherly eye at the distraught girl opposite, a girl who was about the same age as his daughter Kitty. 'I'll get Sergeant Goodenough to escort you home.'

131

For the first time since the disclosure of the photograph, Mavis Brandon brightened. 'Thank you,' she said, but then paused. 'Has Douglas seen it?'

'Douglas?'

'It's Sergeant Goodenough's first name, sir,' said Marriott.

'Oh, is it? No, he hasn't. If you wait here, Miss Brandon, I'll send him down.'

And when Hardcastle told Goodenough to see the girl back to her father's shop on Grand Parade, he cautioned him not to mention the photograph, and that if Mavis should do so, to deny all knowledge of its existence.

Marriott was amazed that his DDI seemed to have a soft side after all.

Thirteen

On the day following the discovery of Hoskins's photographs of nude women – and the one of Alderman Stevenson and Dolly Hancock naked on a bed – Detective Inspector Watson entered the office he had been forced to give over to the London detective.

Nodding briefly to Marriott, he said, somewhat deferentially, 'Mr Hardcastle, I wonder if you could spare me a moment of your time?'

'Mr Watson?' If Hardcastle was surprised at the Brighton man's conciliatory approach, he did not show it.

Uninvited, Watson sat down on the chair adjacent to the desk. 'Sergeant Goodenough tells me that you're having an entry put in the *Police Gazette* seeking the whereabouts of Major Springer, the man who was staying at Mrs Edwards's boarding house.'

'That is so, Mr Watson.'

'I think I may be able to help you there.'

'Really? In what way?' asked Hardcastle. For Watson to be offering assistance was an unusual event indeed.

'I was at a lodge meeting last night—'

'A what?' Hardcastle feigned ignorance. He knew what Watson was talking about – had recognized the device on his watch chain – but he was not a freemason himself and disapproved of policemen who were.

'A lodge meeting. I'm a freemason, Mr Hardcastle.'

'Oh, I see.' Hardcastle allowed the whisper of a smile to cross his face. 'So how does that help me?'

'I was talking to a fellow mason, Councillor Cross. He's a member of the Brighton Town Council, and a well-known antiques dealer in the town.'

133

'Don't tell me he's been offered Fanny Horwood's jewellery, Mr Watson.'

'Good heavens no. He's not that sort of dealer. He only handles genuine antiques: Chippendale, Sheraton, the occasional Hepplewhite, that sort of stuff.'

'I suppose he would,' said Hardcastle drily, thinking that any friend of the Brighton DI would have to be 'out of the top drawer'.

The sarcasm escaped Watson. 'Well, I think, from what he was saying, that he's come across Major Springer in rather unfortunate circumstances.'

'Has he indeed?' Hardcastle took a sudden interest and leaned forward, linking his hands on the desk. 'In what sort of unfortunate circumstances?'

'Councillor Cross told me that a couple of weeks ago, he was attending a reception at the town hall when he was approached by a man who gave the name of Digby. He told the councillor that he was an engineer qualified in geology.'

'So what makes you – or for that matter, Councillor Cross – think that this man was Major Springer? If that's what you're suggesting, of course.'

'I'm coming to that, Mr Hardcastle,' said Watson a trifle tersely. 'This Digby fellow told Councillor Cross that he was raising capital to extend the workings of a gold mine in South Africa, and went on to say that he had a substantial investment in it himself.'

'Oh dear, oh dear,' said Hardcastle, a smile spreading across his face.

'It's not a laughing matter, Mr Hardcastle,' said Watson.

'No, it's not,' said Hardcastle. 'Not if you're daft enough to part with money for a handful of worthless shares, and I presume that's what your friend the councillor did.'

'Yes, I'm afraid he did.'

'Bit saucy that, seeing the town hall's right next door to this police station, ain't it?' commented Hardcastle with a chuckle, further discomfiting the Brighton DI. 'How much did he get taken for?'

'A hundred pounds,' said Watson and, ignoring Hardcastle's

hoot of derisory laughter, added, 'I told Walter that he should have sought my advice first.'

'Walter?' queried Hardcastle, thinking that seeking Watson's advice on such a matter would have been a waste of time.

'Yes, Walter Cross.'

'Oh, I see. And . . . ?'

'Well, last week Councillor Cross – Walter – went to London to attend an auction. Apparently there were some pieces in which he was particularly interested. Having some time to spare, he went to the address he had been given for this gold-mine company in the City, only to find that it was occupied by a reputable firm of solicitors who knew nothing of any gold mines.'

'Not surprised,' said Hardcastle brutally. 'Oldest trick in the book. I don't understand why your friend the councillor fell for it, and that's a fact, Mr Watson. From what you say, he's supposed to be a businessman.'

'Yes, well, be that as it may, he then sent a wire to a professional colleague in Johannesburg, another antiques dealer, with whom he sometimes does business, and asked him to investigate. In short, Mr Hardcastle, there is no such gold mine.'

'Yes, well, that sort of thing's happening all the time,' said Hardcastle dismissively. As a London detective, he was familiar with such frauds. 'But you still haven't told me why Councillor Cross should think that this man Digby and Major Springer was one and the same.'

But Watson was about to reveal that, for once, he was capable of a little detective work. 'He didn't know about Springer,' he said, 'but I made some enquiries at the town hall and questioned the doorkeeper who was on duty that night. Apparently this man arrived claiming to have lost his ticket. He said he was the guest of the mayor and told the doorkeeper that his name was Major Dudley Springer and produced an army discharge book to prove it. Well, as he was properly attired in full evening dress and was wearing medals, including the Military Cross, the doorkeeper let him in without question.' The Brighton detective sat back, a triumphant smile on his face. 'You see, Mr Hardcastle, we know our business down here.'

'Maybe so, Mr Watson,' said Hardcastle, 'but that doesn't necessarily mean that Springer *was* Digby the con man. Although I must admit,' he added grudgingly, 'it does make it seem likely.'

'Councillor Cross's description of this man Digby tallied exactly with the doorkeeper's description of Springer, right down to the medals,' said Watson, enjoying a moment of what he perceived to be ascendancy over the London man. 'The doorkeeper served in the war, but was discharged after Passchendaele – he lost an arm there apparently – so he's familiar with medals. But the point is that there was no Digby on the guest list.'

'And presumably no Springer either,' said Hardcastle, determined not to let Watson have it all his own way.

'Er, quite so.' Watson was clearly unhappy that Hardcastle had spotted that flaw in his investigation, such as it was.

'Did you ask the mayor if he knew Springer – or, for that matter, Digby – given that Springer told the doorkeeper that he was a friend of his?'

'Yes, but the mayor said he'd never heard of him.'

'Don't surprise me,' said Hardcastle, 'and the fact that Springer seems to be a confidence-trickster don't tell us where he is now, does it? Any more than it ties him in with Fanny Horwood's murder.'

'No, it doesn't, but I thought it might help.'

'And how far have you got with this case of yours, Mr Watson?' asked Hardcastle.

'Er, well, I thought that, as you had an interest in Springer, and had had dealings with him, you might—'

But, sensing what was at the back of Watson's mind, Hardcastle interrupted. 'Assuming that a crime has actually been committed, Mr Watson,' he said, 'it was committed in *your* bailiwick against one of *your* town councillors. It's nothing to do with me. My only interest in Major Springer is as a witness in a case of murder.' He had no intention of telling Watson that he had not yet dismissed the major from his list of suspects for that murder.

'Yes, I suppose so,' said Watson wearily, frustrated at having failed to unburden himself of an investigation that was rightly his responsibility anyway. And one that promised to be both complex and protracted, at least in his experience.

'Well, Marriott, what d'you make of that?' asked Hardcastle, once Watson had left the office.

'Not surprised, sir.'

'No, nor me neither,' said Hardcastle. 'I know the army reckoned that Springer was a bit doolally tap, but I've got me doubts about that, and I wouldn't mind betting he worked his ticket. Looks like he's nothing more than a common magsman. And what's more, it wouldn't surprise me if he weren't the sort to pick up women of easy virtue. After all, him and his missus don't seem to be living together, so he's got to get his oats somewhere. I think there might be more to the bold major than meets the eye, Marriott, and I think we'll have to look a bit closer at him.'

'What about the fraud against this councillor, sir?' asked Marriott.

'If there *was* a fraud, Marriott, and *if* we find Springer and *if* he holds his hands up to it, then we'll feel his collar and hand him to Mr Watson on a plate. It's about the only way this lot down here'll get him locked up in their nick.' Hardcastle gave a short chuckle. 'There's something a bit odd about a police force that wears white helmets in the summer, Marriott,' he added, apropos of nothing in particular.

'So, what's next, sir?'

'Next, Marriott, is that we go back up to the Smoke and kill two birds with one stone, so to speak. We'll have another chat with Mrs Springer *and* we'll have a word with Alderman Stevenson. Where's he live, by the way?'

'Down Croydon way, sir,' said Marriott.

'Does he, indeed? Well, that's a bit of a stride from Westminster and no mistake. Still, it has to be done, Marriott. I don't think that the alderman's been quite straight with us, having got himself snapped getting across that Dolly Hancock.'

137

Hardcastle paused to pick up his pipe. 'And while we're about it, we'll nick Master Jack Foster for blackmail.'

'We've only got Hoskins's word that he was involved, sir.'

'Yes,' mused Hardcastle, 'that should set 'em at each other's throats. I can't wait to see Foster's face when we tell him Hoskins'll be giving evidence against him at the Bailey.'

'I didn't expect to see you again,' said Harriet Springer when the two policemen were shown into her drawing room. 'Please sit down.'

'Have you any idea where your husband is, Mrs Springer?' asked Hardcastle.

'No, I haven't. As I told you last time you were here, it came as a surprise to learn that he was in Brighton.'

'Well, he's not. Not any more. And to be honest with you, I'm wondering why he's run.'

'Run? What a strange expression.' Harriet Springer raised an eyebrow. 'What *can* you mean?'

'How long has your husband been pushing bogus gold-mine shares, Mrs Springer?' asked Hardcastle, determined not to waste any more time on a woman he thought was playing him along.

'What a preposterous suggestion, Inspector,' said Mrs Springer with a suitable expression of outrage. 'I hope you have some substantial evidence to support that allegation. I'll have you know that my family is well connected to the legal profession, and I'm sure that such a statement would be regarded by them as highly defamatory.'

But Hardcastle was not to be that easily diverted from his enquiries. 'Does Major Springer own a full evening dress?' he asked. 'White tie and tails.'

'Of course he does.' Harriet Springer's haughty tone of voice implied that it was unthinkable that she could possibly know anyone who did not possess such essential garments. 'Why d'you ask?'

'Without wishing to interfere with the Brighton police enquiry, Mrs Springer, they are dealing with an allegation that, some two weeks ago, a man answering your husband's description defrauded a Brighton businessman – a town councillor, as it happens – of a hundred pounds by selling him shares in a gold mine that didn't exist.' Hardcastle paused for a moment. 'Why did you telephone the major last Saturday, just after Sergeant Marriott and me had left here?' It was a guess, but Hardcastle was fairly sure that it was an accurate one.

With a suddenness that surprised even Hardcastle, Harriet Springer dissolved into tears. 'Oh, it's all too awful,' she sobbed. 'Why has he done this to me?'

Waiting until the woman had at least partly recovered, Hardcastle said, 'I take it you have something to tell me, Mrs Springer?'

At last she looked up. 'It was the war, Inspector. He was all right before it all started. But when he finally came home he was a changed man.'

'Yes, so you said the last time I was here,' said Hardcastle. 'The same time as you denied any rift between you and your husband. Was that the truth?'

'No. Not long after he left the army, a friend of mine saw him in the West End – in Mayfair somewhere, I think – and he was talking to a common street woman, a prostitute. And apparently he went off with her, so my friend said. When next I saw Dudley, which was some three days later, I confronted him with it. Of course, he denied it, but a wife can always tell, you know.'

'So I believe,' said Hardcastle, under no illusion but that his wife Alice would detect any such dalliance on his part in a trice. 'What happened then?'

'I told him that I wasn't going to tolerate such behaviour, and that if that was what he wanted, he'd better go. After all, Inspector, I do have a certain social standing in the community.'

'And did he go?'

'Most certainly. As I said, my family is connected with the law. My father was a high-court judge and my elder brother's about to become a King's Counsel. Heaven knows what he'll think when he hears about this.'

'You still haven't told me why you telephoned him last

Saturday afternoon, Mrs Springer,' said Hardcastle, dismissing
the woman's veiled threat, 'nor how you knew where he was.'

'I didn't telephone him, Inspector. And I've told you already,
I didn't know where he was, and I don't know now.'

And in the face of that flat denial, Hardcastle had no option
but to leave it. For the present.

'What d'you make of that, Marriott?' asked Hardcastle as
they went in search of a cab.

'I'm wondering if they're both at this share-pushing game,
sir.'

'Yes,' said Hardcastle thoughtfully. 'On the other hand, she
might be at a different game. Like entertaining high-class
gentlemen for a fee, if you take my meaning. There's money
there, Marriott, and it has to come from somewhere.'

'Is this Alderman Stevenson connected to the telephone?' asked
Hardcastle when the pair were back at Cannon Row police
station.

'Yes, sir,' said Marriott.

'Well, speak to him and arrange for us to see him. I don't
want to go traipsing all the way down to Croydon if he ain't
going to be there.'

A few moments later, Marriott returned. 'He's there, sir,
and he's willing to see us this evening.'

'Good. How do we get to his place?'

'Train to East Croydon from Victoria, sir.'

Hardcastle glanced at his watch. 'Come along then, Marriott,
there's no time to waste.'

Although the house that Stevenson lived in was nowhere near
as grand as Hardcastle had expected of a man who was both
an alderman and a stockbroker, it was nonetheless a substantial property.

'Well, now, Inspector, I presume that this is about the
unsavoury matter of my involvement with this Dolly Hancock
creature,' Stevenson said, as he invited the two detectives to
sit down. 'Incidentally, you may speak freely. My wife's not
feeling too good, and is lying down upstairs.' He spoke with

all the urbane confidence of his class. 'You've come to tell me that a date's been fixed for the trial perhaps?'

'Not yet, Alderman,' said Hardcastle. 'I'm still in the process of collecting evidence.'

Stevenson, his hand hovering over an array of decanters on a sofa table, turned. 'But surely you have all you need, Inspector?' He paused. 'Can I offer you gentlemen a drink? A whisky perhaps.'

'No thank you, sir,' said Hardcastle, speaking for himself and Marriott. 'But it seems you haven't been telling me the whole truth,' he continued.

Stevenson poured himself a large whisky and sat down opposite the two detectives. 'Well, I can't really think what else there is to tell you,' he said, his face showing no sign of concern at Hardcastle's accusation.

'You paid this unknown man the sum of fifty pounds, I think you said.'

'That's correct.'

'Because he threatened to sue his wife for divorce and cite you as a co-respondent.'

'That was enough, surely?'

'And do you think he would have done, sir?' asked Hardcastle. 'I mean, the word of him and his trollop of a wife wouldn't have stood up against the word of a person of substance such as yourself.'

'Be that as it may, Inspector, I wasn't prepared to risk the publicity, even if the man's case had failed. Whatever the outcome, merely being dragged through the courts would have been enough to ruin me, socially if not professionally. In the Stock Exchange a man's word is all-important, as is the conduct of his private life.'

Hardcastle thought it was a bit late to worry about that. 'Yesterday afternoon, Alderman,' he said, 'in company with other officers, I searched a house in Brighton. The house of a beach photographer.'

'I don't really see what that has to do—'

'And we found some photographs, sir. Photographs that weren't exactly the sort that you'd expect a beach photographer to go about taking. These certainly weren't taken on no beach, and that's a fact.' From his inside pocket, Hardcastle withdrew the print of Stevenson and Dolly Hancock naked on a bed, and proffered it to the alderman. 'That was one of them.'

'Oh my God!'

'You knew this had been taken, of course, didn't you, sir?'

'Yes, I did,' said Stevenson in a whisper.

'It would've been helpful if you'd told us that from the start. We've arrested the man who took it, and we're about to arrest the man who pretended that he was married to the woman you was having your way with.'

'You know who he is?' Stevenson sounded surprised. But then, as he realized what Hardcastle had said, he asked, 'Did you say *pretended* that he was married to her?'

'Yes, I did. The whore who picked you up in St James's Park wasn't his wife. She was a common prostitute with convictions for soliciting. You see, Alderman, you was set up, so to speak. The whole thing was deliberate. Dolly Hancock was sent out to find someone who had all the appearance of a wealthy gentleman, and preferably one who'd imbibed a bit more than was good for him. Then she steers him back to her place, where the photographer's waiting, along with the other man, the man you paid fifty pounds to, and at the right moment, off goes a flash and that's the result.' Hardcastle pointed at the photograph that Stevenson was still clutching. 'There *was* a flash, sir, wasn't there?'

'Yes, there was.'

'And further demands were made, weren't they?' Hardcastle did not know that for certain, but he knew the ways of black-mailers.

'Yes.'

'And did you pay?'

'Yes, I'm afraid I did. A hundred and fifty pounds in all. But once I discovered who this woman was, I came to you.'

'Presumably this man promised to return the photograph and the negative.'

'Yes, that's what he said, but he never did. I think I'd've

had to go on paying. But seeing that woman's photograph in the paper was a lucky stroke for me.'

'You could've come to the police long before that, sir,' said Hardcastle. 'And the next time you met him, we'd've felt his collar, and that would have been that.'

'I suppose so,' said Stevenson, 'but I wasn't thinking straight, I'm afraid. Incidentally, did you find the negative when you searched this man's house?'

'Yes, we did, sir. However, I have to tell you that the photographer concerned also admitted to taking photographs of nude young women – including that Dolly Hancock – and selling them in London pubs. I have reason to believe that he may also have sold some of those.' Again Hardcastle pointed to the photograph in Stevenson's hand. 'There's quite a trade for explicit prints of that nature, you see.'

'Oh, my God! This is terrible. What on earth can I do?'

'Not a great deal, I'm afraid, sir. There's no way of tracing them now. The photographer won't know who he's sold 'em to. They tend not to ask questions in that sort of business, you see.'

'Oh what a mess.' The anguished Stevenson leaned forward and pressed his hands to his forehead. After a few moments, he looked up. 'Did you say you were about to arrest this other man, the man who blackmailed me?'

'That we are, sir.'

'Who is he?'

'His name's Jack Foster and he lives in Combermere Road, Stockwell. And, as a matter of interest, I quite fancy him for a murder in Brighton.'

Fourteen

It was nigh on eight o'clock in the evening by the time Hardcastle and Marriott had made their way from Alderman Stevenson's house in Croydon to Jack Foster's place in Stockwell. A muffin man, a long tray on his head and ringing his bell as he wended his slow way down the centre of the street, gave the two detectives a mournful glance.

'Sounds like he's going to a funeral, Marriott,' said Hardcastle, as he hammered on the door of 5 Combermere Road. After a lengthy pause, it was eventually opened by Foster's wife Lily.

'Yes, what is it?' she asked, failing immediately to recognize the policemen.

'Your man Jack at home is he, missus?' asked Marriott. 'We're from the police.'

'Oh yes, you was here before. I remember you now,' said Lily. 'No, he's down the pub.'

'Would that be the King's Arms?' asked Hardcastle.

'That's right. What d'you want him for anyway?'

'Just a chat, Mrs Foster. Nothing for you to worry about.' Hardcastle had no intention of telling Lily Foster that her husband was about to be arrested on the serious charge of blackmail. 'But while we're here, perhaps we could have a word with you.'

'What about?'

'Might be better if we came in.'

Reluctantly Lily Foster opened the door wide and stepped back. 'I'm just in the middle of getting Jack's supper,' she said.

Hardcastle forbore from telling her she was wasting her time.

144

'Anyway, what d'you want?' Lily asked as she led the two men into the kitchen.

'Just over a fortnight ago, the weekend before Armistice Day, as a matter of fact, was Jack here, or was he away somewhere?'

'What d'you want to know that for? If it's about the money he owes, he ain't got none. Thanks to the army.'

'Well, was he or wasn't he?' persisted Hardcastle.

'No, he wasn't. And it's no good asking me where he was, because I don't know. I never know what he's up to these days. Now, if you don't mind, I've got work to do.'

The badly tuned piano was still playing in the public bar and there was a sing-song in progress, though it was not as fervent as the last time Hardcastle and Marriott had called at the King's Arms.

'Reckon the high spirits of the Armistice has worn off a bit, Marriott,' said Hardcastle as he pushed open the door of the saloon bar.

The landlord spotted the detectives as soon as they entered. 'Evening, gents. Back again, I see. What's it to be?'

Hardcastle gave Marriott a hard look and the detective sergeant bought two pints of best bitter.

'Jack Foster been in tonight?' asked Hardcastle as he drained a good half of his beer.

'Still here, guv'nor, in the public,' said the landlord, absently wiping the top of the bar with a filthy cloth. 'What's he been up to now?'

'Just need a chat with him, but I'll finish my beer first,' said Hardcastle.

'Want me to tell him you're here?' asked the landlord helpfully.

'No thanks. Probably frighten him off. You could just let me know if he's still there, though.'

'Hold on.' The landlord walked a few steps along the bar and peered into the other part of the pub, shielded from the saloon bar by a frosted-glass screen. 'Yeah, he's still there.'

'On his own, is he?' Hardcastle asked casually, as though it were of no importance.

'Yes. Not like him to be on his tod, though. He's usually got that Dolly Hancock with him, but I ain't seen her for a bit.'

'No, and I don't reckon you'll see her for quite a long time.' Hardcastle finished his beer. 'Right, Marriott, let's go and deal with Foster.'

The two walked out into the street and in through the door marked 'Public Bar'. There was an immediate cessation of the singing as the two obvious detectives strode in. Foster, leaning on the bar with a pint pot in his hand, looked round and gazed at the two policemen apprehensively.

Marriott stood behind Foster while Hardcastle placed himself beside the man. 'Jack Foster,' he said quietly, 'I'm arresting you for blackmail.'

'What are you on about, guv'nor?' Foster, looking very alarmed, put his beer down on the bar. 'I ain't done no blackmail.'

Hardcastle turned to face the clientele, who by now were taking a great interest in the proceedings. 'And you lot can get on with your drinking,' he said, 'unless you want to join him.'

Hardcastle and Marriott escorted their prisoner into the street and Marriott hailed a cab.

'Scotland Yard, cabbie,' said Hardcastle, and, turning to Marriott, added, 'No good telling 'em Cannon Row or half the time you'll finish up at Cannon Street in the City.'

'Yes, I know, sir,' said Marriott, who had heard it a hundred times.

'What's this all about?' asked Foster in the dark interior of the cab. 'I don't know nothing about blackmail.'

'You just wait till you get to the nick, my lad, and all will be explained,' said Hardcastle.

'But my Lily's expecting me home for me supper,' whined Foster.

'Well, she'll be waiting a bloody long time,' said Hardcastle. 'About eight years, I should think,' he added, half to himself.

Marriott lodged Foster in the interview room at Cannon Row

police station while Hardcastle went upstairs to his office to get the photographs that he had seized from Danny Hoskins's cellar.

'What have you got say about that?' asked the DDI when he returned. Intent on leading Foster into an admission that he was a party to Hoskins's little money-making scheme, Hardcastle showed him a photograph of the naked Dolly Hancock.

'It's Dolly,' said Foster.

'I know it's Dolly,' said Hardcastle. 'I've got her locked up in Holloway prison. But what d'you know about it, eh?'

'Well, I sort of fixed up for it to be taken,' said Foster, expressing no surprise at the news that Dolly Hancock was in prison.

'And who took it?'

Foster looked miserable. 'Some bloke down Brighton,' he said.

'Name?' demanded Hardcastle.

'Danny Hoskins. He's a beach photographer. I never see no harm in it, guv'nor. And Dolly was all for it. She likes showing off her charms.'

'And this one?' Hardcastle produced the photograph of Alderman Stevenson and Dolly Hancock. 'Showing off her charms there, was she?'

'Don't know nothing about that one,' said Foster, a little too quickly to be convincing.

'Is that so? Well, Danny Hoskins, who took the one of Dolly on her own, says you do. He says you set it up that Dolly went out and picked up a toff in St James's Park, took him back to a room in Perkins Rents, where you and Hoskins was waiting to catch him having his way with Dolly.' Hardcastle sat back and waited.

'It weren't nothing like that,' pleaded Foster. 'I reckoned that Dolly was cheating on me and I wanted proof.'

Hardcastle laughed. 'You'll have to do better than that, Foster. You see, I know that you're lawfully wed to Lily, so, what Dolly Hancock gets up to ain't none of your business. But that didn't stop you relieving this gent of a hundred and

147

fifty quid on the grounds that he'd been having it away with your alleged missus, did it?'

'Ain't got nothing to say,' said Foster, and lapsed into sullen silence.

Hardcastle stood up so rapidly that his chair fell over with a clatter. Leaning over, he seized the lapels of Foster's jacket and dragged the unfortunate prisoner so close to him that he was half bent across the table. 'Don't bloody mess with me, lad,' he said, and just as quickly pushed the man away so that he collapsed into his chair, an expression of stark terror on his face.

'It was Dolly's idea, her and that Hoskins,' muttered Foster hurriedly.

'That's not good enough, not by half,' said Hardcastle, 'and you'll shortly make a statement to my sergeant here, admitting your part in the whole affair. Or I might have to persuade you. Got it?'

Foster nodded miserably, but said nothing.

'Now then,' Hardcastle continued, producing the photograph of the naked Fanny Horwood, 'what about that?'

'That's Fanny,' said Foster.

'I know it's Fanny. I've looked at her dead body in the mortuary, lad. And I want to know who put her there.'

'It weren't me, guv'nor, on my life.'

'On your life, eh? Well, you could well be taking the eight-o'clock walk, Foster, so I should think carefully about what you say. Your missus Lily says you weren't at home the weekend that Fanny got topped, because we've just asked her. And when I saw you before, you said you was in the King's Arms with Dolly Hancock all evening and then spent the night in her bed at Clapham. But your mate Danny Hoskins says you was in Brighton that weekend and you had a drink with him in a pub on the Saturday evening.'

Foster put his hand inside his shirt and scratched his chest. 'Yeah, I was down Brighton,' he admitted eventually.

'And what was you doing down Brighton, eh, my lad?' asked Hardcastle, continuing to hector his reluctant suspect.

'What d'you think I was doing? Kipping with Dolly, of course.'

'Where?'

'We put up in a boarding house, somewhere along the coast, Rottingdean way.'

'Well, we'll check that, but Hoskins said you fixed up with him to have these photographs of Dolly Hancock and Fanny Horwood taken in the altogether. Then you told him where to sell 'em *and* you took half the profits.'

'Yeah, well, I did. There ain't nothing wrong in it.'

'No? Well, I can think of at least half a dozen acts of parliament that I could do you under for that,' said Hardcastle, exaggerating somewhat. 'On the other hand, if you topped her . . .' he added menacingly, and left the threat hanging in the air.

'I never, I swear. Why would I want to do that to a nice girl like Fanny?' Beads of sweat had started to break out on Foster's forehead.

'Because she was two months pregnant, Foster, and you didn't know what you was going to tell your wife Lily, that's why.'

'Knowing Fanny, the sprog could've been anyone's,' whined Foster.

'Come off it, Foster. It was your kid and you know it.'

'Yeah, all right, it was, but that don't mean I done for her.'

'So why tell me all this poppycock about being in a boozer in Stockwell when you was down at the seaside?'

'I thought you was on to me for the killing, guv'nor. It was just bad luck I was down Brighton that same weekend, but I never knew Fanny was down there an' all. An' I know as how innocent people sometimes get nicked for something what they ain't done.'

'Is that so?' Hardcastle fixed Foster with a steely gaze. 'So how come the landlord at the King's Arms reckoned you was in his boozer all that Saturday evening – well, till about half six anyway?'

'I done him a favour and he said he'd cover for me if you came poking around. As soon as I saw that bit in the paper about poor Fanny getting herself murdered, I knew you'd be on to me before long, so I had to fix up an alibi on account of being down Brighton the same time.'

149

'And what about this letter from Sidney Mason? Make that up an' all, did you?'

'Who?'

'You showed me a letter that you said Fanny had received from a Sidney Mason, suggesting that she and him went to live in France.'

'Yeah, well, I got me brother to write that, the day after you come round.'

'D'you know what obstructing the police in the execution of their duty means, Foster?'

'Yeah, sort of.'

'Well, if you weren't in enough bother already, I'd likely be putting that on the sheet an' all. Now, where was this place near Rottingdean you reckoned you stayed at with Dolly Hancock?'

'I don't rightly remember.'

'No, I didn't think you would. Well, we'll just have to ask Dolly, won't we? In the meantime, Foster, you'll be charged with blackmailing this here Alderman Stevenson.'

'I never blackmailed him, guv'nor. He paid me for having his way with Dolly. Straightforward bit of business.'

'What, a hundred and fifty sovereigns just for screwing Dolly Hancock? Ten bob's about the most she's worth. Pull the other one,' scoffed Hardcastle. 'You might call it business, Foster, but I call it living on the earnings of prostitution, and that on its own could score you a few years in the nick. That's on top of what you get for the blackmail.'

'She ain't no prostitute,' said Foster.

'Oh, but she is, and she's been weighed off for it at Marlborough Street police court. As was Fanny Horwood.' Hardcastle stood up. 'You can take a statement from him, Marriott, then you can charge him and put him down. We'll have him up in front of the beak tomorrow morning.' And with a parting shot at Foster, added, 'And you mind you tell the truth in the statement that you're going to make to my sergeant here, or, like I said, you'll have me to reckon with.'

Leaving Marriott to deal with Foster, Hardcastle went

upstairs and called into the detectives' office. 'Is Catto here?' he asked.

'He's gone home, sir,' said Detective Sergeant Wood.

Hardcastle glanced at the clock. It was five to ten. 'Having an early night, is he?' he asked caustically, and turned on his heel. Then he paused. 'Tell him I want to see him first thing in the morning, before Sergeant Marriott and me goes to Bow Street court.'

Detective Constable Henry Catto was waiting for Hardcastle when the DDI arrived the next morning.

'Ah, Catto, come in.'

'Yes, sir.' Catto, always apprehensive when summoned by Hardcastle, followed him into the office.

'You went to the War Office and made some enquiries about Major Springer.'

'Yes, sir.'

'Who did you see?'

'A clerk in the records department, sir, and he got the info from the Royal Engineers records office. Why, is there something wrong?'

'Not with you, Catto, but I don't think the army's being quite honest about this Springer chap. Right, that's all. And send Sergeant Marriott in.'

'Yes, sir.' Somewhat mystified by his short interview, Catto departed to leave Hardcastle pondering.

'Marriott,' said Hardcastle, when the detective sergeant joined him, 'I'm not happy about what Catto turned up at the War Office about this Springer.'

'No, sir?'

'No, Marriott, and I think we'll have to do a bit more digging. But right now, we've got an appointment with the beak at Bow Street court.'

It was all over in the space of about five minutes. The magistrate listened to Hardcastle's evidence of arrest and remanded Jack Foster in custody for eight days.

'And now, Marriott, we're going to Great Scotland Yard,'

said Hardcastle. 'Not our Scotland Yard, the other one down Whitehall.'

'Yes, I know where it is, sir, but what are we doing there?'

'Talking to the military police, Marriott, that's what.'

The cab set them down outside the London Recruiting Office, and Hardcastle led the way up the short flight of steps.

A messenger cast a humorous glance at the two detectives. 'You're a bit late to join up, gents,' he said. 'The war's over.'

'You can keep your jokes for them what appreciates it, cully,' said Hardcastle sharply. 'I want to see whoever's in charge of the military police here.'

The smile vanished from the messenger's face. 'Oh, really? And who might you be?'

'Divisional Detective Inspector Hardcastle of the Whitehall Division.'

Minutes later Hardcastle and Marriott were shown into the office of the assistant provost-marshal, Lieutenant Colonel Frobisher of the Sherwood Foresters.

'Good morning, gentlemen. The messenger tells me you're from the civil police. What can I do for you?'

'I'm investigating a murder in Brighton, Colonel,' Hardcastle began, once introductions had been effected, 'and I'm interested in a Major Dudley Springer of the Royal Engineers. At least, he was until he was discharged on the seventh of July 1918, apparently suffering from wounds received.'

'Is there some suggestion, Inspector, that this Major Springer might have been responsible for this murder?'

'I don't know as yet, Colonel, but it seems fairly certain that he's been involved in some fraudulent share-pushing.'

'Dear me! Murder *and* fraud,' said Frobisher, a half smile on his face. 'So, what d'you want, last address known to the army? Where we send his pension. That sort of thing?'

'Not exactly. One of my officers made enquiries of the War Office and got what you might call the skeleton details. They didn't seem too sure about why he was discharged – said something about a nervous problem – but it could have something to do with this murder I'm looking into.'

'Well, the best I can do is to draw the officer's record file – which may take some time – and then I'll see what I can tell you. Say three days?'

'Three days, Colonel? There is some urgency in this matter.'

'Mmm!' Frobisher stroked his moustache. 'I suppose I could get them here by this afternoon at a pinch. I'll see what I can do. Could you come back at, say, three o'clock?'

Colonel Frobisher was as good as his word, and when Hardcastle and Marriott were shown into his office once again, he had Springer's records reposing on his desk.

'Interesting fellow, this Springer,' he said.

'Thought he might be,' said Hardcastle.

Frobisher riffled through the brief contents of the file and looked up. 'He's not all he seems.'

'I was coming to that conclusion myself, Colonel, but in what way?'

'Let me say at the outset that he won a Military Cross for his involvement in the mining of the Messines Ridge. You know about that, of course.'

'Yes. I'm told them mines rattled the windows of Ten Downing Street when they went off.' And then in an aside, Hardcastle added, 'Time someone did.'

Frobisher smiled. 'But then it would appear that he deserted.'

'Deserted?' echoed Hardcastle. 'What, Springer?'

'Yes, there's quite a bit about it here. Hours after the mines went off, he disappeared, went absent. He was picked up two days later about a mile behind the lines. Seems he was found wandering about in his shirtsleeves. No tunic, no cap, no weapons.'

'So, what happened?'

'At first he claimed to have lost his memory.'

'Typical con man,' muttered Hardcastle.

'But then he said that he was upset by the mine that went off late at Spanbroekmolen and killed half a company of the Royal Irish Rifles who were advancing, but it turned out that it wasn't one of the mines he'd set. Anyhow, it was all hushed up. There'd been a couple of officers shot for cowardice

153

during the war and it caused quite a hoo-ha in the House of Commons. I suspect that the brass didn't want to risk it again, especially with a fellow who'd spent such a long time underground and had got an MC to boot. He was in open arrest for a while, but then they sent him off on leave for a week or two. When he returned, they posted him to a depot near Boulogne somewhere while they thought about what to do with him. Eventually, they wisely decided that he was suffering from some sort of mental illness and discharged him.' Frobisher closed the file and looked up. 'I don't know if that helps at all.'

'Not much,' said Hardcastle, 'although it don't altogether surprise me. Is there anything on his file about his wife?'

The colonel opened the file again. 'Harriet, née Gibson, and an address in Chelsea.'

'Say anything about her parents, Colonel? What her father did for a living, for example?'

Frobisher referred to the file once more. 'Not very much,' he said. 'Only that he was a bank clerk. Why, is that relevant?'

'Might be,' said Hardcastle. 'When I saw her the day before yesterday, she told me her father was a high-court judge and her brother was about to become a King's Counsel. Did it say what Springer did before he joined up?'

'Yes, he was a bank clerk too,' said Frobisher.

Fifteen

The revelation that Harriet Springer's father had been a bank clerk and not a high court judge merely served to deepen Hardcastle's suspicions about the woman's husband.

And the story of his seeking the company of a prostitute – if it were true – moved Springer's status, at least in Hardcastle's mind, from that of witness to suspect. It now became a matter of urgency to find him.

'That notice about Springer in the *Police Gazette* come out yet, Marriott?' asked Hardcastle.

'Yes, sir. And Brighton police have put another in saying he's wanted for fraud. On warrant.'

Hardcastle laughed. 'Well, I'm blessed,' he said, 'so, Detective Inspector Watson's finally got off his arse.'

'So, what's next, sir?'

'Back to Brighton first thing in the morning, see if we can't get this murder sorted out.'

'D'you fancy Foster for it, sir?'

'Yes. And Springer and Danny Hoskins,' said Hardcastle gloomily. 'Where's Catto?'

'Next door, sir. D'you want him?'

'Yes, him and Wilmot. Fetch 'em in here, Marriott.'

When the two detective constables were standing in front of his desk, Hardcastle surveyed them carefully. 'I hope you're up to the job I'm about to give you,' he said, 'because I want you to do an observation.'

'How long for, sir?' Catto asked unwisely.

'For as long as it takes, Catto, and don't interrupt.'

'No, sir.'

'You two are going to keep an eye on Harriet Springer's place down Elm Park Gardens, Chelsea.'

'What exactly are we looking for, sir?' ventured Wilmot.

'If she makes a move, I want her followed. See where she goes and what she gets up to. And if Major Springer turns up, you can have the pleasure of feeling his collar on behalf of the Brighton police. Come to think of it, you can bring her in an' all, but only if you've captured the major. Somehow I don't think she's entirely the innocent party she's holding out to be.'

'Very good, sir.' Catto and Wilmot turned to go.

'I ain't finished yet,' said Hardcastle. 'Either of you know what Major Springer looks like?'

'Er, no, sir,' said Wilmot.

'Then you'll need a description, won't you? Sergeant Marriott'll give you the details. But if you arrest Springer, you bring him here and tell me. I don't want you going off at half-cock and telegraphing that Brighton lot until I've had a chat with him. I think I fancy him for the Fanny Horwood job as much as I fancy Jack Foster. Right, off you go and don't let Mrs Major Springer catch a sight of you, not unless you're in a nicking mood. Got it?'

'Yes, sir,' said Catto.

'Right, Marriott,' said Hardcastle, glancing at his watch, 'just time to go up to Holloway prison and have a chat with Dolly Hancock. And we'll see if this tale of Foster's about going to Rottingdean holds up.'

The fearsome gate-wardress must have weighed at least twelve stones, even though she was little more than five feet six inches in height. 'Who?' she demanded.

'Dolly Hancock, on remand for blackmail,' repeated Hardcastle.

'Oh, that little bitch. Yes, all right, gents, if you like to come in, I'll get her brought up from the wing. Won't keep you a mo'.'

'Not so busy, now you've got shot of the suffragettes, I suppose,' said Marriott, making casual conversation.

156

'They weren't no trouble,' said the wardress dismissively.

'I'll bet they wouldn't have dared,' whispered Marriott as the woman turned away.

'I don't know about you, Marriott,' said Hardcastle, when the wardress had left them in a side room, 'but she terrifies me, so God knows what she must do to the prisoners.'

'Oh Gawd! It's you,' said Dolly Hancock as she was brought into the room by a wardress equally as formidable as the one on duty at the gate. The young prostitute looked drawn and haggard, and was wearing a shapeless, grey cotton dress that seemed two sizes too large for her.

'D'you want me to stay, Inspector?' asked the wardress.

'No, it's all right,' said Hardcastle. 'She won't give no trouble.'

'Well, I'll be outside when you've finished with her.' Leaning close to Dolly's ear, the wardress added, 'And you mind you behave yourself, Hancock, or there'll be trouble.'

'You wouldn't have a flask, would you?' asked Dolly, once she was alone with the two detectives.

'A flask? What are you on about?' Hardcastle asked.

'You know, a drop o' gin, whisky even. I ain't had a drink for a week.'

'No, I haven't. Anyway, it'll do you a power of good going without,' said Hardcastle. 'Now then, we arrested Jack Foster yesterday, and right now he's banged up in Brixton nick.'

'What've you nicked him for?' Dolly seemed genuinely surprised.

'Same charge as you. Blackmailing Alderman Stevenson, and seeing him off for a hundred and fifty quid.'

'*How much?*' screeched Dolly, obviously scandalized by what Hardcastle had told her. 'You're having me on.'

'You heard,' said Hardcastle.

'The swindling little bastard!' exclaimed Dolly angrily. 'He only give me ten bob. And he said that was for the screwing.'

Hardcastle laughed. 'Looks like you've been had in more ways than one.'

'It's not that bleedin' funny, mister,' said the aggrieved Dolly. 'He was always telling me he was on his beam ends.

157

But come to think of it, whenever he come round my place, he always come in some old clothes and he'd change into some decent togs what he kept in my bedroom, to go out like. Then he'd change back again before he went home to his missus.'

'Foster's your pimp then, is he?'

'So what. Anyway, what you here for?'

'Jack Foster says he spent the weekend before the Armistice with you.'

'That's right, he did. I told you last time. We went down the King's Arms, and then we went back to my place in Clapham and spent the night together.'

'Well, Jack's had to change his story now, mainly on account of what someone else told me. So, what did you really do?'

Dolly's shoulders slumped and she shook her head slowly. 'He's a right sod is that Jack Foster,' she said.

'So, what did you do?'

'We went down the seaside, didn't we. Got a train to Brighton on the Saturday afternoon and Jack lashed out on a taxi. It was along the coast somewhere towards ...' Dolly paused. 'He said something about it being near some place called Rottingdean.'

'So why did you tell me this cock-and-bull yarn about having been in the King's Arms at Stockwell till half-past nine on the Saturday, and then going back to your place?'

'That's what he told me to tell you. He said if I didn't I'd be in for a striping.' Even now the thought of Foster's threat to slash her face with a razor made the girl shudder.

'How come the landlord of the King's Arms swears you and Foster was in his pub on the *Saturday* night, then? Did Jack square him up?'

'Sort of,' said Dolly. 'Well, I did.'

'What's that mean?'

'The landlord said he'd only do it for a price.'

Hardcastle laughed. 'Don't tell me. You had to spread your legs for him.'

'How d'you know that?' Dolly pretended to be annoyed that Hardcastle had worked that out.

'Because I've been a copper since before you were born, lass.'

'Yeah, well, that's what happened.'

'I hope you're telling me the truth this time, Dolly.'

'Yeah, I am, honest.'

'So, how long were you in Rottingdean?'

'Till Sunday afternoon.'

'And was he with you the whole time?' Hardcastle asked.

'Yeah! 'Cept for Saturday night.'

'Oh? And where did he go Saturday night?'

'Some pub, I s'pose. I dunno where he went, but he said he had to meet someone.'

'And you didn't go with him?'

'Nah, he said he had to meet this geezer on his tod. Well, that pissed me off, I can tell you, and we had a bit of a barney about it. I asked him what was the big idea of taking me down there and then leaving me on me own. So I told him to bugger off, and I went to bed.' Dolly gave Hardcastle a lascivious grin. 'Again!'

'Did he say who he was meeting?'

'Nah!' said Dolly, 'and I never asked.'

'What time did he get back from this pub, then?'

'Don't ask me. I was dead to the world. All I know is when I woke up next morning about seven, he was kipping beside me. And snoring something awful.'

'What time did you get back to London?' asked Marriott, who was busy taking notes.

'Got home about six o'clock on the Sunday evening, I s'pose. Then we went down the King's Arms for a drink.'

'And did Jack go back to his place in Combermere Road after that?' Hardcastle asked.

'Nah! Stayed the night with me, didn't he? Can't never get enough of it, can't Jack.'

'How many other times did he spring the photograph trick on one of your clients, Dolly?' asked Hardcastle.

'That was the only one, and I never knew it was going to happen neither.'

'Not what Danny Hoskins said.'

'Who's he?'

'You haven't forgotten Hoskins, surely. He's the Brighton beach snapper who took pictures of you in your birthday suit.'

'Oh, him. So, what did he say?'

'That Foster sent you out to pick up a toff so's Hoskins could snap the two of you at it.'

'That's a bloody lie. I never knew nothin' about no pictures being taken. Not till after it was done anyway.'

'Well, there it is,' said Hardcastle, producing the photograph of Dolly with the alderman.

Dolly Hancock studied the photograph for some time. 'That ain't bad of me, is it,' she said with a smile, 'but it ain't so good of poor old Dick. Looks like a frightened rabbit.'

Hardcastle frowned. 'How come you know he was called Dick?' he asked.

'Well, it weren't the first time he'd had me, was it? He must've screwed me at least half a dozen times. He weren't bad at it neither. For a toff.'

'Why didn't you tell me all this before?' asked Hardcastle, infuriated that Stevenson still appeared not to have told him the whole truth about his liaison with the prostitute.

'Never thought you'd believe me, even though what Dick told you was a pack of lies. What with him being a proper gent an' all. Anyway, Jack told me not to let on to the law that Dick was a regular.'

'Tell me about the night the photograph was taken, then, Dolly.'

'Like all the other nights. Dick used to go to some meeting. I think he said he was on the square, whatever that means. And after the meeting he used to come round my place in Perkins Rents for a bit of jig-a-jig.'

'Alderman Stevenson told me that the night that photograph was taken, he was crossing St James's Park on his way to Victoria station and that you accosted him and he foolishly allowed you to take him back to Perkins Rents.'

'Yeah, well, that was a load of tommy-rot. He come down Perkins Rents just like he had before. I never had to go out looking for him. He come round the third Friday of every month, regular as clockwork.'

'How d'you feel about giving evidence against Jack Foster?' asked Hardcastle.

Dolly Hancock picked nervously at the edge of the wooden table. 'I dunno about that,' she said, looking up. 'That Jack Foster can turn bleedin' nasty when the mood takes him. Like I said just now, he threatened to have me striped.'

'Well, the way things are going, he'll be inside for quite a few years. That's if he don't get topped.'

'*Topped*?' Dolly sat up in alarm. 'What would Jack get topped for?'

'That's not your business, Dolly.' Hardcastle remained in thought for a few moments. 'Look, you're due up before the beak again tomorrow, remand hearing, and you'll like as not get another eight-day lay down. But if, come Foster's trial, you're willing to tell an Old Bailey jury what you've just told me, and tell it on oath, I reckon we can count you out of this blackmail. That way you'll be out of here tomorrow.'

'You're on,' said Dolly hurriedly.

'D'you reckon she was telling the truth, sir?' asked Marriott as the pair were on their way back to Cannon Row police station.

'Yes, I do. There's nothing like a few days in a place the likes of Holloway prison to concentrate the mind. What's more, she knows that if she don't come up to snuff, she'll finish up back there. Anyway, now you've taken a statement from her, she can't go back on it, not without getting herself in bother with the judge. And I don't reckon she'd fancy getting sent down for contempt.'

'Don't look like we'll be going to Brighton tomorrow morning, then, sir.'

'Not straight off, Marriott, no. We'll slide up to Bow Street, offer no evidence against Dolly Hancock, and get her sprung. But sometime or other, I've got to have a word with Mister-bloody-Alderman Stevenson. If he thinks he can sell Ernie Hardcastle the pup, then I've got a surprise in store for him.'

Marriott remained silent. He knew that what his DDI said
was true.

The next morning, before the court sat, Hardcastle saw the
chief magistrate in his chambers at Bow Street, showed him
the statement that Marriott had taken from Dolly Hancock and
explained that, in view of that fresh evidence, it was unlikely
that the case against Dolly Hancock would succeed.

Ten minutes later, Hardcastle stepped into the witness box
and told the same magistrate that the police were offering no
evidence against her, and asked that she be discharged.

'You told me that Jack Foster had been in here the night of
Saturday the ninth of November,' said Hardcastle, once the
landlord of the King's Arms had served him and Marriott.

'So he was, guv'nor. Why?'

'Because I've now had statements from Foster, Dolly
Hancock – she's the floozy who was with him – and a bloke
in Brighton, all of which tells me he left London for Brighton
on Saturday afternoon and stayed there the night.'

'But I had a look in me book,' said the landlord, becoming
immediately defensive.

'Well, perhaps you'd better have another look.'

The landlord picked up the book containing details of the
credit he afforded his regular customers, and flicked through
the pages. 'Oh, blimey. I'm sorry, guv'nor, it was the Sunday
evening I gave him half a crown on the slate.'

'So, he wasn't in here on the Saturday night?'

'Not that I noticed, no. Gets very crowded in here of a
Saturday night, so he might have been in. There again, he
might not. I always have a few extra hands working behind
the bar Saturdays, so I can't be sure.' The landlord paused.
'What's it to be, gents – on the house, of course.'

'I'll buy my own beer, thanks.' The furious Hardcastle
leaned across the bar and, putting two fingers in the top of
the landlord's waistcoat, drew him slowly closer. 'Now then,
cully,' he began menacingly, 'when I came to see you the first
time, you said you didn't know the woman who was in here

with Foster. But it seems you knew it was Dolly Hancock all along. And what's more, I have a statement from her, saying that you give her and Foster an alibi for Saturday, on account of which she let you screw her. Well, I hope she was worth it, because in my book that makes you an accessory to murder.' Relinquishing his hold on the licensee's waistcoat, the DDI stood back.

'I never knew it was anything like that, guv'nor, honest,' said the landlord, clearly rattled at Hardcastle's threats. 'Foster said that he was in bother with people he owed money to. He said if anyone come asking, I was to say he was in here on the Saturday with Dolly Hancock. I know what you said last time you was here, but I thought you was after him for money.'

'D'you think I came up the Clyde on a bicycle?' demanded Hardcastle. 'I'm not a bloody debt collector, and right now I've a mind to charge you with obstructing me in the execution of my duty. For a start. Anyhow, the least you can reckon on is regular visits from George Lambert, the DDI from Brixton, and his men, just to make sure you ain't breaking the law. And he might just take it into his head to object to the renewal of your licence.' Turning to Marriott, he said, 'We seem to be wasting too much time on poxy landlords to get on with this bloody murder, Marriott, so when we get back to the nick, telephone Mr X and tell him we're coming to see him again.' And within the landlord's hearing, he added, 'And remind me to have a word with George Lambert.'

Even though Alderman Stevenson was his usual urbane self, he displayed a slight sign of impatience that the two detectives had found it necessary to visit him yet again.

'What is it this time, Inspector?' he asked, as he invited Hardcastle and Marriott to take a seat in the drawing room.

'Dolly Hancock, Alderman,' said Hardcastle.

'What about her?'

'She's been released from custody on account of the police offering no evidence.'

'*What?* What on earth are you talking about?'

'Last time we were here, I told you that we were going to

arrest Jack Foster for blackmailing you. Well, we've done that and he's now locked up in Brixton prison on remand awaiting trial.'

'But I still don't understand why you should have released the Hancock girl.'

'Because, at last, she's told me the truth, and I believe her. You see, Alderman, she didn't pick you up in St James's Park on the nineteenth of July at all. You went to her place in Perkins Rents quite willingly, as you had done on at least six previous occasions.' Hardcastle sat back and waited to see what reaction that allegation would produce. It was predictable.

'That's preposterous. I've never heard such a downright lie in all my life.'

'Furthermore,' Hardcastle continued relentlessly, 'she's willing to give evidence to that effect when Foster's tried at the Old Bailey.'

Stevenson's head dropped so that his chin was resting on his chest. He stayed like that for some moments before looking up at Hardcastle. 'Will my name still be kept out of it, Inspector?' he asked quietly.

'Of course. I told you right at the beginning that your identity would be safe. However,' Hardcastle went on, 'you've made my enquiries much more difficult and you've wasted a lot of my time. Apart from which, Dolly Hancock has been locked up in Holloway prison for a week. A bit harsh that, considering she never had nothing to do with the blackmail.'

'I'm sorry, Inspector, but you must realize my position. That man – Foster, you say his name was? – was bleeding me dry.'

'Yes, well, as I said before, if you'd come to us straight off, we could've knocked it on the head, so to speak.'

'I can only apologize, Inspector, but I was trying to avoid any publicity. To be perfectly honest, I thought you might be able to deal with it without involving me at all.'

'I'd've thought you'd know that we couldn't have proceeded without evidence from the person what was being black-mailed, Alderman. You see, the courts won't accept what they call hearsay evidence.'

'No, I do see that now.'

'What's more, it's possible that Dolly Hancock might take it into her head to sue you for defamation. Even though she's a common prostitute, she still has rights. And you'd been with her several times of your own free will.' Although the giving of slanderous information to the police was unlikely to succeed at law, Hardcastle knew perfectly well that Dolly Hancock would not have the faintest idea about launching such an action anyway, but he saw no reason to let Stevenson off too lightly.

'Oh God!' said Stevenson, putting a hand to his forehead and letting out a deep sigh. 'Is there any chance she might settle out of court?'

'Possible, I suppose,' said Hardcastle, giving the impression that he was affording the matter great consideration. 'I could ask her, unofficially, of course.'

'I'd be most grateful if you would, Inspector. Most grateful indeed.'

Dolly Hancock was almost pleased to see the two policemen. But she was less pleased when Hardcastle told her that he had been to see Alderman Stevenson.

'What did he want this time, then?' she asked, under the misapprehension that the alderman had summoned the police rather than that they had visited him to put Dolly Hancock's account of what had happened.

'He's a bit concerned that you might take him to court for slandering you about picking him up in St James's Park the night the photo was taken.'

'I told you, I never picked him up. He come round Perkins Rents like always.'

'I know, Dolly,' said Hardcastle patiently. 'That's the point. He now agrees that you didn't pick him up, but that's what he told us first off, and that's why you finished up in Holloway for a week.'

'Oh!' It was obvious that Dolly Hancock was having great difficulty in following what Hardcastle was saying. 'So, what happens now?'

'Well, you don't want to go to court and tell the judge about having Alderman Stevenson visiting you half a dozen times so's he could bed you, do you?'

'Blimey, no,' said Dolly. 'I've got me reputation to think of.'

Hardcastle laughed. 'Bit late for that, Dolly.'

Dolly laughed too. 'Yeah, all right, but what am I supposed to do now?'

'The alderman suggested that you might be agreeable to settle out of court.'

'Look, mister, I don't know what you're going on about. What's it all mean?'

'It means, Dolly, that he's willing to offer you a sum of money as sort of compensation for getting you nicked. So how much d'you reckon that's worth?'

Dolly's eyes lit up. 'You mean he's willing to give me money for that? And it'd all be legal?'

'That's it, yes. So, what d'you reckon your pain and suffering in Holloway's worth?'

For several seconds the young prostitute looked pensive. 'Reckon he'd wear ten quid?'

'Make it fifty, Dolly, and he'll come across, have no fear.'

'*Fifty!* Blimey! D'you reckon he would?' Dolly obviously had trouble appreciating what it would be like to possess fifty pounds.

'Leave it to me. I'll have a word with him.'

'You're a toff, Mr Hardcastle, and no mistake.' Dolly paused and looked across the room. 'Would you like a gin, to celebrate?'

Hardcastle glanced at the dirty glasses next to the bottle of Gordon's gin. 'No thanks, Dolly, we're a bit busy right now. But I'll let you know about the money.'

Sixteen

Hardcastle had declined to traipse all the way down to Croydon again that evening, and spoke to Alderman Stevenson on the telephone. He told the stockbroker that Dolly Hancock would agree to settle out of court for fifty pounds and Stevenson acceded with alacrity. A cheque for that amount, he told Hardcastle, would be in the post to the prostitute as soon as his solicitor had received the necessary written assurances from her that that would be an end of the matter.

Hardcastle replaced the receiver on its rest and gazed at the 'candlestick' telephone for a moment or two. 'You know, Marriott,' he said, 'that thing can be quite useful at times. I reckon it might catch on. It's certainly just saved us a couple of hours.'

'Yes, sir,' said Marriott.

'Any news from Catto and Wilmot?'

'Yes, sir.'

'Well, what have they got to say for themselves?'

Anticipating Hardcastle's question, Marriott had already collected the surveillance log from the detectives' office. 'Nothing much, sir. Yesterday was their first full day keeping an eye on Mrs Springer's place at Elm Park Gardens. She went out at half past eleven and walked up King's Road to Peter Jones's shop, where she bought some handkerchiefs and a pair of stockings. Returned home at ten to one. Went out again at five to four, to a teashop in Fulham Road, and spent an hour drinking tea and chatting to a female friend. Then she went home, sir, arriving at ten past five. And that's it, sir.'

'Mmm! I hope I'm not wasting their time,' mused Hardcastle. 'Still, we'll give it a few more days, Marriott. Tell 'em to telegraph Brighton with any important news, because that's where we'll be, come the morning. In the meantime, I think we can treat ourselves to a pint. Then we'll have an early night.'

'Yes, sir.' Marriott glanced at his watch. It was nine o'clock.

Hardcastle's intention of returning to Brighton on the Friday morning was thwarted by the arrival of a telegraph message from Detective Inspector Watson.

'Let's see what the bold inspector has to say this time, Marriott. Has he caught our murderer for us?'

'No such luck, sir,' said Marriott, handing the message form to his chief.

TO DDI HARDCASTLE A DIV METROPOLITAN
FROM DI WATSON A DIV BRIGHTON BOROUGH
POLICE
RE SPRINGER + CALL RECEIVED FROM CITY
OF LONDON POLICE FOLLOWING ENTRY IN
POLICE GAZETTE + STOP + SOLICITOR IN
MOORGATE REPORTED HAVING ANOTHER
CALLER SEEKING SAME NON EXISTENT GOLD
MINE AS CLLR CROSS + STOP + INFORMANT
WAS CLLR MAURICE ISAACS HACKNEY BORO
COUNCIL + STOP + END

'Well, Marriott, it seems that our Major Springer's been at it again. And he seems to specialize in councillors.' Hardcastle let out an exasperated sigh. 'I suppose we'd better go and see this Maurice Isaacs and see what he's got to tell us. Not that he's likely to know where Springer is now. If it was Springer he saw in the first place. There's too many of these con men about for my liking. Still, with sleuths like Mr Watson trying to catch 'em, that's no surprise.'

After half an hour spent on the telephone, Marriott eventually discovered that Councillor Maurice Isaacs of Hackney Borough Council was the owner of a jeweller's shop in Dalston Lane, Hackney.

It was a pokey little shop, dark and forbidding, as befitted an establishment that, in addition to selling items of jewellery, also sported the three golden balls that were the trademark of a pawnbroker. A bell rang as Hardcastle pushed open the door.

A small man, Isaacs wore spectacles with pebble lenses and a yarmulke, and bore a mournful expression. A few tufts of grey hair sprouted from the sides of his head. But he laughed when Hardcastle introduced himself and Marriott, and explained why they were there.

'You've got to get up early in the morning to catch Morrie Isaacs, Inspector.'

'I take it you didn't buy any of these shares then, Mr Isaacs.'

'Hah! Do I look like I was born yesterday?' said Isaacs. 'No, of course not. I led him along like I was interested, got all the details and then made a few enquiries of my own. Well, when I went to where the offices were supposed to be and found that they'd never heard of this gold mine, I knew I'd been right.'

'Did this man give you a name, Mr Isaacs?'

'Yes, he said he was called Digby. Told me some story about being an engineer and said he was qualified in geology. I tell you, Inspector, the only thing that man's qualified in is trying to swindle honest folk like me.'

'How did you meet him?' Hardcastle asked.

'At the mayor's reception at the town hall last Tuesday. There were a lot of people there and I got into conversation with this Digby. Then he tried to sell me some shares in this gold mine. Well, I thought to myself, if this is such a good spec, there wouldn't be any shares for sale. You don't want to sell a piece of land where you're digging up gold, do you?'

'Can you describe this man Digby, sir?' asked Marriott.

'Of course,' said Isaacs, and went on to give a description that exactly fitted Major Dudley Springer.

'One other thing, Mr Isaacs,' said Hardcastle. 'Did you agree to meet this man again?'

'Not on your life, Inspector, and I gave orders that the next time we had a reception at the town hall, the mace bearer wouldn't let him in. And,' he added as an afterthought, 'to call the police if he did show up.'

When Hardcastle and Marriott returned to Cannon Row police station at just after three o'clock, there was a message waiting for them.

'Catto's been in touch, sir,' said DS Wood.

'And what's he have to say for himself?' asked Hardcastle as he seated himself behind his desk and began to fill his pipe.

'He's in Twickenham, sir.'

'What the blue blazes is he doing there?' demanded Hardcastle, laying down his pipe and taking an interest.

'Following Mrs Springer, sir,' said Wood.

'Well, let's have the whole story, Wood, not just dribs and drabs.'

'Yes, sir. Catto and Wilmot saw Mrs Springer come out of her house at a quarter past eleven. They followed her and she took a cab to Clapham Junction and a train to Twickenham from there. She walked from Twickenham station to a house in Arragon Road – it's only a short walk apparently – and she—'

'I don't care if it's a bloody route march, Wood. Get on with it.'

'Yes, sir. She went into this house and she's still there. Catto wants to know what to do next.'

'Did he say whether there was any sign of Major Springer?'

'No, sir.'

'What? There was no sign, or he didn't say?'

'He didn't say, sir.'

'Where did he send this message from, Wood?'

'Twickenham police station, sir. It's in London Road, not far from where they are now.'

'Right, send a message to Twickenham nick and ask for one of their CID officers to go round there and tell Catto and Wilmot to stay put and see what happens.'

But an hour later that message was overtaken by another from Catto to say that he and Wilmot had arrested Major Springer and his wife, and all were now at Twickenham police station awaiting further instructions.

170

'Well, bless my soul. I wonder how he managed that,' said Hardcastle. 'Tell Catto I want both them prisoners brought up to Cannon Row. Meanwhile, I'll have a word with the sub-divisional inspector at Twickenham and arrange for the use of his van. I don't want them running while they're getting off the train at Waterloo. Very good at running is Major Springer.'

In the intervening hour or so – the time it took Catto and Wilmot to bring the Springers back to Whitehall – Hardcastle had given much thought to which of them he would interview first.

Having previously spoken to them separately, he eventually decided that Dudley Springer – despite his war record – was arguably the weaker of the two. Consequently, the complaining Harriet was left in the custody of the police-station matron, and her husband was placed in the interview room.

'Well, Major Springer, we meet again.'

'What the hell is this all about, Inspector? I very much object to being treated like a common criminal.' Far from being contrite, Dudley Springer immediately went on the attack with all the bravado of wronged innocence.

'For a start, Major, it's about gold-mine shares. Or perhaps you'd rather I called you Major Digby.'

'I've no idea what you're talking about, Inspector, and I demand to have my solicitor present.'

Hardcastle smiled. 'Oh, you can demand all you like, Major Springer, but you'll have a solicitor once I've decided it won't interfere with my enquiries. Anyway, I'm not concerned about share pushing.'

'You're not?' Springer looked surprised. 'Then what on earth am I doing here?'

'You've been arrested on a warrant obtained by the Brighton police, something to do with a complaint laid by one Councillor Walter Cross. He seems to think you saw him off for a hundred pounds. But that's not any of my business. You'll shortly be taken back to Brighton, once the police down there can rouse

171

themselves enough to send an escort for you, and doubtless you'll be gripping the rail in the dock at Brighton Quarter Sessions come Christmas. No, Major, my concern is the murder of Fanny Horwood.'

'I've told you all I know about that.'

'Have you? I've heard that you're not above picking up the occasional street woman yourself.'

'Who told you that? It's a lie, whoever it was.'

'It was your dear wife, Major.' Although not in the habit of revealing his sources of information, Hardcastle saw no harm in driving a wedge between the Springers.

Springer gave a mirthless laugh. 'Sheer revenge,' he said. 'She only said that because I left her after finding her in bed with some man when I came home on leave.'

'If you've left her, how was it that my officers found you with her in Twickenham?'

Springer shrugged but said nothing.

'However, I ain't too worried about that, Major. I'm only interested in Fanny Horwood. Do you deny having picked up prostitutes from time to time?'

'I may have done. In France.'

'I'm not talking about France,' said Hardcastle testily. 'Your wife claims that one of her friends saw you with a whore somewhere in the West End.'

'What's sauce for the goose is sauce for the gander,' said Springer, suddenly tiring of Hardcastle's cat-and-mouse game. 'Anyway, what's wrong with that?'

'Nothing, I s'pose, unless you're worried about picking up some nasty disease.'

'Well, I didn't.' Springer pulled out his pipe and, without asking, lit it.

'That's all right then, because the post-mortem on Fanny Horwood revealed that she'd got syphilis.'

'*What?*' Springer, who until then had been languishing nonchalantly in his chair, sat bolt upright. 'Oh my God! I'll have to see a doctor as soon as I can. You've got to get me a doctor, Inspector.'

'So, you did have your way with her then.'

'It was only the once,' said Springer, alarm clear on his face at the thought he may have contracted some dreadful infection.

'When and where?'

'In my room at that boarding house in Brighton.'

'But that wasn't the first time, was it? You'd met her previously in London, and you arranged to meet up with her in Brighton. It was then that she told you she was pregnant and that you were the father.'

'That's not true. Brighton was the first time I met her.'

'And because she was pregnant and you didn't want nothing to do with it, you took her for a walk down the beach on the evening of Saturday the ninth of November, murdered her and left her body under the pier.'

'No, I did not, and if you think you can prove it, I suggest you try.'

'What did you do with the gold necklace she was wearing, and her handbag, Major, eh?'

'I don't know what you're talking about. I went with her the once, and that was in my room at Mrs Edwards's place. It was at about five o'clock, just after high tea.' Springer grimaced. 'Such as it was.'

'Violet Gunn, the maid, said that Fanny Horwood didn't come in until about five.'

'Maybe it was a bit later, then. Anyway, what would that dim little maid know about anything?'

'A lot more than you might think,' said Hardcastle, who had been impressed at how bright the girl was. 'Anyhow, I've a mind to charge you with the murder of Fanny Horwood, and you can make your case at Lewes Assizes.'

'I didn't kill her, I tell you. And I know nothing about her being pregnant. She didn't say anything about that to me. And I certainly wouldn't have gone with her if I'd known she had syphilis either.' It was clear from his nervous demeanour that Springer had suddenly become obsessed with his health.

Hardcastle smiled. 'As a matter of fact, I was just pulling your leg about that, Major. She never had syphilis, so you needn't worry on that score.'

'Damn you,' said Springer, realizing too late that he had been led into a trap.

'Put him in a cell, Marriott,' said Hardcastle, 'and bring Mrs Springer up here.'

'What d'you want with my wife?' shouted Springer as Marriott led him away.

'Just a little chat, Major.'

A few moments later, Harriet Springer, escorted by the matron, was brought into the interview room. There was no doubt that she was an extremely attractive woman, and today she was wearing a fetching costume with a military-style jacket, lace-up boots and a brown velour hat, its wide brim pulled down to the eyes. Like her husband, she immediately went on the offensive.

'I hope you know what you're doing, Inspector,' she snarled, 'because my brother – the one about to become a KC – will be hearing of this. And you can rest assured that legal proceedings will follow.' Her eyes glittered as she issued the threat. 'Thank God my father, the judge, is no longer alive.'

'You have no brother, Mrs Springer,' said Hardcastle mildly. That was a guess on his part; Springer's army record had not mentioned if Harriet had any siblings. 'And your late father was not a judge, he was a bank clerk. As was your husband before the war.'

Just as she had done on the last occasion Hardcastle had interviewed her, the young woman suddenly began to cry.

Hardcastle waited until she had recovered – even though he was convinced that she was play-acting – before posing the next question. 'How long have you been aiding your husband in his share-pushing swindle, Mrs Springer?'

Harriet, her eyes red-rimmed from her tearful outburst, gave Hardcastle a malevolent glance. 'What makes you think I had anything to do with that?' she demanded.

'Your husband said so.' Hardcastle told the lie without any compunction. He had two unscrupulous people in custody, one of whom might well have murdered Fanny Horwood. And although the Horwood girl was certainly a trollop, he saw no reason why she should not have the same protection from the law as the next woman.

'Damn him,' said Harriet vehemently. 'There was no need for him to involve me.'

'But you are involved, Mrs Springer. Anyway, none of this share-pushing is my business. I'm only interested in the murder of Fanny Horwood, and right now I've a mind to charge your husband with it.'

'What on earth can you mean?' Harriet Springer's shock was very obviously genuine. 'Dudley wouldn't murder anyone. He went right through the war. He saw too much death to want to be involved with it any more.'

'Not what you told me before, Mrs Springer,' said Hardcastle. 'If I remember correctly, you drew my attention to the fact that your husband was a trained killer. But if he had nothing to do with Fanny Horwood's death, why did he leave Brighton in such a hurry?'

For the first time since the start of the interview, Harriet smiled. 'That's easy,' she said. 'After you called at Elm Park Gardens, I telephoned him and told him you'd been there.'

'So, you did know he was in Brighton.'

'Of course I did.' Harriet smiled at the belief she had outwitted the police. 'I thought – and so did he – that you'd found out about his frauds and that it would only be a matter of time before you arrested him. I telephoned him and advised him to leave Brighton immediately.'

'So, all this fiddle-faddle about you throwing him out of the house after your friend said she'd seen him with a prostitute was rubbish, was it?'

Harriet shook her head, and gave a convulsive sob as the tears began again. 'No,' she said, 'it was true, but it was also true that Dudley found me in bed with another man when he came home on leave.'

Hardcastle wondered whether the man had paid her for the privilege. 'Well, Mrs Springer,' he said, 'I'm going to send the Brighton police a telegraph message to say that you and your husband are here. I don't know whether they'll want to charge you with anything, but that's up to them.' He thought it unlikely that Watson would want to involve her in the case against her husband. In his view, that might be a bit too complicated for the Brighton detective.

Having told the matron to put Harriet Springer back in a cell while he got in touch with Brighton, Hardcastle made his way back to his office, aware that he was no nearer to discovering Fanny Horwood's killer. Pausing at the door to the detectives' office, he caught sight of DC Henry Catto. 'Come in my office, Catto,' he said.

'Yes, sir.' Catto put on his jacket and followed the DDI.

'How did you come to knock off Major Springer, lad?' Hardcastle settled behind his desk and lit his pipe.

'Easy, sir,' said Catto, risking a grin. 'I took a chance and knocked at the door. If Mrs Springer had answered it, I was going to say something about collecting for army charities and was her husband in, but it was him what answered. So I said, "Are you Major Springer?" and he said he was, so I nicked him. Then his missus come to the door to see what all the fuss was about and we nicked her an' all.'

'You was chancing your arm a bit there, Catto. You might have come unstuck. Do anything to cut short a weary observation, wouldn't you? Still, well done, lad.' And with that rare word of praise, Hardcastle waved a hand of dismissal.

As the delighted Catto left the office, Marriott walked in. 'When I took Springer back to his cell, sir, he said that he had something to tell you. He said it was important.'

'Did he now?' Hardcastle was far from convinced that Springer would have anything of import to tell him. 'We'd better go down and see what he wants, then.'

The station officer, a burly sergeant close to retirement, opened the door to Springer's cell. 'Want me to wait, sir?' he asked.

'No, just give Sergeant Marriott the key. We'll make sure he's tucked up nice and warm when we've done with him.'

Springer was sitting on the wooden bed-plank which comprised the only furniture in the small cell.

'Sergeant Marriott tells me you've got something important

176

to tell me,' said Hardcastle, thumbs tucked in the armholes of his waistcoat.

'I admit I've been share-pushing, Inspector.'

'I know that,' said Hardcastle, 'but I told you that ain't important, not as far as I'm concerned anyway.'

'And I always pick town-council receptions because councillors are a good spec. They're so full of their own importance that they never think that they can be conned.'

'You're probably right about that,' said Hardcastle. He had no high opinion of town councillors himself.

'D'you remember me telling you about the man who'd called at Mrs Edwards's boarding house the afternoon of the Saturday that Fanny Harris or Horwood – whatever her name was – was murdered?'

'Of course I remember.'

'Well, at one of the functions I managed to get into, I saw him.'

'Did you really?' Hardcastle was sceptical about that, and wondered whether it was some ploy on Springer's part to escape prosecution for his fraudulent activities.

'Yes, Inspector, I'm absolutely certain.'

'Another council reception, was it?'

Springer smiled. 'Not this time. It was a charity ball at the Langham in Portland Place.'

Seventeen

'I'm not standing up to listen to all this twaddle, Marriott. Bring the major to the interview room.' Hardcastle turned on his heel and marched down the cell passage. He was unconvinced that what Springer was claiming had any truth in it, and still thought that it was some attempt to talk his way out of the Brighton fraud – or for that matter, the Brighton murder – although he could not work out how.

'So, where did you see this man, Springer?' asked the DDI when he, Marriott and the major were settled once more in the stark little room near the front of the police station.

'I told you, at a charity ball at the Langham,' began Springer.

'How did you gatecrash your way in there, then?'

'I didn't. I bought a ticket.'

'You *bought* a ticket?' Hardcastle raised his eyebrows in surprise.

'Two actually.' Springer smiled. 'Sometimes, Inspector,' he said, 'one has to speculate in order to accumulate.'

'And who was the other one for?'

'My wife, of course. One cannot go to a ball on one's own.' It was a lofty statement, one that implied that lowly individuals like policemen could not possibly know about such things as high-society charity balls.

'So, she helps you with this fiddle of yours, does she?'

'You don't really expect me to answer that, surely, Inspector?'

Hardcastle grunted. 'And did you find a mark?'

'A what?'

'A mark, man, a mark,' said Hardcastle. 'I should have thought you'd've known that word, Springer. It means a sucker

178

prepared to invest in your bogus gold mine. Anyway, get on with it.'

'No, I didn't find a mark, as you call it. But one of the people at this ball was definitely the man who called at Mrs Edwards's boarding house.'

'Describe this man.'

'Difficult to say. About thirty, I should think, and he was nearly six feet tall—'

'That's not what you said when I first saw you,' interjected Hardcastle. 'Give me them notes, Marriott.' For a few moments, he studied the questions and answers that his sergeant had recorded during the interview that they had conducted with Springer about the mysterious caller. 'What you said was that he was about your height. Five feet nine, you said.'

'So, I was wrong. After all, he was standing on the lower step. But this time I had more time to study him. I never forget a face, Inspector.'

'Nor me, Springer,' rejoined Hardcastle before continuing. 'But when you saw him that time, you said he was wearing a belted raincoat and one of them new felt hats, a trilby you called it. So how can you be so sure? Presumably he wasn't wearing them in this charity ball you were casing.'

'Of course not. He was wearing white tie and tails. Everyone was. Apart from the women, of course,' said Springer with a smirk.

'You can keep your sarcasm for them as appreciates it,' snapped Hardcastle, becoming increasingly irritated by Springer's supercilious attitude. 'But you still reckon it was the same man?'

'I'm positive.'

'Did you find out his name?'

'No, I didn't. But I did exchange a few words with him. I recognized the voice as well as the face. I know it was the man who asked for Fanny Harris.'

'Horwood,' muttered Hardcastle absently.

'Well, whatever, but it was him, Inspector, without a doubt.'

'When was this ball you was at, then?'

'Last Monday.' Springer paused, calculating. 'That would have been the twenty-fifth.'

'And what name did you use this time? Digby, was it, same as last time?'

'Yes, as a matter of fact it was. However, there's another ball tomorrow, and this man told me he'd be there.'

Hardcastle stood up. 'Well, thank you for your assistance, Major,' he said sarcastically. 'Put him down, Marriott and then come up to the office.'

'D'you think he's having us on, sir?' asked Marriott when he joined Hardcastle a few minutes later.

'He's definitely having us on, Marriott, and that's a fact. I don't know what his game is, but if he thinks I'm delaying sending him back to Brighton to face the music, he's got another think coming.'

'But d'you think it's worth following up, sir?'

'Of course it is, Marriott. After all, we've bugger all else, and this murder of ours is beginning to get whiskers on it.'

'So, where do we start, sir?'

'We start at the Langham Hotel in Portland Place, Marriott, that's where.'

On their arrival at the Langham, first thing the following morning, the two detectives made straight for the hall porter. Hardcastle's long experience in criminal investigation had told him that the hall porter was the one man who knew everything that went on in a hotel.

'It's about the charity ball you had here last Monday,' said Hardcastle, once he had introduced himself and Marriott.

'Oh yes, sir, and how can I help?' enquired the hall porter, whose name, he told them, was Jenkins.

'Was there a guest here name of Digby? Although his real name's Major Dudley Springer.'

'I'll have a look, sir. I've got a list here somewhere.' Jenkins rummaged in a drawer beneath his counter and produced three sheets of foolscap. 'Yes, he's on here. Major and Mrs Dudley Digby.'

'Any chance that you can let me have a copy of that list,

Mr Jenkins? It's rather important. I'm investigating a murder, you see.'

'Not here in the Langham, sir, I hope,' said Jenkins with a false concern softened by a smile.

'No, not here,' said Hardcastle, who had long been accustomed to the wry sense of humour possessed of hall porters in major West End hotels.

'You can have this one, sir,' said Jenkins, handing the sheets of paper to Hardcastle. 'I shan't be needing it again.'

'And this is the lot, is it?' Hardcastle asked, folding the list and putting it in his inside pocket.

'Not necessarily, sir. Some of 'em turn up on the night and pay at the door.'

'I've been told there's another junket being held here tonight, Mr Jenkins.'

'That there is, sir,' said the hall porter. 'But this one's special like, to celebrate the Armistice.'

'Same people coming, are they?'

'I don't know about that, sir,' said Jenkins, 'but I do know that it's fully booked, so there won't be any latecomers wanting to buy tickets at the door this time.'

'Well, there's a few hundred on there, Marriott.' Hardcastle waved a hand at the list of those who had attended the charity ball on the previous Monday. 'Of course, this bloke that Springer says he saw might be going tonight, or he might not. The fact that he told Springer he was don't mean that he will. And if he was on the same game as Springer, he might have used a duff name an' all. Not that we know what his real name is, let alone any alias he might have been using. It's a waste of time.'

'If he doesn't turn up tonight, are we going to have to see all those people, sir?' Marriott could foresee an unending number of visits and late nights.

'See them?' scoffed Hardcastle. 'I haven't even bothered to read the names, because from what the hall porter said, our man mightn't be on it. I doubt we'd know any of them anyway. No, it'll have to be up to Springer. There's no addresses on

this list, so we can't go dragging him halfway round the Metropolitan Police District knocking on doors on the off-chance of him picking this bloke out. Not that I would anyway.'
For several seconds, Hardcastle pondered the problem confronting him. 'Get Catto in here fast, and then get on the telephone and ask that hall porter if he can get three of us into this do tonight, on the sly like. You, me, and Major Dudley Springer MC. I'm not paying for tickets, not to a junket like that. The Commissioner would have a blue fit if I put in a claim for that.'

'Yes, sir.' Marriott, as usual amazed at the speed with which his governor's mind worked, left to do his bidding.

'You wanted me, sir?' asked Catto, hovering nervously inside Hardcastle's office door.

'You can drive a motor cab, can't you, Catto?'

'Yes, sir.'

'Right, get on to the transport people and tell 'em I want to borrow that cab they keep for observations. Tell them the DDI of the Whitehall Division wants it tonight to do a special job. And don't stand no nonsense from 'em. If they cuts up, just refer 'em to me.'

When Marriott returned, Hardcastle had taken off his shoes and was massaging his feet.

'All arranged, sir. The hall porter says to have a word with him when we get there.'

'Good,' said Hardcastle as he replaced his shoes. 'And now get a telegraph off to DI Watson at Brighton. Tell him we've nicked Springer, but I'm holding him till Sunday in connection with the murder of Fanny Horwood, then he can send an escort to pick him up and take him back to the seaside. Oh, and you'd better tell him we've nicked Mrs Springer an' all. Ask if he wants her on account of she tipped the major off when he was staying at Mrs Edwards's place, and that she went to this ball with him, so I reckon she's an accomplice. Not that I think he'll know what to do about that. And tell Wilmot to get Springer up here.'

'What is it now?' asked Springer in a tired voice when Wilmot brought him into Hardcastle's office.

'Where's your soup and fish, Springer?'

'My *what*?'

'Your dressing-up togs. Your white tie and tails.'

'At Chelsea. Why? Don't tell me I'm supposed to wear that in court to answer this trumped-up charge of yours.'

'No, you don't. You're going to the Armistice charity ball at the Langham Hotel. Tonight.'

At six o'clock, Hardcastle, Marriott and Springer set off for Chelsea in the cab driven by Catto. It was a taxi like all the other London taxis, but Hardcastle, ever mindful of saving the commissioner's money, knew that it would be cheaper to use the police cab than to charge for one off the rank. Apart from which, he did not want to risk his prisoner escaping.

Having let the detectives into his house in Elm Park Gardens, Springer went upstairs to change.

'Go with him, Marriott,' said Hardcastle. 'I don't want him jumping out of no window and doing a runner.'

Ten minutes later, elegantly attired in full evening dress complete with miniature medals – which caused Hardcastle to comment that it was the only genuine thing about him – Springer returned to the sitting room. 'Now, perhaps, you'll tell me what this is all about, Inspector,' he said. He was half suspecting that Hardcastle was taking him to the Langham in the hope that someone would pick him out as the fraudsman who tried to swindle him, rather than looking for a suspect in a murder case.

'You're going to have a good gander round and see if you can spot this customer you reckon called at Mrs Edwards's place, Springer.' Hardcastle had no great hopes that the major would be successful. Indeed, he still harboured suspicions that Springer had committed the murder, and that his tale of seeing the caller was intended to shift those suspicions away from himself. After all, no one else had either seen or heard of the man.

The foyer of the Langham Hotel was filled with couples in evening dress. The men in obligatory white tie and tails, the

women in a breathtaking variety of the very best that London
– and indeed Paris – had to offer. To one side of the huge
vestibule, a queue of people waited to deposit fur wraps and
capes and silk opera hats and canes.

The hall porter spotted Hardcastle and Marriott as soon as
they escorted their prisoner through the main door. 'Go on
through, sir. It's in the main ballroom.' He pointed at the
ornate entrance to the ballroom, from which the sounds of a
band playing ragtime could be heard, and made an arcane
signal to the uniformed attendant who was checking tickets.
Then, seeing Springer, he added, 'Evening, sir, nice to see
you here again.'

'Right, in you go, Springer. Sergeant Marriott and me'll be
right here at the door. We ain't coming in on account of we'd
stick out like sore thumbs, what with being in our everyday
whistles. But don't you try making a run for it, or the whole
of the Metropolitan Police'll be on your tail before you can
say Jack the Ripper.'

'Trust me, Inspector,' said Springer.

'That'll be the day,' muttered Hardcastle.

Minutes later, Springer returned. 'He's there, Inspector,' he
said. 'He's standing in front of the band with a glass of cham-
pagne in his hand, and he's talking to a rather good-looking
flapper in a gold brocade dress with a train. You can't miss
her, she's wearing a bandeau with an ostrich feather in it.'

'Good God!' said Hardcastle as he took a pace into the
room. It was more a comment on prevailing fashion than one
on Springer's apparent success. 'Point him out.'

'He's over—' Springer stopped suddenly. 'He's gone,
Inspector. He was there a moment ago.'

Hardcastle turned to face Springer. 'I don't know what your
game is, Springer,' he said, 'but I'm not buying it.'

'You can think what you like, Inspector,' said Springer,
'but I'm telling you that he was definitely there.'

'It's a bugger us not wearing soup and fish, Marriott,' said
the furious Hardcastle. 'But get in there with Springer and
find the bloody man. And if you can't find him, bring out the
girl he was talking to. Springer here'll point her out.'

But it was to no avail. Despite there being nigh-on five hundred people in the huge ballroom, it took only minutes for Springer to satisfy Marriott that their quarry had disappeared. And an open fire exit that led ultimately to Chandos Street suggested that the suspect had escaped that way. If, Hardcastle later angrily commented, the suspect had been there in the first place.

'Marriott, get outside and ask Catto if he's seen anyone in soup and fish legging it down the road.'

Hardcastle turned to face the young woman – she was probably no more than twenty – whom Marriott and Springer had conducted to the foyer. 'Now then, young lady, I'm Divisional Detective Inspector Hardcastle of the Metropolitan Police.'

'How exciting.' The girl flicked open a Spanish-lace fan and waved it gently in front of her face.

'That man you were talking to just now, in front of the bandstand.'

'What about him?' The girl smiled sweetly at Hardcastle.

'Who was he?'

'I haven't the faintest idea, Inspector. I'd only just started talking to him when he ran away. Very strange behaviour, I thought.'

'And you've not met him or seen him before?'

'Never. Why? Has he done something awful?'

'Don't you worry your pretty head about that,' said Hardcastle gruffly. 'What did he say, when he was talking to you?'

'Nothing very much really. He said what a nice frock I was wearing and then he asked if I was with anyone.'

'And what did you say to that, miss?'

'I told him it was a silly question. Ladies do not attend charity balls on their own. But then he glanced across at the door and ran out of the fire exit.' The girl gave a gay laugh. 'I thought the place had caught fire,' she added.

'Thank you, miss,' said Hardcastle. 'Sorry to have bothered you.' And with that, he and Springer crossed to the hall porter's counter just inside the main door of the hotel.

Minutes later, Marriott joined them with the news that Catto

185

had indeed seen a man in full evening dress running down the road, but had thought nothing of it. It was, after all, the West End, Catto had said with a shrug, and these days anything goes. It was a remark that Marriott thought unwise to repeat to his DDI.

'D'you have a list of them who's here tonight, Mr Jenkins?' asked Hardcastle wearily.

'Indeed I have, sir.' Jenkins produced the list from beneath his counter.

Hardcastle ran his eye quickly down the several hundred names. 'Well, I'll be buggered,' he said. 'There's a Richard Stevenson on here.'

'D'you reckon he's our man, sir?'

'Don't be daft, Marriott, he's nothing to do with Fanny Horwood getting topped,' said Hardcastle, but even as he spoke, he began to wonder whether the urbane alderman had been pulling the wool over his eyes. After all, he had been less than truthful about his association with prostitutes, and Dolly Hancock in particular. 'Mr Jenkins, was this man Stevenson here tonight?'

'Can't help you there, sir,' said Jenkins. 'I don't check them in. That's Alf's job. He checks the tickets.' Pointing towards the ballroom entrance, he indicated the uniformed flunkey to whom he had signalled earlier. 'The list's only sent down so's we can verify any gent who's forgotten to bring his ticket.' He gave a cynical laugh. 'They might run big businesses or command armies, sir, but expect them to remember their ticket, well, that's something a bit different. Take their secretaries and their staff officers away from them and they're done for, I can tell you.'

Alf was no help either. 'I don't ask their names, sir,' he said. 'I just make sure they've got tickets.'

'Well, if that don't beat cock-fighting, Marriott,' said Hardcastle. Having returned to the police station by way of Chelsea so that Springer could change again, the DDI and his sergeant were seated in Hardcastle's office. It was now ten o'clock.

'D'you reckon it was him, sir?'

'Well, Springer certainly seemed sure enough, but I'm beginning to wonder about the major.'

'Could be he's throwing a dummy, sir,' said Marriott.

'That's what I think, Marriott. He's a devious bugger is Springer, and he is a con man after all. Well, he ain't conning Ernie Hardcastle, and that's a fact. I don't know what his game is, but it ain't going to help him out of his spot of bother, is it? No, Marriott, there's something a bit queer going on here, if you ask me. The more I see of Major Dudley Springer, the more I fancy him for the topping.'

'On the other hand, sir, Springer might be genuine. Supposing he really had seen this bloke who called at Sussex Street. And supposing the bloke recognized Springer, then caught sight of us in the doorway. If he guessed the game was up, that'd be enough for him to sling his hook. And Catto did see someone legging it.'

'You might be right, Marriott,' said Hardcastle, loath to believe that Springer had been telling the truth. 'A villain would suss us out for busies without a second glance.'

'So, what do we do, sir? Front the alderman with it and ask him if he was at that jolly tonight? Fanny's topping might be down to him, knowing that he likes the occasional cheap tart.'

'Not straight off, no, because I don't think it's down to him. After all, the description that Springer gave us don't tally. Not that that means much. Anyway, we'd have to go a bit softly-softly, seeing as how Stevenson's a stockbroker and an alderman. To say nothing of being a freemason.' Hardcastle stood up. 'Anyhow, that can wait till Monday. Have we heard anything from Brighton?'

'Yes, sir, they're sending an escort for Springer tomorrow.'

'What, on a Sunday, Marriott? Bless my soul. What did they say about Springer's missus?'

'As far as Mr Watson's concerned, sir, he said we can let her go. He reckons she hasn't committed any offence.'

'He don't try hard enough, that's his problem.' Hardcastle paused. 'Get on the phone to Brighton right now, Marriott, and tell them I want urgent enquiries at the better-class hotels

187

in Brighton. There can't be too many of them. And tell 'em I want it done this minute, not on Monday morning. And I want an answer within the hour. Oh, and you'd better tell 'em to belay sending an escort for Springer. I might need him for an identification parade.'

'But hasn't Mr Watson got a check of the hotels in hand, sir?' said Marriott, busily taking notes.

'Maybe, but he said there were a lot of hotels and pubs in Brighton, and for once he was right. But if – and it's a big if – Stevenson was down there, he'd've put up at a decent place.'

'What have they got to look for, sir?'

'Tell them to ask if Richard Stevenson was staying there at the weekend of the ninth and tenth of November.'

'But I thought you said that Stevenson had nothing to do with it, sir.'

'I don't think he had, Marriott, but in a case of murder, you have to go down every street till you come to a dead end. Then you go back to the crossroads and start all over again.'

'Right, sir.'

'Then, once we've got an answer, we'll get a warrant and search Alderman Stevenson's house. See what that turns up.' Hardcastle reached for his pipe. 'And tell Catto a cup of tea wouldn't go amiss while we're waiting.'

'Yes, sir,' said Marriott.

Eighteen

It had gone three on Sunday morning before Hardcastle received an answer from the Brighton police. And for once he had no cause to criticize them.

Richard Stevenson had stayed at the Grand Hotel in King's Road on the night of the ninth of November.

'I think the bold alderman's got some explaining to do, Marriott,' said Hardcastle, stifling a yawn. 'But I think we'll call it a day. We need to make a few more enquiries before we tackle him, and I don't reckon he's going anywhere in a hurry.'

After rising at about ten o'clock on the Sunday morning, Hardcastle spent an untroubled day with his family in Kennington, and Mrs Hardcastle prepared the usual roast beef and Yorkshire pudding for lunch.

Kitty – no longer working on the buses now that the men were coming home from the war – her sister Maud and her young brother Walter, were all at home. Sunday lunch was, after all, a family event.

That afternoon, Kitty, the Hardcastles' eldest, announced that she had a new boyfriend, a City of London policeman, and was going out for a walk with him in Kennington Park.

'Well, you mind you behave yourself, my girl,' said Hardcastle.

'What *do* you mean, Pa?' said Kitty with a gay laugh, her eyes twinkling.

'I don't know why you can't find a proper policeman to go out with,' muttered her father. In his view the City police was little better than the Brighton force.

Glancing in the mirror over the fireplace, Kitty adjusted her hat and departed, slamming the front door as she did so.

'We should never have let her work on the buses, Alice,' said Hardcastle, shaking his head in dismay. 'I don't know what'll become of the girl.'

The only other jarring note of the day was Mrs Hardcastle's complaint that they hadn't been to the seaside for ages, and that it was time she and her husband took a charabanc ride to Brighton and spent the day there. The suggestion was sharply dismissed, and Hardcastle passed the afternoon in front of the fire, reading the *News of the World* and dozing in his armchair.

On Monday morning, the head of A Division's CID was in the office at his usual time of half-past eight. Marriott was waiting.

'An escort arrived from Brighton yesterday, sir, to take Springer back.'

'What? Weren't they told I'd be hanging on to him for a bit?' Hardcastle's tone was accusing.

'Yes, sir,' said Marriott, risking a grin, 'the message was sent but it seems it didn't get through to whoever was arranging it. Anyhow, they went off empty-handed.'

'Seems to me, Marriott, that the left hand of the Brighton force don't know what the right hand's doing. What about the major's missus?'

'As Mr Watson had decided not to charge her, sir, she was released on Saturday evening.'

'I knew that'd be a bit too tricky for the seaside inspector, Marriott,' growled Hardcastle as he searched his pockets for his pipe. 'Send Wood in here, there's a good fellow.'

'You sent for me, sir?' Wood appeared, moments later, in the doorway.

'I've got a special job for you, Wood,' said Hardcastle. 'I've cleared it with the chief constable of the Croydon Constabulary for you to take a gander at the station occurrence book there, and then have a chat with his CID officers and his beat men. See if anything a bit odd's known about this here Alderman Stevenson.'

'Very good, sir.'

'Know anyone in the City?'

'Got one or two contacts there, sir.'

'Good. Well, when you've done down at Croydon, see what they can tell you about him. He's on the Stock Exchange.'

When Wood had set off on his enquiries, Hardcastle turned to Marriott. 'You're a freemason, Marriott, aren't you?'

'Yes, sir.'

As he had frequently said, Hardcastle did not approve of policemen being freemasons, but nevertheless did not shrink from taking advantage of Marriott's membership of that organization. 'Have a word with your mates in this club of yours, Marriott, next time you have one of your pow-wows, and see what you can find out about Stevenson. He belongs to some lodge in St James's, so he says.'

'It's a bit tricky, sir,' said Marriott. 'We're not supposed to reveal anything about our fellow—'

'Who pays your wages, Marriott?' demanded Hardcastle. 'The Commissioner or your secret society?'

'All right, sir,' said Marriott, 'I'll see what I can do.'

The following morning, DS Wood was able to report that the Croydon police believed that Alderman Richard Stevenson occasionally picked up prostitutes. In fact, one or two patrolling officers had seen him from time to time talking to street women, and even though Stevenson was a lay preacher, the police had cynically assumed that he was not engaged in trying to persuade them of the error of their ways, or to convert them to the path of Christianity.

'That makes sense, Marriott,' Hardcastle said. 'We know from Dolly Hancock that he saw her regular like for a bit of nookey. But he's a damned fool doing it on his own doorstep. Anything else, Wood?' he asked, turning to the other sergeant again.

'I had a word at Vine Street nick, sir, just off Piccadilly—'

'God Almighty, Wood, I know where Vine Street is. I used to be a sergeant there.'

'Yes, sir. Well, some of the PCs there reckon that a man fitting Stevenson's description has been seen occasionally chatting to the local whores.'

'Don't mean much,' said Hardcastle. 'Hundreds of men look like him.'

'I was going to ask around Shepherd Market and that area to see if any of the women knew him, but, not having a photograph, I reckoned I'd be wasting my time.'

'Probably right, Wood,' admitted Hardcastle. 'Anyway, you and Catto get back there and put yourselves about. See if any of these women knew Fanny Horwood when she was on the game, and ask them if Fanny had ever mentioned Stevenson.'

And then he and Marriott went to Clapham to see Dolly Hancock once again.

'Hello, Mr Hardcastle.' Unlike the previous occasions upon which she had been visited by the two detectives, Dolly was clearly delighted to see them. 'I got the cheque from Dick,' she said, almost bubbling over with excitement as she led them into her untidy sitting room. 'Fifty smackers. Ta ever so much for fixing that up for me.'

Hardcastle took out his handkerchief and ostentatiously flicked the seat of the only armchair before sitting down. 'Well, now, Dolly,' he said, 'perhaps you can help me.'

'Just say the word,' Dolly said.

'Did you know Fanny Horwood who sometimes called herself Harris?'

'What, her what got snuffed out down Brighton, you mean?'

'That's the one. You see, Jack Foster knew her – in fact, he was the father of the nipper she had in March.'

'I never knew she had no baby,' said Dolly.

'You did know her then.'

'Yeah, I did.'

'You should have told me before, Dolly,' Hardcastle said, not unkindly.

'Jack said I shouldn't say nothing about knowing her.'

'Well, Jack's inside now and it'll likely be a long time before he gets out.' But in view of what he had recently learned about Alderman Stevenson, Hardcastle was less sure of that than he had been before. If Foster's barrister bothered to find out what Hardcastle's officers had discovered, he would be able to destroy Stevenson's reputation the moment the alderman stepped into the witness box. And if Stevenson got wind of it in advance, it was likely to result in him withdrawing his allegation of blackmail.

'Jack fixed up with that Danny Hoskins, down Brighton, to take pictures of me without nothing on, see.' Dolly was not at all embarrassed at admitting that she had posed naked for the Brighton beach photographer.

'I know he did, you told me that in Holloway, and I've seen them,' said Hardcastle.

'Good, weren't they?' said Dolly with a cheeky grin. 'And there ain't nothing wrong in it. Anyhow, one weekend, Jack brought Fanny down an' all, and he wanted me and her to have our photographs took together, doing things like what women shouldn't never do with each other. I wouldn't have minded having me picture took having a tumble with Jack, but not with another woman. Well, it ain't natural, is it?'

'Yes, well, never mind all that, Dolly. Did she ever mention that she knew Alderman Stevenson?'

Dolly Hancock paused long enough for Hardcastle to know that he was about to learn something else about Stevenson. 'Yes,' she said eventually. 'Fanny used to work Haymarket and St James's. She reckoned she was picked up by Dick Stevenson one night and taken to a hotel where he had his way with her.'

'You should have told me all this before, Dolly,' said Hardcastle again, shaking his head. 'Did she say when this was?'

Dolly gave that some thought. 'It must have been round about June, I reckon,' she said.

'And was that the only time Stevenson met her?'

'Far as I know,' said Dolly. 'There might have been more times, but she never said. Matter of fact, I never saw her again.'

'Did you see her the weekend you were in Rottingdean, the weekend she got murdered?'

'No, I never.'

'Did you see Alderman Stevenson down there that weekend?'

'No, I never saw him neither.'

Detective Sergeant Wood returned to Cannon Row at about nine that evening. 'I found several women who knew Fanny Horwood, sir,' he told Hardcastle, 'but none that'd ever heard her mention Alderman Stevenson.'

'Never mind, Wood,' said Hardcastle cheerfully. 'I think we've got enough to beard the alderman in his den, so to speak.'

'There was one other thing, sir,' said Wood. 'I had a word with an informant of mine in the City. Seems that Alderman Stevenson is in a spot of financial trouble. I don't know if word's got out about his shenanigans with prostitutes, but it seems he's 'lost the confidence of others on the Change'. That's the phrase they use when someone's going down.'

'Can't say I'm surprised, given what he was shelling out to Foster for keeping that photo to himself. Not that Foster did. To say nothing of the fifty he's just handed over to Dolly. And for all we know, it might have been more than that.' Hardcastle chuckled and rubbed his hands together briskly. 'I do believe it's starting to come together, Marriott,' he said, glancing at his first-class sergeant.

'Doesn't mean he killed her, though, does it, sir?' said Marriott. 'I mean, a lot of men – even gents like Stevenson – pick up street women, but they don't necessarily top 'em, do they? And Springer's description of the caller at Sussex Street doesn't fit Stevenson.'

'I can see you're a bit of a Job's comforter, Marriott, but blokes like Springer have been known to make mistakes. Anyhow, I still reckon we've got enough to go down to Stevenson's place and have a bit of a chat with him.' Hardcastle paused. 'Did you get anything from your freemason chums?'

'No, sir, nothing. You see, my lodge is in Pimlico, but

Stevenson's is in St James's. Not that I reckon I'd've learned anything anyway. Freemasons don't even talk about their wives, let alone their mistresses. And they'd never mention if any of them was picking up a prostitute.'

'And nothing about him going under, either, I suppose,' mused Hardcastle before lapsing into thought. 'There's one other thing we can do, Marriott. It's putting money on an outsider, but you never know your luck.'

'Yes, sir,' said Marriott, having no idea what Hardcastle had in mind.

'Get Wood, Catto and Wilmot in here, a bit *tout de suite*.'

When the four detectives were assembled in his office, Hardcastle set out the task he wanted them to undertake. 'Marriott, you take Catto and get yourselves round the West End,' he began. 'Start with the pawnbrokers and see if anyone has hocked the jewellery that Fanny Horwood was wearing when she got herself strangled. Have a look at the snap Hoskins took of her. The gold choker she was wearing ought to be easy to identify, it being quite a handsome piece by all accounts. And I want you, Wood, to take Wilmot and do the same down Croydon. I know it's a tall order, lads, so don't waste any time. I'll give you all day tomorrow, but if you can come up with the answer, I reckon we'll have Mister-bloody-Alderman Stevenson right where we want him: in the condemned cell.'

But Hardcastle's four officers did not need all the next day. At noon, Marriott returned and triumphantly handed Hardcastle what was undoubtedly the late Fanny Horwood's choker.

'Looks like you struck gold, Marriott,' said the DDI, chuckling at his own joke. 'What's the story, then?'

'A West End jeweller took it, sir, along with these.' Marriott laid two cheap rings on Hardcastle's desk. 'He only took the rings as a favour because the necklace was worth more than he gave for it.'

'That reckons. So, who sold them?'

Marriott grinned. 'A man called Richard Stevenson, sir. The jeweller showed me his book, so I know it was kosher.'

'Well done, Marriott.' Hardcastle was delighted. And so was Marriott, who had rarely received such praise from his

DDI. 'Right then, we'll go and see Alderman Richard Stevenson this evening and see what he's got to say for himself. Get on that telephone thing and fix it up.' He paused. 'And we'll get a search warrant on the way, just to be on the safe side.'

'Well, Inspector, don't tell me that you're seeking yet more evidence. I should imagine that you've more than enough with which to go to court.'

'I think we have, Alderman,' said Hardcastle enigmatically, barely able to conceal his elation.

'Do sit down, Inspector. You too, Sergeant, and tell me all about it.'

'I have caused certain enquiries to be made, Alderman,' began Hardcastle pompously, 'and I have learned that you're not above picking up prostitutes in both the Croydon area and the West End of London, Haymarket in particular.'

'*What?* That's an outrageous suggestion, Inspector.' Stevenson gave a masterful performance of indignation. 'I shall make a complaint about your slanderous accusations personally to Sir Nevil Macready, whom I know rather well.'

'That is your right, sir.' It was not the first time that Hardcastle had been threatened by suspects of standing who believed that he could be diverted from his duty by promises of a word with the commissioner of police, even one so recently appointed as Macready. 'However, I have several reliable witnesses who are prepared to testify in court to that effect. Some of them police officers, I may say.' But he was not too sure about the reliability of the street women that the Croydon police claimed to have seen Stevenson talking to. By the very nature of their trade, their testimony was regarded with some scepticism by the courts, even if they could be persuaded to appear. 'I also have evidence that on one occasion you went with Fanny Harris to a hotel after picking her up in the Haymarket area.'

'I defy you to produce any evidence of that, Inspector,' said Stevenson calmly. 'This is all utter nonsense.'

'You might have got away with it if you hadn't come to

me trying to gild the lily, so to speak, by making allegations of blackmail. I wouldn't have known who to look for, or where. But I have another witness, an army officer, who will tell the court that you called at a boarding house in Brighton on Saturday the ninth of November asking for the same Fanny Harris.' Hardcastle had some doubts, not only about the disparity in the descriptions, but about Springer's probity in the eyes of a jury, given that by the time the murder trial began he would probably have to be escorted from prison to give his evidence. 'But this is going to take some explaining, ain't it?' He took the gold choker necklace from his pocket and placed it on the low table that separated him from Stevenson.

'What's that supposed to prove?' asked Stevenson, still unruffled by the inspector's allegations.

'That necklace, which several witnesses will state was Fanny Harris's, and that she was wearing right up to her murder, was sold by you to a Mayfair jeweller on Tuesday the twelfth of November, along with other items. Detective Sergeant Marriott here seized it as evidence this morning, and the jeweller was in no doubt that it was you what sold it, on account of you giving him your name.' Hardcastle sat back in the soft cushions of Stevenson's plush sofa and waited. 'To be honest, I don't know why you never just threw it in the river.'

'The pieces I sold, including that necklace, belonged to my late wife, Inspector.'

'Your *late* wife?' Hardcastle recalled that, on the first occasion he had visited the alderman, Stevenson had told him that his wife was upstairs resting. 'And when exactly did your wife die, Alderman?'

There was a pause before Stevenson answered. 'Eleven years ago.'

'*Eleven years ago?*' Hardcastle was unable to conceal his surprise. 'But the first time we came here, you said your wife was ill in bed and we could speak freely.'

'So, I lied,' said Stevenson with an arrogant sneer.

'You didn't marry again, then.' It crossed Hardcastle's mind that Stevenson might have been stupid enough to have brought a prostitute into his own home, and that it was she who had been upstairs in bed.

'No.'

'So, what were you doing in Brighton on the ninth of November?' asked Hardcastle.

Stevenson laughed. 'It's only you who is suggesting that I was in Brighton on the ninth of November. I was not there then, nor at any other time recently. In fact, Inspector, I haven't been to Brighton since before the war.'

'An officer of the Brighton police made enquiries at the Grand Hotel on King's Road, Alderman. There is a record of your staying there that weekend.'

'You've been very thorough, Inspector, I must say. Very well, I decided to have a weekend away. What of it?' Even in the face of proof that he had been in Brighton, Stevenson showed no signs of guilt at having been caught out in his lie.

'If you deny knowing Fanny Harris, why did you call at this boarding house in Brighton asking for her?'

'I deny that I called at any boarding house.'

'As I said before, Alderman, I have an army officer who is prepared to give evidence that at about half-past four on Saturday the ninth of November, he answered the door to you. He alleges that you asked for Fanny Harris and when you was told that she was out, you left a message with this here army officer asking Fanny to meet you, and that she would know where.'

'I don't know who this phantom army officer of yours is, Inspector, but I can assure you that he was mistaken.'

'This witness subsequently saw you at a charity ball at the Langham Hotel in Portland Place a week ago last Monday – that'd be the twenty-fifth of November – and states that he recognized you as the man who had called at the boarding house. He says that he engaged you in conversation.'

'Attending a charity ball is hardly a crime, is it, Inspector?' Stevenson continued to maintain his insufferable air of superiority. 'But I don't recall speaking to anyone of that sort. After all, if he'd recognized me, it's reasonable to assume that I would also have recognized *him*.'

'Sergeant Marriott and I took the witness back to the Langham last Saturday and, seeing you there again, he confirmed that you was the man.' Hardcastle was by no means certain that Springer had seen the alderman there, but Catto had seen someone running away, for what that was worth. However, Stevenson's name had certainly appeared on the guest list.

'Well, of course he did. He'd seen me there on the Monday and saw me again on the Saturday. I don't deny that I was there, Inspector, but I do deny calling at Mrs Edwards's boarding house in Sussex Street.'

'How did you know it was in Sussex Street and that it was Mrs Edwards's boarding house, Alderman, if you say you never went there and you was staying at the Grand anyway?'

'You mentioned it just now, that it was Mrs Edwards's place in Sussex Street,' said Stevenson, but spoke with less confidence than when he had disclaimed knowing Fanny Harris.

'I didn't mention Mrs Edwards or the address,' said Hardcastle. 'I deliberately never mentioned them. So, how come you know her name and where she has her boarding house?'

'I think it would be unwise for me to continue this conversation, Inspector, until my solicitor is present.'

'I think you're probably right, Alderman,' said Hardcastle, 'and if you give Sergeant Marriott his address, he'll arrange for him to be sent for.'

'I'm perfectly capable of calling my own solicitor, Inspector,' snapped Stevenson. He stood up, signalling, in his view anyway, the end of the interview.

'I'm afraid that won't be possible,' said Hardcastle as he and Marriott stood up too. 'Richard Stevenson, I'm arresting you for the wilful murder of Fanny Horwood, otherwise Harris, on or about the ninth of November 1918.' He glanced at Marriott. 'Caution the prisoner, Sergeant.'

'Richard Stevenson,' Marriott began, 'you're not obliged to say anything, but anything you do say will be taken down in writing and may be used against you.'

Stevenson sat down again and ran his hands through his hair. 'I suppose you could call it a crime of passion,' he said quietly.

Sensing that Stevenson was about to confess, Hardcastle and Marriott resumed their seats too, but Hardcastle thought it unwise to mention that a crime of passion was not recognized in English law as a defence to murder.

'Fanny told me that she was expecting my baby, Inspector.' Stevenson looked up, the pathetic expression on his face clearly an attempt to invoke Hardcastle's sympathy. It was an expression Hardcastle had seen many times before on the face of a murderer trying to justify his crime. 'She wanted a substantial sum of money from me, far too much in my view. God Almighty, she was a common tart and pregnancy's a risk such women take. Anyway, I foolishly agreed to meet her and suggested Brighton. It was easy to get to from here, but sufficiently far away for me not to be recognized by anyone I knew.'

Hardcastle was mildly amused that a man who had just confessed to what he was sure was premeditated murder had worried about his reputation. Particularly as he had been known to consort with prostitutes much closer to his home.

'Fanny told me she knew a cheap boarding house in Sussex Street run by this Mrs Edwards,' Stevenson continued, 'and I agreed to call on her there. I made it quite clear that she should not come to the Grand Hotel. After all, what would people think, having a woman of that sort asking for me? But she was out when I called at Sussex Street, so I left a message saying that she would know where to find me.'

'How would she have known that?'

'I'd told her I was staying at the Grand, but as I said, I didn't want her calling there, so I waited outside the hotel, in King's Road, until she turned up.'

'And what time would that have been?'

'About seven o'clock, I suppose.'

'What did you do, once you'd met her, Alderman?'

'I took her for a drink in some low pub along the seafront, and I bought her a meal, all in the hope that I might make

200

her see reason. Then later on we went for a walk on the beach. But she threatened to expose me to the newspapers. Then she put forward this outrageous demand for two hundred pounds. I don't know where she got that figure from. Someone must have put her up to it, I should think. Probably the man Foster, the man you say you've arrested.'

'And so you strangled her.' Hardcastle's accusation brooked no denial, and none was forthcoming.

'Yes,' said Stevenson in a whisper. 'But it was a terrible accident. I didn't mean to kill her. She'd become hysterical and started pummelling me with her fists. I tried to restrain her and the next thing I knew she'd collapsed at my feet. And it was then that I realized that she was dead.'

'Tried to restrain her by putting your hands round her neck, did you?' observed Hardcastle drily. 'If all that's true, why did you take the poor little bitch's jewellery? You wasn't that hard up, was you?'

'As a matter of fact, money is a bit tight, but that aside, I thought I'd make it look like a robbery. I didn't think anyone would believe it was an accident.'

'You're right there, Alderman,' said Hardcastle, now using Stevenson's title sarcastically, certain in the knowledge that he had his man. 'But I'm afraid you was had there. It was Jack Foster who put Fanny up the spout. And now,' he continued as Stevenson slumped back in his seat, ashen of face at that latest twist, 'I have a warrant to search these premises. Not that I need it.'

Nineteen

Not wanting his prisoner to escape, or subsequently to be accused by him of planting evidence, Hardcastle insisted on Stevenson accompanying them during the search.

Pausing at the top of the stairs, the DDI looked at the four doors facing him. 'Which is your bedroom, Alderman?' he asked.

'That one,' said Stevenson, indicating a door. But after a cursory search, it was apparent that the room contained nothing of evidential value.

Returning to the landing, Hardcastle put his hand on the knob of another door. 'What's this one?'

'It's a spare room, and so is that one. And that one's the bathroom.' Stevenson pointed to each in turn.

Hardcastle opened the door. Judging from the disorder, it was clear that the room was occupied by someone. 'So, no one sleeps here, eh?' he commented drily. 'Have a look round, Marriott.'

The sergeant opened the wardrobe. Among the clothing that was hanging there, he found a set of full evening dress, a belted raincoat and a trilby hat. In the pocket of the raincoat was a receipt for one night's stay at the Grand Hotel in Brighton on the ninth of November.

Hardcastle took the receipt, examined it and showed it to Stevenson. 'Is this yours?' he asked.

'Yes,' said Stevenson, nodding.

In the deep drawer beneath the wardrobe, Marriott discovered an army uniform carefully folded and wrapped in tissue paper.

Hardcastle took the uniform from Marriott, spread it out on

the bed and examined it slowly and carefully. 'A second-lieu-
tenant in the Middlesex Rifles,' he mused, glancing at the
collar badges and running his fingers over the single star on
the cuff of the tunic. 'Whose is this?'

'My son's,' said Stevenson quietly.

'I take it he was killed during the war.' Hardcastle relinquished his hold on the uniform and turned to face the
alderman.

'Yes.'

'No he wasn't,' said a voice from the doorway.

'Dickie, I thought I told you—' But Stevenson got no further.

'I'm Richard Stevenson, Alderman Stevenson's son,'
announced the young man who now stood on the threshold
of the room.

'And you're an army officer?'

'Obviously,' sneered the younger man, nodding towards the
uniform on the bed. 'What the army calls a temporary
gentleman.'

'There are no medal ribbons on this tunic,' said Hardcastle.
'Have you only just been commissioned?'

'On the contrary, I was commissioned in 1914, but I didn't
stay long enough to acquire any medals.' With a gesture that
emphasized his effete character, Dickie Stevenson flicked a
lock of long golden hair from his eyes. 'I wasn't going to
fight a bloody war for those stupid bastards,' he said as he lit
a cigarette. 'I was in at the start – Mons – and saw almost all
my friends killed. And for what? For nothing. So, I decided
that if idiots like French and Joffre wanted to fight the Huns,
they could bloody well fight them without my help.'

'So, you deserted?'

'My, my, you coppers do catch on fast.' And with that
sarcastic comment, the younger Stevenson crossed the room
and rolled the ash from his cigarette into an ashtray on the
dressing table. 'So, what are you going to do? You can't arrest
me, not now.'

'That's just where you're wrong, my lad,' said Hardcastle.
'Not only will I arrest you, but you'll be handed over to the
military, who'll probably execute you for deserting your post

203

in the face of the enemy.' But even as he uttered the words, he thought it unlikely. The assistant provost-marshal, Lieutenant-Colonel Frobisher, had told him that there was disquiet in Parliament about similar draconian sentences that courts martial had imposed during the war. It was, however, sufficient to unnerve the young renegade army officer.

The sneer vanished from Dickie Stevenson's face and he went an ashen white. 'Don't be bloody silly,' he said. 'The war's over.'

'But it wasn't when you ran like a rat, was it?' The death of his nephew Harold in the battle of the Somme, and of young Kimber at Neuve Chapelle, did little to generate any sympathy in Hardcastle for the cowardly specimen of manhood who now stood before him. 'Is this your raincoat and trilby hat?'

'Yes, it is.'

'And this receipt is yours also?'

'Yes.'

'What were you doing in Brighton on the ninth of November?' Hardcastle was now convinced that it was the younger Stevenson, rather than his father, who had killed Fanny Horwood.

'Fancied a weekend away,' said the youngster nonchalantly. 'I often have weekends away.'

Hardcastle nodded. 'Richard Stevenson, I'm arresting you for being a deserter from military service, and I must warn you that more serious charges may follow.'

At the police station, the young Richard Stevenson was placed in the interview room with a uniformed constable to guard him.

Minutes later, Hardcastle brought in Dudley Springer. 'Do you recognize this man?' he asked, pointing to Stevenson.

There was no hesitation. 'That's the man who called at Mrs Edwards's boarding house,' said Springer. 'And the man I saw at the Langham on Saturday.'

'You're quite sure?'

'No doubt of it, Inspector.'

'Thank you, Major.' Hardcastle waved a hand at the

204

constable. 'You can take Major Springer back now,' he said.

'Was that little charade supposed to prove something?' asked Stevenson sardonically, as the door closed behind Springer and his escort.

'Why did you call at Mrs Edwards's place on Saturday the ninth of November?' Hardcastle asked.

'To see Fanny Horwood. She was expecting my baby.' The young man seemed finally to tire of his posturing.

'I'll tell you what I told your father, Stevenson,' said Hardcastle. 'A man called Jack Foster has admitted putting her in the family way himself.'

'I don't believe it.' The younger Stevenson looked aghast at that information.

'But it had nothing to do with any baby, had it? You weren't worried about that, and it probably wasn't the first child you'd fathered anyway. No, Stevenson, Fanny had learned about you running from the army and she threatened to shop you to the authorities unless you paid her a substantial sum of money. Money you hadn't got and which your father refused to give you. That was much worse than making her pregnant. If she'd shopped you it would have meant a firing squad, so you took her for a walk along the seafront – quite late at night – and you murdered her.'

There was a long pause before the young man replied. 'It wasn't murder,' he said eventually. 'It was an accident.' He then went on to give his version of the way in which Fanny had met her death. It was an account identical in every particular to that which his father had given earlier.

Hardcastle shook his head. 'It was no accident, Stevenson, as the pathologist will testify, and I shall now charge you with the murder of Fanny Horwood on or about the ninth of November.'

Recovering himself from the initial shock of facing a second capital charge, Stevenson sneered yet again. 'You won't be able to prove it,' he said. 'There were no witnesses.'

'Oh, I'll prove it, Stevenson, don't vex yourself about that,' said Hardcastle.

Once the formalities had been completed and Stevenson

had been placed in a cell to await his appearance at Bow Street police court the following morning, Hardcastle returned to his office.

'And now you can send a telegraph message to Mr Watson at Brighton, Marriott. Tell him we've solved his murder for him.' Hardcastle took off his shoes and began to massage his feet.

Seconds later, the station officer appeared in the doorway. 'There's an Alderman Stevenson waiting downstairs, sir. He says he wishes to see you.'

'Bring him up then,' said Hardcastle, sighing as he replaced his shoes.

As Stevenson was shown into the office, it was apparent that the alderman had lost much of his former arrogance. 'Thank you for seeing me, Inspector,' he said.

'Sit down, Alderman,' said Hardcastle. 'What can I do for you? Incidentally, we have charged your son with the murder of Fanny Horwood.'

'I imagine you have,' said Stevenson listlessly. 'The damned young fool only showed himself because he thought he couldn't be arrested for desertion now the war's over.'

'Well, *he* might not have known, but I'd've thought you would,' said Hardcastle, choosing not to afford the alderman too much comfort.

'I did, Inspector, but he wouldn't listen. He never listened.' Stevenson took a silver cigarette case from his inside pocket. 'D'you mind if I smoke?'

'Not at all.' Hardcastle pushed an ashtray across the desk so that it was close to where Stevenson was sitting.

'I've come to apologize, Mr Hardcastle,' Stevenson began, blowing a plume of smoke into the air. 'I'm afraid I led you a bit of a dance.' He paused, collecting his thoughts. 'Young Dickie has been the bane of my life ever since his mother died back in oh-seven,' he said, sighing deeply. 'He got thrown out of his school for misconduct in his last term. Nevertheless, I managed to get him a place at Oxford, but he was sent down in his first year.'

'What for?' asked Hardcastle.

'I'm afraid he assaulted a bulldog.'

'What did he do? Kick it?' Hardcastle smiled at the thought that someone could be banished from university for attacking a dog.

'A bulldog is Oxford slang for a proctor's attendant, Inspector. A sort of college policeman.'

'Oh, I see.'

'When the war started, he joined up immediately,' Stevenson continued. 'I think he believed what we all believed: that it would be over by Christmas, and that it would be a bit of a lark. To be honest, I thought the army might have been the making of him, but no sooner had he joined up than he deserted. I suppose the horror and the reality of war became apparent all too soon. I hate to say this, but I don't think he had the guts for it.'

'He certainly didn't strike me as a hero,' Hardcastle commented drily.

'No, he certainly wasn't,' said Stevenson. 'Nevertheless, it's a natural instinct for a father to try to protect his only son. I gave him money and denied having seen him when the military police called. But he was a wayward boy, Inspector.' The alderman leaned forward to tap his cigarette on the edge of the ashtray. 'He got into the wrong company, and despite my warning that he would almost certainly be found and shot at dawn, he insisted on frequenting the fleshpots of London. And he often came home in the small hours, more often than not drunk. When he came home at all, that is. How he wasn't picked up in London is a miracle. Incidentally, the reason I pretended my wife was upstairs the first time you called was in case you heard Dickie moving about up there.'

'And I presume telling me that it was you who'd gone to Brighton on the ninth of November was an attempt to throw me off the scent?'

'Yes, it was. The trouble with Dickie is that he was so cock-sure of himself that he probably thought that you'd never find out he'd been to Brighton, even though he was stupid enough to use his own name at the Grand. But I was so sure that you knew, that I pretended it was me who'd been there, and I was hoping that you'd charge me. You see, Inspector, I have a cast-iron alibi for that weekend, which I wouldn't have revealed until I went for trial. In that way, I'd hoped to give Dickie a chance to get away. I warned him to go to America perhaps, or Africa. Somewhere where he'd be out of the way. I can tell you it came as a dreadful shock when I learned that he'd been responsible for that poor girl's death.'

'And how did you discover that?' asked Hardcastle.

'It was on the Sunday evening before Armistice Day. Dickie came home with scratches on his face and hands, and when I asked him about them, he told me he'd spent the weekend in Brighton and got involved in a fight. But once I learned from the newspapers that a girl had been murdered there, I started to put two and two together.' The alderman afforded Hardcastle a bleak smile. 'You see, I'd already found out from Dolly Hancock that Dickie knew Fanny Horwood, and had taken her to a hotel in London sometime previously.'

'Seems you had quite long chats with Dolly, then,' observed Hardcastle.

'We knew each other rather well,' said Stevenson with a smile. 'Anyway, I confronted Dickie with it and he admitted killing the girl. But he assured me it was an accident. I got all the details from him, about the boarding house and Mrs Edwards, so I could keep telling you half truths in an attempt to spin out your investigation.'

'And the blackmail?'

'Ah, yes, the blackmail. It wasn't the photograph of me with Dolly Hancock. I didn't really care about that. Why should I? I'm a widower, after all, and I can sleep with whosoever I like.' Stevenson was being quite open about his relationship with the prostitute now. 'But, like a fool, I let slip to her one night that young Dickie was on the run from the army. I suppose she must have told Foster and that's what he was blackmailing me about. He said the photograph was his insurance against me not paying up. But that didn't matter. Had it not been for Dickie, I'd've said what Wellington said: Publish and be damned. I only came to you after I'd learned that the death in Brighton was being treated as a murder. It was an attempt to lay a false trail and protect the boy.' He paused, shaking his head slowly. 'It was my own stupidity in telling Dolly about Dickie that's put him where he is.'

'Only partly,' said Hardcastle. 'Do you still intend going ahead with the charge of blackmail?' he asked.

'Most certainly,' said Stevenson. 'I've nothing to lose now.'

'Did your son know that you were doing all this in an attempt to protect him?'

'No, of course not. Perhaps I should have told him and insisted on his going abroad, rather than just suggesting it. Then none of this would have happened.'

'It might have been better if you'd handed him over to the army as soon as he came back from Mons,' said Hardcastle. 'At least that way Fanny Horwood would still be alive.'

'Maybe you're right, Inspector.' Stevenson shook his head sadly. 'But I didn't want to see him shot as a coward.'

'Instead of which, you'll see him hanged as a murderer, Alderman,' said Hardcastle brutally.

The trial of Richard Stevenson, junior, took place at Lewes Assizes some months later.

Hardcastle testified to having searched Stevenson's house, and produced the receipted bill for the young man's stay at the Grand Hotel in Brighton on the Saturday night of Fanny Horwood's murder. He also produced the raincoat and trilby hat that Springer later identified as the clothing Stevenson was wearing that fateful weekend.

After much soul-searching, Councillor Walter Cross had withdrawn his charges against Major Dudley Springer on the grounds that to admit in open court that he had been swindled would damage his reputation and standing in the Brighton business community. But this decision was, no doubt, influenced by the return of the hundred pounds that he had 'invested' in Springer's bogus gold mine. Although Hardcastle muttered something about it coming close to compounding a misdemeanour, he was nevertheless pleased that, for the purpose of Stevenson's trial, the major's integrity had been restored sufficient to make him a credible witness. In cross-examination, defence counsel tested Springer's evidence rigorously, but the major was unshaken in his assertion that it was young Stevenson who had called at Sussex Street and asked for Fanny. And Stevenson's barrister fared no better with the receptionist at the Grand Hotel, who would not be moved from his statement that the accused had spent the night there.

And among a succession of damning testimonies, a Mayfair jeweller positively identified young Stevenson as the man who had sold him Fanny Horwood's gold necklace. And a confident Mrs Dyer swore that it *was* Fanny's necklace. 'I'd know it anywhere,' she said adamantly.

In dry medical language, the pathologist told the court that Fanny Horwood had been killed by manual strangulation. He described finding skin beneath her fingernails, undoubtedly the result of attempting to fend off her attacker, and concluded by saying that his examination of the woman's body indicated that she had put up a spirited struggle for survival.

Dolly Hancock cheerfully admitted to being a prostitute, and related what Fanny had told her about spending a night in a hotel with Stevenson the previous June, despite defence counsel's attempts to have such evidence excluded as irrelevant hearsay.

In his closing address – a brutal display of forensic demolition – counsel for the Crown negated Stevenson's pathetic denials and excuses one by one and, in the process, completely destroyed his defence that Fanny's death had been an unfortunate accident.

Two hours after the closing speeches, the jury returned a verdict of guilty.

The judge donned the black cap and sentenced Richard Stevenson to death, the only penalty the law allowed.

And with awesome finality, the chaplain's sonorous tones completed the proceedings: 'And may the Lord have mercy on his soul.'

Finding no grounds for commuting the sentence, the Home Secretary, Sir George Cave, scrawled his damning decision on the front of the docket: 'Let the law take its course.'

Three weeks later the young Richard Stevenson was hanged at Pentonville prison.

Two weeks after the end of Stevenson's trial, the indictment of blackmail was put to Jack Foster and Danny Hoskins at the Old Bailey. At its close, Foster was sentenced to eight years penal servitude and Hoskins to eighteen months. They began their sentences on the day that Mr X's son went to the gallows.

And it was also on that day that Detective Sergeant Douglas Goodenough of the Brighton Borough Police announced his engagement to Miss Mavis Brandon.

'Seen this bit in the paper, Marriott?' asked Hardcastle as his sergeant entered the office.

'What's that, sir?'

'Alderman Stevenson threw himself under a train at East Croydon station yesterday morning.' And with that, Hardcastle took off his shoes and began to massage his feet.

Glossary

'A' FROM A BULL'S FOOT, to know: to know nothing.

ALBERT: a watch chain of the type worn by Albert, Prince Consort.

ALL MY EYE AND BETTY MARTIN: nonsense.

ANTECEDENT HISTORY: details of an accused person's address, education and employment, etc.

BAILEY, the: Central Criminal Court, London.

BARNEY: an argument.

BEAK: a magistrate.

BIRD LIME: time (rhyming slang).

BLACK ANNIE or BLACK MARIA: a police or prison van.

BOB: a shilling (now 5p).

BOOZER: a public house.

BRADBURY: a pound note. From Sir John Bradbury, Secretary to the Treasury, who introduced pound notes in 1914 to replace gold sovereigns.

BRIEF, a: a warrant *or* a police warrant card *or* a lawyer.

BROLLY: an umbrella.

BULL AND COW: a row (rhyming slang).

BUSY, a: a detective.

CARNEY: cunning, sly.

CARPET: three months' imprisonment.

CHESTNUTS OUT OF THE FIRE, to pull your: to solve your problem.

CHOKEY: prison.

CID: Criminal Investigation Department.

CIGS: Chief of the Imperial General Staff.

CLINK: prison. Clink Street, London, was the site of an old prison.

CLYDE (*as in* D'YOU THINK I CAME UP THE CLYDE ON A BICYCLE?): to deny that the speaker is a fool.

COLDSTREAMER: a soldier of the Coldstream Guards.

COMMISSIONER'S OFFICE: official title of New Scotland Yard, headquarters of the Metropolitan Police.

COPPER: a policeman.

COPPER-KNOBS: people with auburn hair.

CO-RESPONDENT SHOES: brown & white shoes, reputed to be worn by philanderers.

CRACKLING: an attractive woman.

CRACKSMAN: a safe-breaker.

CULLY: alternative to calling a man 'mate'.

D: a detective.

DDI: Divisional Detective Inspector.

DEKKO: a look (*ex* Hindi).

DICKY BIRD: a word (rhyming slang).

DOGBERRY: a policeman or watchman (*ex* Shakespeare).

DOLLAR: five shillings (25p).

DOOLALLY TAP: of unsound mind (*ex* Hindi).

DOXY: a woman of loose character.

DRUM: a dwelling house.

DSO: Distinguished Service Order.

DUMMY, to throw a: to set a false trail.

EARWIGGING: listening.

EIGHT O'CLOCK WALK, to take the: to be hanged.

EWBANK: proprietary name of an early type of non-electric carpet sweeper.

EYEWASH: nonsense.

FEEL THE COLLAR, to: to make an arrest.

FIVER: five pounds sterling.

FLEET STREET: former centre of the newspaper industry, and still used as a generic term for the Press.

FLIM or FLIMSY: a five-pound note. From the thin paper on which it was originally printed.

FLORIN: two shillings (10p).

FLOUNDER: a cab (rhyming slang: flounder and dab).

FORM: previous convictions.

FOURPENNY CANNON, a: a steak and kidney pie.

FRONT, The: theatre of WWI operations in France and Flanders.

GAMP: an umbrella (from Sarah Gamp in Charles Dickens's *Martin Chuzzlewit*).

GILD THE LILY, to: to exaggerate.

GLIM: a look, a shortening of 'glimpse'.

GREAT SCOTLAND YARD: location of an army recruiting office, not to be confused with New Scotland Yard.

GROWLER: a taxi.

GUV *or* GUV'NOR: informal alternative to 'sir'.

HALF A CROWN *or* HALF A DOLLAR: two shillings and sixpence (12½p).

HAWKING THE MUTTON: leading a life of prostitution.

HOLLOWAY: women's prison in North London.

IRONCLAD: a battleship.

JILDI: quickly (*ex* Hindi).

JOANNA: a piano.

JUDY: a girl.

KC: King's Counsel – a senior barrister.

KETTLE: a pocket watch.

KIP, to have a: to sleep.

KNOCKED OFF: arrested.

LAY-DOWN: a remand in custody.

LINEN DRAPERS: newspapers (rhyming slang).

LONG BOW, to draw the: to exaggerate *or* to tell unbelievable stories.

MAGSMAN: a common thief.

MANOR: a police area.

MBE: Member of the Order of the British Empire.

MC: Military Cross.

MI5: counter-espionage service of the United Kingdom.

MILLING: fighting.

MINCES: eyes (rhyming slang: mince pies).

MONS, to make a: to make a mess of things, as in the disastrous Battle of Mons in 1914.

NAPOO: no good; finished. Bastardization of the French: *il n'y en a plus* (there is none left), usually in answer to a soldier's request for more beer.

NICK: a police station or prison.

NICKED: arrested.

OBE: Officer of the Order of the British Empire.

OLD BAILEY: Central Criminal Court, London.

OLD CONTEMPTIBLES: name assumed by survivors of the Battle of Mons in response to the Kaiser's condemnation of the British Army as 'a contemptible little army'.

ON THE GAME: leading a life of prostitution.

ON THE SLATE: to be given credit.

ON THE SQUARE: a freemason.

OUT OF THE TOP DRAWER: of a superior class.

PEACH, to: to inform to the police.

PETER JONES: a London department store in Sloane Square, Chelsea.

PIP, SQUEAK AND WILFRED: WWI medals, namely the 1914–15 Star, the British War Medal 1914–18 and the Victory Medal 1914–19, so named after newspaper cartoon characters of the period.

POLICE GAZETTE: official nationwide publication listing wanted persons, etc.

PREVIOUS: prior convictions for crime.

PROVOST, the: military police.

QUID: one pound sterling.

RAINING CATS AND DOGS: raining heavily.

RECEIVER, the: senior Scotland Yard official responsible for the finances of the Metropolitan Police.

RECORD: record of previous convictions.

ROZZER: a policeman.

SAPPERS: the Corps of Royal Engineers (in the singular, a member of that corps).

SAUSAGE AND MASH: cash (rhyming slang).

SCREW: a prison warder.

SCRIMSHANKER: one who evades duty or work.

SELL THE PUP, to: to attempt to deceive.

SEXTON BLAKE: a detective hero of boys' stories.
SHILLING: now 5p.
SILK, a: a King's Counsel (a senior barrister) from the silk gowns they wear.
SKINT: broke.
SKIP *or* SKIPPER: an informal police alternative to station-sergeant, clerk-sergeant and sergeant.
SMACKER, a: a pound sterling *or* a kiss.
SMOKE, the: London.
SNOUT: a police informant.
SOMERSET HOUSE: formerly the records office of births, deaths and marriages for England & Wales.
SOVEREIGN (or SOV): one pound sterling.
SPIT AND A DRAW, to have a: to smoke a cigarette.
STAGE-DOOR JOHNNY: young man frequenting theatres in an attempt to make the acquaintance of actresses.
STONEY: broke.
STRETCH, a: one year's imprisonment.
SWADDY: a soldier (*ex* Hindi).
SWEET FANNY ADAMS, to know: to know nothing.
TANNER: sixpence (2½p).
TATLER, The: a society magazine.
TEA LEAF: a thief (rhyming slang).
TICKETY-BOO: all right, perfect.
TITFER: a hat (rhyming slang: tit for tat).
TOBY: a police area.
TOD (SLOAN), on one's: on one's own (rhyming slang).
TOM: a prostitute.
TOMMING: pursuing a life of prostitution.
TOMMY: a British soldier. From the name Tommy Atkins, used as an example on early army forms.
TOPPED: murdered or hanged.
TOPPING: a murder or hanging.
TROUBLE-AND-STRIFE: wife (rhyming slang).
TUBE: The London Underground railway system.
TUMBLE, a: sexual intercourse.
TWO-AND-EIGHT, in a: in a state (rhyming slang).

UNDERGROUND, The: London Underground railway system.

UP THE SPOUT: pregnant.

VAD: Voluntary Aid Detachment – wartime nursing auxiliaries.

WATCH COMMITTEE: a provincial police authority.

WAR OFFICE: Department of State overseeing the army. (Now a part of the Ministry of Defence.)

WET ONE'S WHISKERS: to take a drink.

WHISTLE: a suit (rhyming slang: whistle and flute).

WHITE-FEATHER JOHNNY: man avoiding military service.